TERMINAL WARNING

Grief and rage exploded in Bandit's heart, but she did not delay even to look at her fallen comrade. She dove for the assailant in a desperate drive to reach him before he could strike again and assure the end of his dying or already dead victim.

The renegade was confident of his victory. He smiled coldly and raised his weapon, steadying it to make certain of the Commando-Captain's death . . .

Ace Books by P.M. Griffin

STAR COMMANDOS
STAR COMMANDOS: COLONY IN PERIL
STAR COMMANDOS: MISSION UNDERGROUND
STAR COMMANDOS: DEATH PLANET
STAR COMMANDOS: MIND SLAVER
STAR COMMANDOS: RETURN TO WAR
STAR COMMANDOS: FIRE PLANET
STAR COMMANDOS: JUNGLE ASSAULT
STAR COMMANDOS: CALL TO ARMS

P.M. GRIFFIN

ACE BOOKS, NEW YORK

This book is an Ace original edition,
and has never been previously published.

STAR COMMANDOS: CALL TO ARMS

An Ace Book / published by arrangement with
the author

PRINTING HISTORY
Ace edition / August 1991

Cover art by Kang Yi.

ISBN: 0-441-78048-2

Ace Books are published by The Berkley Publishing Group,
200 Madison Avenue, New York, New York 10016.

PRINTED IN THE UNITED STATES OF AMERICA

10 9 8 7 6 5 4 3 2 1

To my friend,
Father Michael Kelliher,
who lived his life in service
to God and humankind
and who gave that life
to save another's.

CALL
TO ARMS

ONE

COMMANDO-COLONEL ISLAEN Connor's eyes narrowed as she followed the progress of the small sailing vessel through her distance lenses. The boat was very far out for a craft of that size, and Thorne's ocean was uncommonly rough in the wake of the previous day's fierce storm.

Disapproval hardened her expression. They encountered danger often enough as it was in the general course of their work without courting it needlessly.

She forcibly quelled the tension rising in her. Commando-Captain Varn Tarl Sogan was no shooting star, nor was he some scramble-circuited fool of a boy with the need to prove his manhood with ridiculous stunts. The best on the water of all the elite guerrilla unit she commanded, he knew full well what he was doing.

All the same, her hands tightened on the lenses as she continued to watch him. The former Arcturian Admiral had been driving himself and every vehicle at his disposal like this ever since they had returned from Amazoon of Indra. He made no complaint, gave no other outward sign of impatience, but he wanted the vengeance she had promised him. He wanted it badly.

All of them did.

They had been sent to the jungle planet to retrieve or destroy a large shipment of Navy arms stolen in a daring, well-planned raid from the docks on Alpha Gary. Because of the awesome slaughter those weapons could cause, her team, acknowledged the best Commando unit in the Federation forces, had gone after them. They had succeeded, despite the loss of their on-world support force and assault equipment in the crash of the transport taking them to their target.

Islaen's great brown eyes darkened. It had not been a pleasant journey, and they had suffered heavily, both from Amazoon's vile climate and from her wildlife; the leeches that were the lords of her treelands and the stinging and biting insects. All the hard work and the perils they had encountered had seemed acceptable by comparison with that unremitting persecution.

They would have been a galaxy worse off had Sogan not been able to shield them. He and Islaen Connor were mutants from their respective races, possessing similar though by no means identical gifts. They could speak mind-to-mind, as no others of their species could do, and they each had other differing gifts which had served them and their comrades well in the past. One of Varn's was the ability to detect, with varying degrees of sensitivity, the emotions radiating from a large portion of the animal universe and, in many instances, to influence the behavior of certain of those creatures. He had been able to exert a particularly strong control over Amazoon's nonhuman denizens, even those on a low intelligence level, and he had drawn upon that power to keep their tormenters away from them. In the end, that control had given them their victory; a dark success none of them cared to recall.

A shudder passed through the woman. They had reached their target too late. The renegades were all but ready to lift with the arms, allowing her party no time in which to utilize the guerrilla tactics which had proven so effective against the forces of the Arcturian Empire during the recently ended War. With their heavy assault gear burned in the crash, it had seemed that they could only acknowledge their defeat until Varn had acted. In order to prevent the massacre which would almost inevitably follow the escape of those weapons, the Captain himself had initiated a massacre.

While his comrades had blown the energy picket guarding the camp, he had called out with his mind. Crown wasps, swarm upon swarm of them, had answered that summons, descending on the spacers in a vast, viciously stinging cloud.

That attack had been terrible to watch, but it was no worse in its way than the lasers and missiles of a conventional military assault and would have left them the witnesses Intelligence required—had a second army not accompanied the flying insects.

Leeches in inconceivable number had massed around the camp, hungering for the blood their instinct told them was within and utterly frustrated in their desire for it by the deadly, glowing wall. When that went down they, too, had poured into the base in numbers that defied counting.

Varn had known they would come, but as he had been able to keep the blood suckers away from his own party, he also had believed he would be equally successful in driving them off from the base. He fought to do so, in the end very nearly draining himself of his own life, but his efforts had been useless. The leeches' primal excitement, amplified by the smell of the blood the wasps were drawing, proved too powerful, and when some of the host attached themselves and began feeding, he was beaten. Their transmissions overrode anything he attempted to do to counter them. He was finally forced to break off his battle and concentrate on guarding himself and his comrades.

Even then, the slaughter should not have reached the magnitude it did. Sogan had seen the river flowing nearby as a refuge for most of his victims. He had not realized that a school of sawmills was in possession of that stretch of it. In less than thirty seconds, the voracious fish had stripped every shred of soft tissue from the skeletons of those who had taken to the water to escape the torment on land.

Islaen's eyes momentarily closed. When her team had at last been able to enter the ravaged clearing, not one of the sixty-odd men and women who had been working there an incredibly short time before remained alive.

Her head lowered. Varn Tarl Sogan had never tolerated butcher work. He had lost his rank in the Arcturian Navy and his place in his own caste, had seen his consort, concubines, and his children die, and had very nearly died himself at the hands of his people's executioners because he refused to obey the order of his insane commander. He had become involved with her unit because he could not stand by and watch the innocent peoples of his former enemies slaughtered by human vermin who sought to build wealth from the chaos following the close of the War, threatening to destroy from within what so many Federation soldiers had perished to preserve. Now, albeit in a great part unwillingly and to prevent a worse atrocity still, he had brought this nightmare to pass.

The revulsion he himself felt for the blood suckers magnified his sense of guilt, and even more so the fact that he had been forced to utilize her strength to help power his summons; thereby, in his mind, sullying her as deeply as he had himself.

That was dark, indeed. An Arcturian officer could not while preserving his honor turn on an enemy a weapon he would either be unwilling to face himself or would protest if sent against his own command. Those who had done so, out of what they had held to be military need in the ever-increasing pressures of the great War, were to a greater or lesser degree disgraced among their own, and few if any of them had compounded their shame by directly involving any of their comrades in the deed save as instruments acting under order. In the face of that stern ethic, nothing he had done to prevent or mitigate the extent of the slaughter was of any consequence. His condemnation of himself was complete, and it had very nearly proven fatal.

She and his other companions had not been of much use in dispelling that conviction, either, Islaen thought bitterly. Numbed by the horror they had just witnessed, they had been aware only of that. Jake Karmikel and even Bandit had openly blasted him. She and Bethe had not actively turned on him, but neither had they been able to rouse themselves to say or do anything in his defense. Sogan had accepted what he believed to be their corroboration of his own judgment of himself and had taken leave of them. When Jake went after him moments later, he overtook Sogan barely in time to prevent him from turning his blaster on himself.

That had been a near thing, and it remained a danger. Suicide was acceptable for a member of the Arcturian warrior caste, which Varn remained despite having been stripped of his place and privileges. It was the only appropriate course for one who had dishonored himself. If his condemnation of himself still held in his heart and mind when this was all over, he might well claim his right to take that path; almost certainly would do so if he did not also believe he would thereby be damning her for her active role in the nightmare as well.

For the moment, however, he would stay his hand. All the unit—Varn, second to her in command and her husband since their meeting on Visnu of Brahmin; herself, the team's field CO; her long-time friend, comrade, and fellow Noreenan, Commando-Captain Jake Karmikel; the space-bred demolitions expert,

Commando-Sergeant Bethe Danlo, who was Jake's wife and copilot on the *Jovian Moon;* and Bandit, the gurry who had bonded with her and Varn on Jade of Kuan Yin and come with them into space—they all recognized that what had happened on Amazoon affected the entire company, not merely the man who had been its focus. The ultimate guilt for all the suffering and danger, for the crash and the deaths of the on-worlders who had perished in it, for everything that might yet follow, lay with the person who had masterminded the arms grab which started it all. None of them would feel really clean again until he and his associates were either dead or rotting in a galactic penitentiary for the remainder of their natural lives.

She had petitioned her commander, Navy Admiral Ram Sithe, for the right to take them, a request he had been quick to grant, although he had not been aware of the depth or the cause of the hatred driving her. In her report, she had merely stated the physical facts—that the Amazoonan creatures had rushed the base as soon as the energy picket went down and had left nothing living in their wake. Because of the unique nature of their mind talents, all her unit was very careful to keep its leaders' gifts a close secret. In this case, they would have concealed that part of it anyway. Varn was flogging himself enough without having to face the possibility of official censure.

The Commando-Colonel stiffened as the boat she had been watching veered suddenly and came broadside to a great, white-topped wave. The little craft went over. Her sail was parallel to the water, and it seemed for a moment that only a miracle could save her, then she righted again.

Varn, come in now! Islaen ordered in thought, the mode of communication they most commonly used between themselves. She realized how sharp that sounded and quickly added, *I've just been on the transceiver with Admiral Sithe.*

His thought answered in the same moment. *He has what we want?*

. . . Aye.

Despite herself, she had hesitated before replying. Sithe had given her a name, a name and a location that had turned her heart to ice.

As quickly as she had covered herself, the Arcturian felt her uncertainty and something of what lay behind it. *What is wrong, Islaen?*

Patience, Admiral, she said, making herself speak lightly. *I've called Jake and Bethe back. Let's wait until they get here before starting any explanations. I'd just as soon not have to go over it all again.*

TWO

VARN TARL SOGAN wasted no time in bringing his boat ashore.

He went at once to the small room they had chosen for their office. His eyes ran over the intricately engraved walls and marvelously carved, finely proportioned Thornen furniture without noticing them and fixed on his consort. Islaen Connor was a beautiful woman, comfortably tall, her slender body lithe and carried with the grace of one well familiar with space.

Her features were delicately chiseled, her eyes large and thickly lashed. Her hair, tightly confined in the braid that was the almost universal style of women who ranged the starlanes, was a rich auburn color, and her complexion was exquisitely fair, the mark of all those born of Noreen of Tara.

When he had set out two hours previously, she had been wearing Thornen costume, as she often did when at liberty on this planet that had become both their home and their base. Now, she was clad in spacer's garb—tunic, close-fitting pants, and high boots capable of giving good support and purchase either on the deck of a starship or in a surplanetary wilderness. Around her narrow waist was clasped a heavy, multipouched utility belt, and its holster was not empty.

The small, winged creature perched on her shoulder whistled excitedly at his entrance. *Good! Varn's here!—Islaen's unhappy! Bad mission!*

"Bandit!" the Commando-Colonel corrected sharply, speaking aloud as she and Varn nearly always did when addressing her, save when they were in the presence of strangers.

The little feathered mammal looked to be nothing more than an exceptionally delightful mascot, barely seven ounces in weight and brown in color, apart from the black stripe circling her head and crossing the equally dark, merry eyes like the mask of a pre-space Terran thief. Her bright yellow bill was supple, giving her a wide range of facial expressions. Her legs and feet were also a vivid yellow, and the prehensile toes functioned as did a human's finger.

She was appealing, aye, but she was also a great deal more. The gurry was intelligent as humans defined the term, and she could communicate in thought with those to whom she was bonded, as well as understand the verbal speech of anyone using a language comprehended by them. Beyond that, she could broadcast an enormous volume of goodwill, influencing anyone not totally depraved or gripped by some overpowering, usually violent emotion to respond favorably to her and to her companions—all facts Islaen's unit guarded as closely as they did their commanders' equally strange abilities.

As for her love and her courage, those had been proven time and again since she had met and joined with Islaen and through her, with Varn on her homeworld, Jade of Kuan Yin.

Sogan looked somberly at the Jadite. "I am aware that she is disturbed, small one." His eyes flickered to his commander. *What is this about a bad mission, Colonel?*

It's not bad, really. It just has some . . . unexpected aspects.

She, in her turn, studied the former enemy she had come to love even as she had battled his forces as head of Thorne's Resistance and whom she had once believed dead—executed by his own people for giving the world he had invaded her life at the great War's end.

He was moderately tall, by the Federation's broad standards, and slight of build. At the moment, he was too thin. He had been hard hit on several of their assignments, and one had followed the other too quickly to allow him to put back those lost pounds, although he was otherwise fully recovered.

He carried himself like the soldier he was, with the balance and lightness of movement of one who had spent a large portion of his life in space. The air of command rested on him like a cloak, as it should. He had been bred to lead a fleet in time of war and to rule star systems in peace.

His hair and eyes were the same dark brown color, a trait found only in the ranking officers of the Arcturian warrior caste, and among them only in those whose families were closely linked with that of the Emperor himself. He had the olive skin of his people and their well-formed, rather harsh features; features that could mean his death should they be recognized for what they were, given the deep hatreds engendered in the recent War. On several occasions already, his life had been threatened when suspicion of his race had been aroused in the wrong place.

Islaen sighed to herself. That was a threat they would have to go on facing, probably for the remainder of their lives, whatever the services he rendered to the people of the Federation ultrasystem. A mob or hate-maddened individual assassin rarely gave time for the description of such deeds before striking.

Her love for this man suddenly surged into her conscious awareness, and she came into his arms, *Oh, Varn,* she whispered, in his mind, *how much darker my life would have been if we had not met that day on Visnu.*

Sogan held her close, startled by the strength of the emotion on her. He was also concerned by what he had detected earlier. The very fact that the greater part of her mind was closed confirmed that worry, that fear, was still present within her. *Can you tell me nothing of what is troubling you?*

Immediately, the shields already in place over her thoughts tightened still further.

He sighed. *Do not wall yourself off from me, my Islaen.*

You do it often enough.

That is why I know the cost so well, Varn said quietly.

Before she could answer him, she felt the approach of two familiar minds and turned toward the door. *A few more minutes. Our friends are here now.*

The two remaining members of the unit came into the office upon receiving their commander's permission to do so.

Commando-Captain Jake Karmikel was also a citizen of Noreen. He was a relatively big man, more than a head taller than Sogan and considerably broader of shoulder, although he was by no means muscle-bound. He was handsome by his own race's and by Terran standards. His eyes were a clear, bright blue and his hair a fiery red.

The woman beside him looked particularly diminutive by comparison. Commando-Sergeant Bethe Danlo was, in fact, exceptionally small, but no one knowing her doubted her right to her place with the famed guerrillas.

Her features were regular and of a Terran cast that proclaimed the origins of the spacer clan into which she had been born. There was the steadiness of one willing and well able to bear responsibility reflected in her slate blue eyes. Her tightly braided hair was blond.

Both newcomers were dressed in Thornen fashion, for they had been en route for Lan City, Thorne's capital, when their Colonel's summons to return had reached them. Now, they eyed her curiously, waiting for her to start.

The Noreenan woman hesitated, as if she were seeking a way to begin, then she unconsciously squared her shoulders and raised her head.

"Intelligence had given Admiral Sithe a lead at last," she said, confirming what the others already knew or had guessed.

Jake frowned. "A lead, not a definite answer?"

"A lead, unfortunately, though it's a good one. Amazoon's wildlife didn't leave us anything in the way of live witnesses, remember."

She sighed to herself as she felt Sogan cringe, although there was no visible change in either his expression or his stance.

She went on as though she had detected nothing. "About half of the bodies left on land belonged to the freighters. They were the usual well-mixed crew, with records as long as an interstellar voyage." Those who had gone into the river had been reduced to skeletons, of course, and their antecedents could only be surmised. "The rest apparently belonged to the brig, and every last one of them was an Albionan."

"Anything on them?" Bethe asked.

"Not from the Navy, but the Stellar Patrol had plenty and Albionan authorities even more."

"The buyer's crew?"

Islaen nodded. "Almost certainly. That ship was too big for a rim freighter, and one simply would not entrust a cargo like that to yet another set of middlemen."

"They were a bad lot?" Sogan inquired almost unnecessarily. What other sort would be dealing in stolen arms or with vermin of those spacers' ilk, subbiotics who sought out charters no one fit to bear the title of human would consider touching?

"Nothing like the freighter hands, but bad enough. They had all been members of the now-defunct Albionan Justice Department Auxiliaries."

Her companions' lack of response did not surprise her. She had known nothing about the planet's on-world situation before hearing Ram Sithe's briefing and reading the more detailed material he had faxmitted to her.

"The Arcturians never hit Albion's quadrant, but its planets had to fight for their survival all the same. Pirates had always been a problem in Queen Sector, and as the War dragged on, they multiplied and grew so daring that they were operating openly on even the major starlanes. Undermanned and ill-equipped as they were, and with the whole ultrasystem to cover, the Stellar Patrol could do almost nothing to check them, and the Navy could spare neither soldiers nor warships to fight wolf packs, not while the Empire was pressing us on every side. Nearly every colony there would literally have been annihilated or starved out had it not been for the battle put up by the freighters servicing the area."

All three of her comrades nodded. The Federation's merchantmen had been compelled to become battlecraft in order to stay in space, but those of Queen Sector had won particular fame both because of the odds they had faced and the degree of success they had achieved. Not only had they continued operating, but by the great conflict's end, they had brought pirate activity down to very nearly its pre-War level. That was high enough, and they would probably have to continue their fight for many long years to come, although the Patrol was at last regaining the strength to give them some real aid.

"Albion of Scotia's the most centrally located as well as the most highly developed of the quadrant's colonies, and she has been the general capital of local spacer activity since that region first opened up. She's also basically industrial, with a large population for a rim world, the bulk of it working in lower-grade jobs, people as tough as the space hounds frequenting her port."

Islaen stopped. Her expression remained somber, but she glanced at the several high-backed, wooden chairs placed about the room. "Pull some of those closer," she told her comrades. "We'll probably be at this a while, and we might as well make ourselves comfortable."

When all were settled, the Commando-Colonel continued her briefing. "The planetary police have always had their hands full between the port visitors and their own citizens. About four years back, four almost to the day actually, a new Minister of Justice took office, one Lloyd George Thatcher, or L. George Thatcher, as he prefers to be called. He brought with him and quickly implemented the idea of supplementing the regular police with an auxiliary force to handle routine patrols, crowd control, traffic management, and the like, freeing the others to see after more serious matters."

"What of that?" Bethe asked. "A lot of planets have done the same thing, especially among the inner-systems."

"Aye," Islaen responded, "that they have, but with a number of significant differences—the caliber of those they took on to do the job, for one. None, and I mean not one, of the fine, high-achieving youths graduating from the schools and none of the soldiers returning home after demobilizing and in need of a job were accepted. The roughest thugs crawling the capital's lanes and hanging about the spaceport were recruited instead. At the same time, older, experienced police officers were eased out of the regular service and were either not replaced at all or else had their positions taken by candidates whose histories would bear little close scrutiny. In every instance, it was made very clear to the newcomer to the Justice Department Auxiliaries who was responsible for the appointment."

"His own private army," muttered Karmikel.

"Right on course, friend."

"This was permitted to go on?" her husband asked rather contemptuously. He still had little patience with the Federation's apparent willingness to bear with an obvious cancer until it had taken such root that it was difficult if not impossible to eradicate.

"He moved cautiously and kept his curs on a tight tractor, at least overtly."

Jake snorted. "I've never known rim folk to be utter fools. That kind don't survive long enough to establish a colony."

"The Auxies, as they quickly became known, were highly unpopular," she agreed, "and distrusted as well, though that remained gut feeling until recently, even after the accidents began." Her voice was deadly serious now, and cold as the depths of interstellar space. "A number of police officers, younger men not near retirement age and not the type to be bought or frightened into submission, died in mishaps of one sort or another, and so did some of the returned veterans—officers, chiefly—people who could lead a resistance or take charge in an emergency. Their kin usually went out with them."

"Son of a Scythian ape!" swore Karmikel. "None of it could be pinned on Thatcher, I take it?"

"Not a damned thing, and not a thing on any of his cohorts. He conducted his campaign with great subtlety. Thatcher never was liked, but it took a long time for real suspicion to rise, and even at that, it was an off-worlder who put it together, not any Albionan."

"If he was disliked, how'd he manage to get elected in the first place?" the demolitions expert asked curiously.

"He wasn't. On Albion, the governmental department heads get their places through competitive examination followed by heavy public interviewing in case of a tie or near tie. That last wasn't necessary in his case. There's no denying Thatcher's brain or his long-term determination. He legitimately placed well ahead of every other candidate, and there was a good many of them."

She frowned slightly. "L. George Thatcher is an interesting study, an almost classic example of major potential thoroughly warped.

"He comes from a very old and prominent Terran financial family. When he was three, his father was transferred to Albion to manage his firm's main branch in Queen Sector. Phillip Thatcher did extremely well both for his house and for himself personally, and his son grew up a wealthy young man.

"Comfortable or not, he must have had a lonely childhood and youth. His mother was killed in a flitter crash shortly after their arrival on Albion, and his father never seemed to forgive the planet for that. He never remarried or mingled with the locals apart from the association demanded by business, and his son was raised strictly in the company of the few other Terrans stationed there like themselves. He was educated via tapes from Terra and was sent to the mother world for his university work, at which he excelled."

"How did he manage socially?" Bethe asked.

"Surprisingly, he made out equally well. He had in truth been raised for that sort of life, and he fitted in. He liked Terra and the ways of the group in which he was moving—not wild, but very exclusive and sophisticated.

"Thatcher probably should have stayed, but in his final year he became involved with a woman, a fellow student, the only serious attachment he's known to have formed. Unfortunately, she was a particularly bad example of the old northern Terran aristocracy, and she let him know—publicly—in no uncertain terms that she had no intention of burying herself on any backwash colony planet with some banker, amply funded or otherwise. It was a cruel blow to his heart and to his ego alike."

"So he went home?"

"Aye, immediately following graduation, and probably regretted it almost at once, although he continued to work diligently for his father for the next eight years until the elder Thatcher's death.

"He promptly requested a transfer to a Terran branch of the firm, or at least to one in the inner-systems, but he was denied. There were no openings or projected vacancies on a level that would interest him. Besides, he was doing very well for the firm right where he was, and no one was particularly interested in shifting him.

"The following year, he took the exam for the Justice Department position. Once his appointment was secured, he showed his true character. Thatcher quit his position with the firm outright. That would be necessary for one assuming such responsibility, but he also completely severed contact with his family. He found his former staff other comparable jobs and promised them large annual stipends—he is independently wealthy, you recall—to leave their places and to refuse to give their erstwhile employers any information concerning what they had done while with the old company. A most suspicious fire in the office followed, which destroyed all the records kept there. There were backups of most stored off-site, of course, but none of his private files, and those contained a great deal of the most critical data. It proved a terrible blow to his replacement, and the firm hasn't fully recovered even now, especially since its representatives were kept reeling under a nearly constant barrage of legal questions and requirements."

"Nice man," Bethe Danlo remarked dryly. "Who finally figured out what he was about? You said it was an off-worlder."

"Our old friend Patrol-Commander Marta Florr. Her *Free Comet* was sent in to check out the local pirate activity. She took one look at the Auxies and decided it was the surplanetary situation that most required immediate Patrol attention. As you can imagine, once Commander Florr started ferreting around, all sorts of things began coming to light.

"Thatcher's very care in keeping so low a profile actually worked with her at the start. Since there were no serious suspicions against him, just dislike in plenty both for him and for his bullies, she had no trouble getting people to talk to her and her crew. They quickly realized the magnitude of the danger that was threatening Albion.

"Fortune seemed to reverse itself at that point. Just as no one was afraid to talk to her people, neither did the informants hesitate to mention that they had done so, and it wasn't long before Thatcher learned about the investigation."

"And he promptly guarded his fins?"

She nodded. "All too efficiently. If some of his lesser satellites hadn't gotten spooked and overreacted right into the Patrol's nets, he and his organization might have had to be left sit exactly as they were. One particularly vacuum-brained thug made an attempt on Florr's life that was thwarted before he had been able to draw his blaster, and that was followed by a potentially deadly try against a man who was a logical key witness. That one was well planned and nearly succeeded, but the hit men were taken in time. In both cases, the would-be killers proved true to type. The penalty for attempted assassination is the same as that for a successful strike according to Albionan as well as Federation law, and they tried to take every one of their associates that they could with them."

"Including the honorable Minister of Justice?" drawled Karmikel.

She shook her head. "Apart from an apparently obvious total lack of ability to judge character, nothing whatsoever could be discovered to connect L. George Thatcher personally with any of it. So much did come out about his Auxies, though, in the ensuing official investigation and the scandal accompanying it that the unit was disbanded and Thatcher himself was forced to resign."

The Noreenan woman grimaced. "With no evidence against him, the Patrol was powerless to hold him when he announced that he was going to quit the planet and people who had so doubted and insulted him. The best they could manage was to demand that the Patrol be kept informed of his whereabouts in case his help should be required during later phases of the investigation."

Both Sogan and the Commando-Sergeant swore at that, and Islaen signed. "I know, but the law's the law."

"He got away clean, then?" the Arcturian demanded in disgust.

"Aye, he and a number of his associates, all of them ostensibly in the clear like himself, in the sense that they got off Albion. He hasn't dropped out of sight, not yet."

Varn's fingers stroked Bandit, but his eyes were hot with anger and barely reined impatience. "So much for Albion's troubles," he said. "What do we have to connect him with the Alpha Gary arms?"

"That's the point, friend. All we have are some pretty solid suspicions."

"The brig? Her crew was Albionan."

"Aye, and that's her registry. The *Homeworld*'s a government ship—the best they have. She delivered mail and dispatches among her other duties, and Thatcher had her manned by his Auxies on her last voyage since she was carrying official documents." Her mouth tightened. "A ship-late report and a request for information about her had just been quite properly filed when everything hit the jets."

Jake Karmikel nodded. "He 'borrowed' her to transport the weapons, figuring once he got his claws on them, he wouldn't have to explain anything to anyone again?"

"That's the way Intelligence has it worked out. They believe he was just about ready to strike when the *Free Comet* arrived and he lost everything."

Sogan shook his head sharply. "They are off the charts on that last part of it," he said somberly. "Your L. George Thatcher is a man I can readily despise on many levels, but I do not read him as one who would be content with flight and saving no more than the skin on his bones, not with the way he managed his conspiracy throughout, the way he covered and preserved himself. I would put down every credit I have that he provided not only an escape route but the means of securing a comfortable future for himself should his plot fail."

"How, man?" Karmikel demanded irritably. "He lost the arms, his brig, and the bulk of his army on Amazoon."

"Not quite, Jake," Islaen Connor told him. "He'll have to forget planetary conquest and raids against major, well-defended colonies, right enough, but we very much fear he's a long voyage from being entirely helpless. For one thing, it's nearly certain the *Homeworld* took a lot more than those needed to handle her off Albion."

"Where . . ."

"Some were probably brought to his lair, and the rest to a hidden base somewhere off the starlanes." Her eyes swept over her companions. "There's reason to believe he's been purchasing or otherwise acquiring the use of ships—fighters, two-man mostly with maybe a couple a class larger. Estimates vary as to their number as well as their size, but he could have as many as thirty—"

"Thirty fighters!" the redhead exploded. "Spirit of Space! That's not a wolf pack. It's a bloody baby fleet!"

"Where could he get ahold of so many, Islaen?" the demolitions expert asked. "I don't care how rich he is, he couldn't collect and outfit that number of battlecraft in the span of a year or so, not without raising all sorts of uncomfortable questions. Besides, how in space could he man them?"

"Some, he siphoned off from the legitimate surplanetary forces. That wouldn't be as hard as it first seems, since he's the one who ultimately processes the reports of such losses and he had the whole Auxiliary Force to take care that not many were declared missing in the first place. You can be sure he conducted his diversion of matériel with the same restraint and care that marked the rest of his plotting. The remainder of the ships were probably acquired with the aid of some of his Auxies' less savory contacts.

"As for the hands, that was simple. Albion of Scotia's a spacer world. A full quarter of her citizens wind up in the starlanes at one time or another. He made a special effort to recruit as many as he could with good space skills, and you can put credits down that he didn't ask the kind of trade in which they learned them. There's also the likelihood that he hired outright pirates to round out his muster. He would have the contacts to reach some of those as well."

The Commando-Colonel flexed her shoulders. Her muscles felt tense and sore, as if she were supporting a heavy and unwieldy burden. "If any part of this is accurate, he does still have the power to cause a lot of trouble, and he must strike somewhere soon if he's to keep his hirelings satisfied so that they don't turn on him."

Bethe nodded slowly. "A quick raid against one of the lesser colonies, a lightly populated planet possessing some product easily transported in small ships, very salable, and worth the trouble."

"Precisely. Our job's to discover his target, when she'll be hit, and what he has to throw against her in time to thwart the attack. In the process, we hopefully get to take our payment for Amazoon out of his hide."

Her husband's dark eyes narrowed. "That is a job for Navy

Intelligence, not a Commando unit. They have been handling the investigation efficiently enough until now. Why is your Admiral Sithe sending us in at this stage?"

Islaen's head lowered. It was a moment before she replied. "Because L. George Thatcher's headquarters is on Noreen of Tara."

Bethe Danlo stared at her. "Have you blown every circuit in your skull?" she demanded. "Commandos are never sent to fight on their own worlds, and for some pretty sound reasons. It wasn't a pack of inner-system bleeding hearts who made that particular rule."

"Commandos are rarely sent to their native planets," she corrected. "It does happen when circumstances warrant the exception, as they do in this case. Our cover's just too good to be ignored on this one."

Jake's already-deep frown darkened still further. "Say what you mean, Colonel. I don't like games."

"It's no game," she said quietly. Too quietly. The assignment troubled her, and she could not completely conceal that unease. She was not really attempting to do so. "Almost immediately following the refusal of his request for a transfer to Terra, Thatcher rented an old house on a farm called Dunbrityne. It's an adjoining neighbor to Kinkora, my father's place. In fact, Father owns it as well."

"Son of— Islaen . . ."

She sighed. "I know, Jake. It could turn real nasty all around." Her head raised. "Your participation is strictly voluntary, the same as mine. If you want out, say so now."

"If you're in, I'm in!"

"Good. —Bethe?"

The spacer shrugged, although the disapproval in her expression did not clear. "Noreen's not my homeworld. I'll fight there. I just think it's damn poor planning to involve you two."

The Colonel braced herself for a battle and faced Sogan. To her surprise, instead of the open hostility to the plan which she anticipated, she found his inner mind tightly shielded and his face a mask. "Varn?"

"It is hardly necessary to ask, is it?" he responded coldly. "I am unequivocally opposed to this violation of your Navy's usual policy." *—We have to talk. Alone.*

This is a war council. Make your point here. All of us have a right to hear it.

No. Not this.

She frowned. *Very well. As soon as our friends leave us.*

She turned back to the others. "It'll be best if we start at once."

"Can we take both ships, or are we all going to be jammed on the *Maid* again?" Jake asked. He was still not happy about any of this, although neither was he going to withdraw from it and leave Islaen to carry his part as well as her own. Since he had yielded, he figured he might as well do it gracefully.

The Noreenan woman smiled faintly. "Do I detect a preference there?"

"Quite possibly."

"Use the *Jovian Moon* by all means. We can put her new steering system and the *Maid*'s to the test en route. I'd rather find any gremlins that way than wait for them to show up in the midst of a disagreement with some wolf pack."

Islaen Connor held her peace until their comrades had gone before turning to the Arcturian. *All right, Varn, let's hear your objections.*

They are valid, he replied stiffly, stung by her manner.

She softened. *I know. I probably share them. This proposal was made to me. I didn't originate it.*

She walked over to the table. Bandit was there, sitting quietly on the papers stacked by the guerrilla leader's place. Too quietly. The gurry was patently miserable.

She shot a quick look at her husband. She herself was not transmitting the kind of emotion to spark this, and there was no hard feeling between them to upset the Jadite. It had to be something in Sogan that was doing it, something he was keeping from her. Islaen could not read his closed thoughts, no more than he could read those she locked behind her shields, but those barriers did not exist for the gurry, a fact which would not have been any comfort to Varn Tarl Sogan should he ever become completely aware of it.

Islaen was troubled now. She had been prepared to face logical opposition and anger, but this seemed to be something different, and she had learned not to ignore such a reaction to a mission in him.

Varn? she asked softly. *What is it? Surely, you have to realize*

I believe there are powerful reasons for taking on the assignment.

He seemed to gather his courage, but as he did, his mind shut completely. "Are you doing this because of me?" he demanded abruptly, reverting to verbal speech as he nearly always did when he feared to reveal too much through more intimate contact. His mouth twisted. "What happened on Amazoon is done. I cannot erase my deeds there, only seek satisfaction after the manner of my kind for being pushed into such a situation. That is not worth what you might have to endure if we go on with this."

Islaen gripped her temper. She could not ream the man when it was worry for her that was driving him. "No. Ram Sithe is asking a lot, but he's right. We can't just throw away the cover chance has given us. We'll have open access to the whole region for any length of time that we need to be there."

"The cover and Sithe both be damned! It is what may happen to you that concerns me. —Get back to your commander and tell him you have reconsidered, that some other unit should be sent in."

"That doesn't sound like Admiral Varn Tarl Sogan."

"No? I think otherwise." Both his eyes and his voice were grim. "That any Arcturian world should ever be threatened with invasion was unthinkable to us, yet our Ruling Command planned against the eventuality. Under no circumstance was an officer from the involved planet or system to have part in either the defense or the fight to regain lost territory, and even the Yeomen were to be spared that trial as much as was feasible. Our Navy does not coddle its soldiers, but such conditions were considered unacceptably detrimental to efficiency in either the planning or the conducting of a battle. You Commandos might have performed the superhuman at times, but I seriously doubt that any of you, including Commando-Colonel Islaen Connor, are so beyond mortal limitations as to be exempt from that judgment."

"We aren't being sent to Noreen as a penetration team," she told him patiently. "We're to gather intelligence and make an arrest if our discoveries warrant it—not fight a war, at least not there."

"You are not a damn fool. Do not talk like one."

"Even if we do have to fight, as is likely I suppose, given the character of our targets, Dunbrityne house is six miles from Kinkora—"

His fist slammed down on the table. "Put that debris on freeze, Colonel! Name me one, just one, of the assignments we have shared together that has not involved a major battle or contained the threat of ultimate destruction for a large number of innocent people. Why should this one turn out any differently? If Ram Sithe thought this was going to be an easy slide, he would have sent someone else, and you know it!"

A new note entered his voice. "What if the worst does happen, my Islaen? Kinkora could become a battleground, with your people caught in the crossfire."

Her eyes wavered. "That . . ."

"Islaen, listen," he said desperately. "Please. I was responsible for the deaths of my closest kin. You do not forget that, not ever again in your life do you forget it. I-do not want that for you."

She looked up at him, taking great care to shield both thought and feeling. He loved her that much—enough not only to lay aside his desire, his need, for revenge but to open this wound to her.

"What if they're hurt, and I'm not there?" she countered in a voice so tight that she scarcely recognized it as her own. "What if my parents or the others are killed while I'm safe here on Thorne, having refused to so much as try to defend them because of my fear?" Her eyes closed. "I'm damned either way, Varn. I'd rather it happen if it must while I'm at risk myself and fighting for them—for them and for Thatcher's target planet."

She drew herself erect. "We are the best choice for this job. There's no real arguing around that. Apart from the excuse my connection with Kinkora gives us for coming to the region and remaining there, I know every inch of that countryside. I could just about conduct a war on it blindfolded if it came down to that."

"I admit all that. Logically, I would pick our unit as well, but think, Islaen. Think well before you answer me. If the worst comes to pass and a major contest is necessary, a battle involving Kinkora and its inhabitants, will you be able to order it and conduct it as it must be fought? Would Jake?"

She nodded slowly after several moments' silence. "Aye, Comrade. We might not enjoy it, but we'd pull our part. It's no more than the Thornen Resistance had to do and the populations of how many other planets your people overran. That was true in just about every war Terrans fought in pre-space and early space times, and it must have been the same with Arcturians as well. It's only since we reached ultrasystem size that either of our peoples gained the ability to avoid sending soldiers to fight on their homeworlds."

He sighed. "I am with you, Islaen. You know that. I am merely afraid for you."

The woman smiled. "What we love, we want to protect. That's a fairly basic need of our species."

His fingers reached up to touch and brush the side of her face. *We shall make that our business in this case, Islaen Connor,* he said in her mind, *to see that your Noreen does not have to suffer to save the colony L. George Thatcher has chosen for his victim.*

THREE

VARN TARL SOGAN'S eyes fixed on the *Fairest Maid*'s visual observation panels, gazing at the universe beyond the starship until he seemed to meld with it.

It was so fair, he thought, so exquisitely beautiful. Beautiful and more than beautiful. Those distant sparks of light and the black infinity between them held a peace for which every fiber of his being hungered.

His expression changed, darkened. During the black years between his disgrace and his meeting with Islaen Connor on Visnu of Brahmin, he had time and again longed only to set course for one of them or for the great void beyond them all. The temptation to do so had been powerful, and he would have yielded to it had it not been for the stubbornness and anger burning inside him—an narticulate fury over the cruelty with which he and his had been used. That, and a genuine acceptance of the apparent will of his mpire's savage gods, had combined to move him to refuse the ate he desired—the fate expected of one of his caste who had allen so irredeemably from his place.

He sighed as he felt something akin to that old ache stirring vithin him, the wish that he, that they all, might remain out here n the clean infinity of the starlanes, free from the filth and the orror and the brutal responsibility of the work to which he had iven his oath.

The Arcturian forced that thought out of his mind. It was nworthy in itself, and this was not the time to be indulging imself. Islaen had been strong for him since their first encounter, ut now it was his turn. She would need his support in the days head, whatever eventually came to pass on Noreen of Tara, and that he was determined she would have—that and all the help it lay within his power to give.

Reluctantly, he switched his attention from the distant stars to one that loomed large enough in the *Maid*'s screens to require filtering for direct observation. It had been a peaceful, idyllic voyage, a pleasure in itself and in the performance of his starship during the stringent tests through which he had put her, but now he must set that satisfaction behind him. They were rapidly approaching their destination and would soon have to take up the work they had been sent to perform.

His mind sought out and found his consort's. *Islaen, we are entering Tara's system.*

We'll be right up!

True to her word, the Commando-Colonel swung off the core ladder moments later and darted onto the bridge. An excited-looking Bandit was riding her shoulder.

Islaen's eyes did not leave the observation panels as she dropped into the copilot's seat. Even in the minute span of time it had taken her to reach the bridge, Tara and her clutch of four planets had come to dominate the whole field of vision.

The sun-star herself was magnificent—a glorious yellow, large and bright for her class.

The first of her planets, Leanbh, was a dwarf orbiting Tara so closely that the little metal on her surface was molten. Beside her at about ninety-five million miles was Noreen, their target, and her nearest sister, the ice world Deirdre, glittering like an immense diamond in her near space. Farthest out lay Fion, a gas giant with a crushing gravity and a frozen atmosphere comprised of congealed gases inimical to human life. A distance that might comfortably have supported two planets the size of the tiny Leanbh separated her from the rest.

Satellites were comfortably plentiful in the system. The inner world had none, but Noreen and Deirdre each boasted of one the size of Terra's famous Luna, and Fion was escorted by fourteen, most of them quite small.

His attention narrowed on their destination. By any standards Noreen of Tara presented a fine view from space. The cloud cover was considerably heavier than that marbling either Thorne or Terra, as was only to be expected considering the planet's really abominable weather. —He had seen the sun only once during the visit he and Islaen had made following their marriage and their battle for Astarte's life against that pirate armada. He smiled briefly to himself. He had no complaints about Noreen's climate. He was not forced to live long-term with it, and it was responsible for the exquisite if rather sun-sensitive complexion that he so loved on Islaen Connor.

As for the world beneath that veil of clouds, Noreen was blue-green rather than the pure blue of Thorne. Like most Terra-normal planets, a large portion of her surface was under water, but her seas were shallower and less extensive than those of many other planets, and her continents' contribution to her near-space image was proportionally greater.

Bandit whistled her approval. *Pretty!*

Varn Tarl Sogan sighed to himself. Noreen was pretty, particularly among the softly rolling, high hills of Islaen's home region, but she lacked the grandeur, the wild glory, of many other worlds, and large stretches of her surface were dead flat, with little visual appeal or interest at all.

His head lowered. It was the thought of associating for a relatively long stretch of time with her people, not her tame appearance, that was bothering him.

The fault was his. The Noreenans were a fine race, and he had liked most of those he had met, but he was uncomfortable among them. Being who and what he was, that was well nigh inevitable. A war prince simply had little place on a planet of farmers.

The gurry looked up at him, and he hastily altered the direction of his thoughts. The little Jadite was incredibly sensitive to the moods of her humans and rarely kept silent when he would have preferred that she do so. He did not want to cast any shadow over this part of Islaen's homecoming.

His expression softened as he turned to watch his consort. She was sitting slightly forward, her face alive with the excitement and eagerness radiating from her. Her attention was locked on the scene beyond the panels, as if she were seeking a glimpse of details still rendered invisible by distance.

Sadness, and also guilt, welled up in him. She wanted this visit so badly, the Arcturian thought. He should have realized before that she was longing to see her kin and her birth world again and brought her here instead of actively postponing the journey until they were forced to make it by the circumstances currently driving them.

This was not his first error in his relationship with the

Commando leader. Sometimes, it seemed to him that for every time he read her needs accurately, he failed utterly on a dozen other occasions. How she continued to bear with him, she who never ceased to give . . .

Islaen's happy, Varn!

"Aye, small one," he agreed quickly to forestall anything more Bandit might say to his shame. "You should be pleased yourself. Once her family meets you, they will have you so spoiled and well-fed that you will have to inhale to fit through the the *Maid*'s hatch."

Nooo! Bandit's always careful!

Islaen smoothed down the gurry's ruffled feathers. *Varn! Stop teasing her!—You're turning into a regular demon, Admiral Sogan.*

Sorry, Colonel, he said with a smile. *Perhaps you would prefer that I resume my old ways?*

Not on your life, friend! It's taken a lot of time and effort to loosen you up this much.

Nooo! Bandit agreed in real distress. *Varn can't go back! Happier now!*

"I suppose I am," the man said, with no good humor.

His commander laughed. *You asked for that one, Admiral. Besides, you should have known better than to give her an opening like that if you didn't want the subject at hand broadcast to the universe at large.*

Bandit didn't mean . . .

"You did no harm, love. I'm just jinking Varn for jinking you."

She fell silent again and watched the ever-nearing planet for a few moments, then she turned back to him. *Varn?*

The war prince was surprised by her tone, and more so by the worry he saw and felt in her. *Aye?*

You . . . She took a deep breath. *You don't have any bad feeling about this one, do you?*

No!

Sogan gripped himself. Islaen more than half believed that he could sense exceptional danger or trouble in an upcoming mission, an ability he was most unwilling to own. His mutation itself was hard enough to accept for one of a race that totally condemned all major alteration from their own prototype without adding the exotic element of foreseeing the future to it, however dimly. That gave him no right to snarl at her, particularly since it was nothing less than her duty to question him. Islaen Connor commanded their unit and had to draw upon every potential source of information that might reflect upon their activities.

Duty? Could he think of nothing else? Noreen of Tara was her birthplace and the home of those dearest to her in all the universe. She had to be concerned about what might come.

My objections are those we discussed, he told her, *but I have no particular fear about going there.* Varn frowned. *What made you think it might be otherwise?*

Your mind had been shut so often during the voyage, and it was closed now. I was afraid of what you were keeping from me.

His own guilt and uncertainty . . . *I was only doing some thinking.* He made himself smile. *It is not always easy to find the privacy for that when one's companions can pick the thoughts from his outer mind before they are half-formed.*

You are all right? the Colonel asked sharply. She knew full well the kind of mental activity that Varn Tarl Sogan usually tried to keep concealed.

Aye. The former Admiral's tone hardened. *What happened on Amazoon is not troubling me now. I want this L. George Thatcher, right enough, if he is the one who grabbed those arms, but that is the extent of it.* He shook his head, dismissing the doubt he felt begin to rise in her. *We are on a mission. I will not permit my attention to be diverted from that.*

His reassurance was not very far from the truth, and he was relieved to see that it seemed to satisfy her.

Sogan settled back in his flight chair. *Strap in, both of you,* he ordered. *As soon as we get planeting permission, I am going to set her down.*

FOUR

VARN TARL SOGAN watched while Jake Karmikel brought his *Jovian Moon* into the center of her bay with a precision that would have wrung praise from the toughest technical drill Sergeant in his old fleet.

He activated his transceiver as soon as the other starships's engines quieted. "Nice job, Captain—Are you two about ready to disembark?"

"Completely ready. I suppose you have the flier loaded and prepared for us?"

"Everything's aboard except our packs and our persons," Islaen interjected. "I saw to that before coming to the bridge. We'll meet you outside and start for Kinkora at once."

The Colonel waited by the Commando flier that was their preferred method of surplanetary transport while her husband set the final guards on his ship.

Once, she had been almost embarrassed by his precautions, but she had not been in his company for long before realizing that, far from displaying a mild paranoia, he was merely practicing a very sensible survival discipline in a universe all too unfriendly to one like him. Indeed, Jake had promptly adopted a great many of those same safeguards for his *Moon* as soon as he had seen them.

Sogan joined her, and a couple of moments later, Bethe and Karmikel emerged from their vessel, their packs swinging on their arms.

The team took their usual places—Varn, Islaen, and Bandit in the front, the others in the rear. The Arcturian claimed the controls as he nearly always did, a right he had gained in acknowledgment by his comrades of the skill he had acquired in managing the vehicle.

All four humans would have their turn driving on this journey. It would be a good six hours and probably longer before they reached Kinkora, even flying at high planetary speed and with the winds continuing to favor them. Fortunately, it was early enough in the day that they would still have a couple of hours of reasonable light left when they reached their destination. Islaen would not want to wait until morning for at least a brief look around her old home.

Everything seemed to be working with them, Sogan thought. The weather was glorious. The air was brisk enough to be invigorating but still warm enough that he felt no need of his jacket. The sky was a vivid blue dotted with high, white clouds, and all the world was awash with Tara's light. They had enjoyed nothing like this during his previous visit.

He drew in a deep lungful of air and held it, savoring the perfume it carried. Once they had left the immediate environs of the spaceport, they were in the midst of Noreen's farmland, and the harvest of the golden-stemmed, purple-crowned grain that was this part of the planet's chief crop at this time of year was in full swing. The wonderful, heady scent of it was everywhere.

He stole a glance at Islaen and wished that he might see her face. She looked like a little girl, grasping the side of the vehicle with her two hands as she peered eagerly at the passing countryside. He would have liked to share her excitement but held his peace, fearing to embarrass her and kill the mood entirely.

Was Jake equally moved? he wondered, although he resisted the impulse to turn around to study his fellow Captain. He had to be, he supposed. Noreen was the redhead's home as well, and he also had family living here. Sogan sighed to himself. The Spirit of Space knew, he would feel that way if by some miracle his old place and rights were restored to him and he could once more return to the planet of his birth, and he had no immediate blood kin left to draw and hold him.

He sighed again, then turned his thoughts to the planet Noreen herself and to the race and society she supported.

Their first ship charter had declared Noreen of Tara to be a low-tech, low-populace, low-impact agrarian colony, and that philosophy and the laws and customs supporting and stemming from it had been unanimously ratified when the planet attained full member status in the Federation the usual ten generations later. It had not changed significantly in spirit in all the centuries which followed, and there had been many. Noreen was an old world for this part of the ultrasystem. Her farms were run by labor-intensive methods, with transports being used for the heaviest chores only because the people believed it wrong and potentially cruel to force such service from beasts. Despite that, and their aversion to most synthetic ground additives and air sprays, crop yields were high, and the planet's farms met her own basic food needs with plenty left over for export.

Noreenan grains lent themselves well to nearly all the uses to which Terrans and their offshoots put such products and were in steady demand throughout the ultrasystem. Terra herself and Albion were but two of the planets heavily dependent upon them.

Other field produce enjoyed a good export market as well, but it was for her angora cattle that the blue-green world was really known. The big creatures' silky, long coats were combed out each week, and the gathered hair was sorted by color and quality, bagged, and delivered to one of several regional processing centers where it was cleaned and either spun into thread or woven into cloth for home use or export, or exported raw. Their dairy products were used only locally, on the farms owning the animals, a lack of market that surprised the former Admiral, although he knew such goods were plentiful throughout the Federation. He had found Noreen's dairy products rich and of a fine flavor.

The planet was somewhat metal poor, and there was little mining, barely enough to meet her people's limited needs. Mechanized industry was not encouraged. Little existed apart from that connected with the angora hair, and none of it was on a large scale.

The populace did not suffer because of the lack of industrial occupations. Noreen was not a wealthy planet, but she was a very comfortable one, with a trade balance that was the envy of most of her sisters. Apart from the ubiquitous jakek, whose seed plants did not grow well on-world, just about everything basic to the life of an average Federation citizen was made and sold locally. Only luxury-class items had to be imported.

The spaceport handling those goods was very well maintained and equipped with the most current instrumentation available to a civilian installation. The superbly trained staff manning it were all on-worlders.

It was a small port for all its quality, both the planeting field itself and the support facilities surrounding it. Relatively few starships visited the quiet, agrarian world—chiefly small freighters holding the charters to carry the planet's animal and vegetable produce, which also brought in imports and passengers. The surplanetary police, the Garda, owned two five-man fighters, which they used to run down the occasional smugglers trying to slip in a cargo of untaxed opaline. They also handled rescue work; vessels running into difficulty in the surrounding starlanes made for Noreen, the closest inhabited planet, and often required assistance. A Stellar Patrol ship called irregularly, but Noreen and the space around her were quiet and received little attention from the harried interstellar service.

Almost the only other visitors using the port regularly were freighters from Kimberly, Hope, and Motherload. Noreen lay approximately in the center of a triangle formed by the three mining planets, and they sent their rough gemstones for storage in the vaults constructed to hold them adjoining the planeting field, where they were kept for the Hedonite merchants who came several times a year to take delivery of them. The pickups occurred frequently enough that the stockpile never became sufficiently large to tempt raiders, or so valuable that the insurance firms or Noreen herself would be beggared making restitution should surplanetary thieves succeed in getting through the stringent guards protecting the stones.

The spaceport and the off-worlders utilizing it played little part in the daily existence of most of the population, save for those actually employed there. Though well able to turn their hands to just about any task, high-tech or low, Noreen's people preferred to continue with the quietly fulfilling lifestyle bequeathed to them by their ancestors.

Hard labor was an inescapable part of it. Noreenans did not enjoy work more than did any other people, but they believed it to be best for the individual and the race in the long run, as seemed to be borne out by their physical and cultural vitality.

The excellent surplanetary communications system was supportive of and probably essential to that last. It would have been hard to maintain the level of general spiritual development and excellence they attained without it. Farmhouses were widely spaced, and there were no massed urban centers. There was no need for them. The population was tightly controlled, with no excess over the established ideal limit being permitted. Anyone reaching adulthood and completing his or her education who did not have a farm or other place either by inheritance or through marriage, or an active position in one of the service professions, was compelled to emigrate off-world. Families like Islaen's with three offspring had been fairly common during the decades of the War when it was necessary to replace those lost in the fighting, but that would no longer be the case. Noreen's people had a horror of bringing children into being who would be doomed to almost inevitable exile once they were grown.

The hours passed by, not unpleasantly, but all the Commandos were weary of their cramped positions and of the traveling itself. Even Bandit had quit sight-seeing and had gone to sleep on the Colonel's lap.

Varn flexed his shoulders, trying to ease his back without calling attention to himself. The scar tissue pulled when he was tired like this or when the weather was cold or damp, sometimes more sharply than he cared to admit to Islaen. The Navy physicians on Horus had done all they could for him, but he had received treatment too late for anything like complete healing to be possible, either physically or cosmetically. There was no point in worrying her with these minor residual twinges. He simply had to live with them.

He gave a mental shrug. It was not even worth his own consideration. If he suffered no worse than this in the course of the mission, he would have reason indeed to be grateful to Noreen's numerous, generally friendly gods.

The journey would soon be over. That in itself would be a relief. He had just reclaimed the controls from Bethe Danlo. Only a few miles remained, but he had wanted the others to be free to disembark as soon as the flier came to a stop. Islaen, of course, would scarcely wait for that, and Jake, an old and familiar visitor at Kinkora would delay little longer. Neither would Bethe. She was a total stranger, but her husband would want to pull her forward and introduce her. He was not precisely an outsider himself, but he was the best fitted at the moment to postpone the exchange of greetings long enough to at least secure the brake on their vehicle.

There was a small gasp of delight, half-mental, half-verbal, from Islaen, and the war prince smiled. They were in the final stretch now. She knew and loved every inch of the area over which they were flying, and his own sense of happiness rose with her joy.

They crested yet another hill, one taller than most. There, on the rise following it, stood a large two-story house fashioned out of fine-grained, blue-gray stone. Blue-painted shutters stood on either side of the comfortably large windows, and a structure like the battlement of a pre-explosive castle followed the line of the roof.

He eyed it thoughtfully. Kinkora was very old, he knew. *Was there some sort of surplanetary war here once?* he inquired curiously. He had never heard either of his Noreenan comrades mention anything of the sort, and the Britynon threat had arisen and been thwarted too quickly for such defenses to have been put into effect. He had seen similar structures on the other houses they had passed en route here, so he knew it to be a general practice and not just the whim of this single family or locality.

No. Noreen was settled peacefully. Her gaze followed him. *The battlement? Didn't you notice it when we came here before?*

Aye.

The woman laughed. *You just weren't asking questions then?*

Not too many unnecessary ones, he admitted.

It's there because of the banshee. She had told him about Noreen's fierce windstorms that struck almost without warning out of the north a number of times in the year on his last visit, and she saw him nod now in recollection. *We watch from up there before it gets going full force, to be sure everyone makes it home and the animals are bedding down all right, without being blown halfway around the planet.*

She did not elaborate further. The flier had been spotted, and people were coming out of the house to stand on the neat lawn in front of it.

Sogan brought the vehicle down beside them, moving carefully so that the air jets would not strike anyone with excessive force. They were more than strong enough to knock one of the two children in the gathering.

As he had anticipated, he had not completely cut the engine before his consort leaped from the machine into the arms of the young man who ran forward to meet her.

Will Connor, the younger of Islaen's brothers, was as tall as the Arcturian and of a similar light build. He had his sister's brown eyes, but there was considerably more red in the auburn of his hair. He had the striking good looks that characterized all his family.

Beside him, watching his exuberant performance before joining in themselves, were his pretty wife Jeanie and their children, a boy of about six and a girl a year or so younger.

Islaen's parents waited until the others were done before coming forward. Theirs was a quieter, more reserved welcome, but there was great tenderness in it, and Varn lowered his eyes. He felt as if he were intruding upon a personal and private moment.

Sinéad Murchu was an attractive woman bearing a strong general resemblance to her daughter, although the two were not images of one another. Her hair was tawny blond and her eyes a deep, startling black. They were large like Islaen's, with a steady, perceptive expression, and revealed more than any other feature the strength that was within her which she could draw upon when life demanded it. She was short for one of her race, though still a good three inches taller than Bethe Danlo, and her body was thicker than those of the younger women—a mark of her life and the work she did rather than a sign of self-indulgence.

Paud Connor was close to an inch taller than Will and had the same wiry build. His shoulders were slightly rounded, but his head was carried high, even as was Islaen's. His kinship to the Commando-Colonel was evident in his features as well, although, of course, they lacked the feminine delicacy of hers. His eyes were proportionally smaller and closer set, but they, too, were brown; his hair was the same rich auburn, blurred at the temples by a shadowing of gray. Most older Noreenan men chose to permit that as a mark of distinction. Since science had defeated senescence, it was no longer a sign of decay.

There was none of that in either of these people. Both could have been taken as being of one generation with their offspring or near enough to it. Sogan recalled his surprise at that on their first meeting. His consort had described them as being on in years and in need of help on their place, but she had been alluding to Noreenan custom rather than actual physical state. On this world, a couple worked hard to raise their young, but they were then entitled to the aid and labor of their heir and of his or her spouse in the running of their large, heavily stocked farm, holding that as only just. The younger couple had their own house, known as the heir house, on the land and would eventually inherit the whole. It was right by their way of thought that it should be earned.

The war prince felt a movement beside him and glanced down. Bandit looked up at him inquisitively. *Why do you not join Islaen, small one?* he asked her, surprised to still find her here. She had been eager to meet the on-worlders, especially after his half-jesting buildup. *Go on. Islaen wants to introduce you to everyone. She has been telling them about you in every letter and transmission she sends.*

Varn doesn't need Bandit?

He touched her lightly with the tips of his fingers. It had become almost a duty for the gurry to act as a buffer for him when he ventured among strangers. Not only did the goodwill she projected deflect or at least soften any suspicion aroused by his appearance, but her very presence seemed to declare ridiculous the idea that he might be an Arcturian. None of his kind had ever been known to concern themselves with animals of any sort, much less involve themselves with a minute, odd-looking little being like this.

The man let his appreciation pour into her. His own sense of dignity was no less overbearing than that of any other member of his caste and former rank, and he still could not understand in the rare moments when he considered the matter how he had come to forget himself so much as to allow himself to fall under the gurry's spell.

He smiled. No matter. It had been a glad day for him when he had, and if that indicated some sort of weakness or folly in him, he should rather welcome more of the same than shun it.

Once more, he touched her. *Go, Little Bandit. I have met these people before. They are no danger to me.*

The gurry needed no further encouragement. She streaked from the flier and settled on Islaen's shoulder, purring loudly and looking very pleased with herself.

"Well, there you are!" the Commando said, chiding her comrade as if she were indeed talking to a pet. Even with these loved and closely related people, she was determined to preserve the secret of the Jadite's intelligence. "I was wondering what was keeping you!"

The on-worlders gathered around her curiously. "So this is the little creature you're always describing!" Will exclaimed in delight. "She's ever better than you said, Islaen."

He fished around in his overall pocket and came up with a gold-covered square. Under the wrapping, which he proceeded to remove, was a dark brown substance. Bandit's ear-piercing whistle of pure rapture identified it for her companions. "Look at her go at it! I don't even have to break it up for her!"

"Space!" his sister moaned. "Varnt was right. She'll be as big as an aged steer before we get her off-world again." "Varnt Sogan" was what the war prince's rescuers on Dorita had thought he said when the semiconscious man had mumbled his name in response to their questions, fortunately in Basic, the language in which he had been addressed. Transparent as the alias was to anyone suspecting his true identity, he had feared to try to alter it at that point, and so had been forced to adopt the name.

Will looked guilty. "You did say she liked chocolate," he explained defensively. "I wanted her to feel welcome, too."

Sogan laughed softly at the three of them. He felt the others' eyes on him then and quickly came out of the flier. He went first to the elder Connor, extending his hand in the Terran fashion. The gesture was totally alien to his race, but he had grown enough accustomed to it since his arrival in the Federation that it came almost naturally to him now. "It is good to see you again, Mr. Connor."

The other gave him a quick, sharp look, then nodded almost imperceptibly in approval. His daughter's husband had spoken in flawless if oddly accented Noreenan. "A hundred thousand welcomes to you, Captain," he responded in the formal greeting of his planet. Something about this dark-eyed Commando made it seem more natural to address him by his rank than by his given name. Paud was not alone in that feeling. It was the same with the rest of the surplanetary family and with those neighbors who had met him. This Varnt Sogan of Islaen's was a fine man, right enough, easy to respect and likeable in his own way—he had certainly won everyone's favor and approval during the pair's brief stay following their marriage—but there was that about him which did not encourage familiarity.

The farmer sighed. Jake Karmikel was a different sort entirely, one of their own kind, and he had always hoped . . .

He pushed that out of his mind. His daughter had made her choice. As long as the man was good to and for her, he had no call to complain. Islaen probably would not have come home in any event, no matter whom she married. She had gotten a taste of the stars, and no planet could hold her now, not even the merchant world, Thorne of Brandine, though she seemed to come closest to calling it her home.

Sogan had finished his greetings by then. Paud glanced in the direction of the house. "We held up the final dinner preparations since we didn't know exactly when ye would be arriving," he said in Noreenan. Bethe Danlo spoke it as well, albeit less perfectly than his son-in-law, and he decided it would be more comfortable to revert to that language. They did not use Basic often here, and it was an effort to converse for any length of time or in any depth in it. "It'll take a little while to finish up, and I know my daughter would like to see at least the current crop of calves." He chuckled. The brightening of her expression was answer enough to any doubts he might have had with respect to that.

"Go ahead," Sinéad told them, "but remember that those calves have had their supper. We haven't."

Her black eyes turned to Sogan. "Captain, I leave it up to you to get them back here within thirty minutes. Islaen's likely to forget all about things like food and time when she's in a pasture full of young animals, and her father will go right on and indulge her."

"I shall do my best," he promised, "but she can be stubborn, as you probably well know."

Jake laughed. "You may be putting your charge in the wrong hands if you're concerned about indulgence. Varnt would let us all fade away into oblivion rather than see Islaen Connor's pleasure curtailed."

Bethe gave him a rabbit punch to the side sharp enough to make him gasp, but Varn only smiled. "I will remember that one, Captain Karmikel," he promised.

Islaen just tossed her head, ignoring them all, and started for the calf field, whose location she knew full well.

Her mind touched her husband's in the next moment. *You really don't have to come, Varn. You're tired, and I know you're not particularly interested in livestock.*

I have had a commission laid on me, Colonel, and I am hungry enough to be diligent in fulfilling it.

The guerrilla leader glanced back at their vehicle. *Join us later, then. I'd like to get the flier stored someplace safe first. It's too much of a temptation with the children around, and some of the adults for that matter. My folk won't bother it, but with us here, more than my family may be coming around Kinkora to see us.*

She switched to verbal speech. "Varnt should bring the flier up to the roof if you don't mind, Father. It's a Commando vehicle, and we're required to travel with our gear."

"It's no toy for curious little hands," Paud agreed quietly. "Put it by the door, Captain. There's good shelter there at any time, and it should fit fine if we get a surprise call from the banshee and have to close off the vestibule. You'll have no trouble coming down again," he added. "The door's not locked."

Sogan nodded and returned to the little machine, bringing it quickly to the designated place on the roof. He was not long in securing it and in mounting the powerful laser they had brought with them. His hand slid over the weapon in a kind of caress. It was artillery class, and if they had had its like on Amazoon of Indra, maybe they could have prevented the escape of those accursed arms without . . .

The Arcturian put that out of his mind and turned his attention to studying the roof area, a flat expanse of closely laid stone covered with a rough-textured sealant. The whole was obviously carefully tended, a necessity on a planet as wet as Noreen of Tara if the damp was to be kept out of the building.

It was equally apparent that the battlement, striking as it was, served a real and serious purpose. Like the walls of the house itself, it was fully three feet thick, carefully constructed throughout and well-buttressed to withstand great pressure and violent hammering. It was also effective. Not a breath could be felt of the strong breeze blowing over the world beyond.

The entrance, too, was well-defended. The door he would be using, that giving access to the small landing inside and the stairs leading down through the Connor dwelling, was of average size and strength, but a large stone-roofed porch extended out from it. This was open at the moment, but a metal wall could be pulled down from the roof, completely enclosing the structure. This was pierced by a door, one which Islaen had once told him could readily admit the flier if opened to its full extent, even under conditions preventing precision maneuvering. Anyone caught outside a little too long in the face of the banshee's approach required the insurance offered by as large an escape hole as possible.

His dark eyes grew somber. It was difficult for a spacer like himself to appreciate the need for such precautions. He understood the power of water and fire, but to him, wind was merely the movement of air. He could not, at gut level, attribute to it the same potential threat present in so many other surplanetary natural phenomena, apart from the hazard it could occasionally represent for flying machines and small-class starships trying to planet or lift. Still, he realized that the danger must be there. Noreen's people were not alarmists, and they had plenty to do in the normal course of their lives without taking additional heavy labor on themselves. If they felt these safeguards to be necessary, he could not doubt the reality of the peril sparking them.

He turned away with a mental shrug, dismissing the matter. This, at least, was not likely to become a problem for his unit.

The off-worlder went down through the house. He had spotted the others from the roof and was not long in locating them at ground level.

The female cattle and their current year's offspring, all but the very youngest, were gathered in the huge field behind the house awaiting the currying session scheduled to begin the following morning. Not even an active harvest interfered with or delayed that task. The steers, and finally the bulls, would be brought in for combing when these first had been released again.

Islaen Connor was sitting on the topmost of the three large rails of the fence confining them. She was studying the cattle intently, with the practiced eye of one born among those who raised the creatures. "A fine herd," she declared in admiration. "Your breeding program's bearing out well."

"Aye," Paud replied with satisfaction. "It took time, but we're finally getting the results we want. We're not hurting confirmation or general condition for those coats, either."

"I can see that."

"Which of them do you think's the best?"

"That little black, of course. —You'll be keeping him entire?"

The farmer sighed. "That I don't know. He's good, all right, but there's not a big market for black hair. I don't want to strengthen that gene in the herd. I'll wait and see how he comes on. If he continues to develop like this, I'll given him a crack at the cows, for a year or so anyway."

Varn's attention drifted away from the two Connors. Jake was a few feet to his right, standing with Bethe and Will. He, too, appreciated the quality of the herd and was explaining the characteristics marking their excellence to the spacer.

He himself did not join either conversation. The cattle were fine in their way, and the calves had the appeal of most young things, but Islaen was right in saying that they aroused little interest in him.

Varn paused in his thought. He realized suddenly that a good part of the reason for that lack of enthusiasm was the minimal degree of communication he was able to establish with them. These were mammals, basically high-level with the intelligence for a broad scope of individual personality development, yet he had attained a closer bond of understanding and a greater power of influence with reptiles and even insects on some other planets. Testing the strength and possibilities of that interaction had become one of the challenges and the pleasures of visiting new worlds for him, discovering the differences and similarities each planet had imparted to the creatures she had nurtured. It was unfortunate that he could establish so little meaningful contact with those of Noreen.

If he could not receive thought or transmit his will to the cattle, he could receive general feelings from them, and that quite strongly. It was pleasant to do so. Cows and calves alike were contented and at peace. Their stomachs were full, and they were growing drowsy as the day drew to its close.

The Arcturian straightened. The former was true of most, but one was in pain. It was more than discomfort or soreness, and he strove to hold the transmission and center upon its source.

Islaen, he called sharply. *One of these animals is injured.*

Her head snapped in his direction. *Which one?*

I do not know yet.

The colonel excused herself and left her father to join him. *Any luck?*

No.—Aye, I believe so. That cream one with the lighter patch on her shoulder.

It was a heifer, last year's calf. Islaen thought she moved a little stiffly, but could not be certain. She tried to use her mind to examine the animal, but her ability to diagnose injury and some illnesses did not extend beyond her own species and those of a similar mental level. She linked with Varn, thereby accessing his talent, but that aspect of her gift was too specific in its nature, and the attempt proved as futile as her initial effort had been.

"Father," she called. "Varnt thinks there may be something wrong with the cream heifer. He could be right."

More to humor his guest than from any feeling of alarm, the farmer climbed over the fence with the ease of a lifetime's practice and approached the animal. His son and Jake went in with him to help him isolate and hold her.

Paud Connor's strong, knowledgeable fingers ran over the heifer's head and down her back, then under the long, dense hair of her sides. Suddenly, she bellowed and sidestepped to get away from him.

He looked up. "You've got a good eye, Captain. We owe you.—All right, lads, let's drive her into a crusher where I can get a proper look at her."

A half dozen very narrow, high-walled rectangular enclosures fashioned of well-spaced metal bars stood in a row just inside the fence where they were gathered. The Noreenan men urged the injured animal into the pen nearest the fence and closed its gate behind her. With her thus confined, Paud could examine her thoroughly.

He drew the hair away from the sensitive place and swore bitterly. "Look at this bruise! That third rib has to be cracked."

"How . . ." began Karmikel.

"Those maggot's spawn over in Dunbrityne, may the banshee sweep them!" Such fury radiated from him that Islaen winced mentally under its lash. "Some of them probably got drunk and tried to ride or throw her—our lads do that with the steers at times," he explained for the benefit of Varn and Bethe. "They're a good third bigger, and they have the temperament to match that sort of sport. These females are different. They're ladies clean through. There's nothing rough in them." He swore again. "She's all right with Will and me, but see how she shakes when Jake and the Captain come near her—a mild, gentle, trusting animal that never knew any abuse before this!"

Varn Tarl Sogan's hands balled by his sides. Anger was hot in him as well, that and worry. Islaen's mind was momentarily unguarded, and if she was this upset over violence done to a cow, what would it be for her if any of her kin . . .

He quelled both emotions. Neither would serve any good purpose. *Bandit, help me,* he commanded the nearly forgotten gurry. *I cannot reach the poor thing well enough to reassure her.*

The Jadite's mind, the soothing force she transmitted, touched and joined with his sending. Immediately, the beast relaxed perceptibly. The channel between them was still imperfect, but it was sufficiently clear for him to give comfort to her, to let her experience for herself that all strangers were not the evil, hurting beings she had encountered on Dunbrityne land. The pathetic trembling stopped, and her long tongue reached out to lick the back of his hand.

"She appears to be calming down," he observed. "Are there any other injuries?"

"More bruises. Nothing major," the farmer answered after completing his examination. "The legs are all right, praise our gods. That's why she wasn't limping."

Thanks, Varn, Islaen whispered. "Keep her here. We've got a portable renewer in our gear that'll fix her up fast."

The ray was one of medicine's greatest discoveries, providing almost instantaneous, complete regeneration of damaged or destroyed skin, muscles, blood vessels, even nerves and bone. Only the organs of the chest and abdominal cavities could not be so repaired, requiring treatment with the much newer and far more complex regrowth equipment.

At the War's beginning, only a few of the great experimental hospitals could support the then-massive renewer systems, but development had progressed quickly until they became standard equipment on every major battleship, and then on the medium and many of the smaller-class vessels as well. Now Federation scientists had produced a model compact and light enough to be used by individuals or small, mobile parties such as her unit, which was one of the first teams chosen to benefit from and test it in the field. It had saved their lives and permitted them to continue as an effective unit on more than one mission already and would handle a relatively minor injury like this in a matter of minutes.

"A renewer that small?" Paud exclaimed. "Fetch it, Daughter! She's suffered too long now."

"I know," Islaen Connor replied grimly, whirling and running for the farmhouse even as she spoke. Aye, she thought, she would bring healing now. Later, she would as certainly bring vengeance.

FIVE

THE CHAMBER RESERVED for dining in the Connor household was large enough to be comfortable even with extension tables expanding the main board at either end to better accommodate the family and their guests.

The furniture was made of one of the dark Noreenan woods, fine-grained and readily taking a high polish. It gleamed beneath the white, lacy covering laid over it.

Sinéad seated herself after setting out the last of the foods she had prepared for the main meal. "Tam will be here tomorrow," she apologized. "One of his patients went into labor early, and he figures it'll be all hours before she finishes delivering."

"The perils of a physician's life!" Islaen said sympathetically.

"What about the heifer?" the older woman inquired. "Will she be all right?"

"Oh, aye. The renewer took care of her."

"Do you think any of the others are hurt as well?"

"There may be some more bruises," Paud replied. "We won't know for sure until we examine them tomorrow, but there doesn't look to be any problems."

Bethe Danlo nodded to herself as she listened to them. It was the cattle themselves that concerned these people, not just valuable property that happened to be alive. No wonder Islaen was like she was, coming from this household.

"It can't be allowed to happen again," Sinéad declared flatly.

"It won't," her husband affirmed with equal certainty. "They're off-worlders, and I've got the standard right-of-eviction clause in my lease. First thing tomorrow, I'm getting on the transceiver and informing Mr. L. George Thatcher that he's to clear and take his garbage with him, and if he doesn't shift real fast, I'll have the Garda over to help him do it."

"Hold up, Father," the Commando-Colonel said thoughtfully. "Report the incident to him and inform him that he's out if there's any further trouble whatsoever, then get your stock—all the animals including the fowl—over to Planet's Glory. Uncle Angus can hold them for a while. Also, tell our neighbors abutting Dunbrityne to move any cattle they have grazing in the bordering fields nearer to home."

The older man frowned. "Just what are you thinking is going to happen, lass?"

"Perhaps nothing, but you've mentioned these tenants of yours before, nearly every time we've been on the transceiver or when you've faxmitted a letter since the day they came here. I've never liked the sound of them, even though you haven't had, or given me, any concrete complaints. This incident seals it as far as I'm concerned, at least as far as the underlings go. I've run into the type before, and nearly every one of them would happily take out a grudge on a man's property, particularly on stock or a valued pet. I'd rather overreact at this point and be safe, than risk having any more animals injured. Besides," she added, as if in an afterthought, "I'm curious about your Mr. Thatcher. This might just flush him over here."

"Don't count on that, little sister," Will told her. "That son wouldn't demean his cultured person by dealing directly with a bunch of cattle-combing farmers, even if we are threatening to toss him out on his nicely formed ear."

"He's that kind, is he?" Jake drawled in a manner whose threat his comrades readily recognized despite the seeming quietness of his tone.

"A proper aristocrat, or so he imagines." Paud scowled, then his expression cleared again. "Ah, forget Thatcher," he said. "Just thinking about him spoils my appetite for a very fine meal."

He stood up and opened the first of the two wine bottles holding the place of honor at his end of the table. He carefully distributed the contents to each of the adults.

Varn raised his glass without enthusiasm. Officers of his caste rarely drank at all, and when they did, it was only fine wine. The vintages produced and sold on the rim planets of the Federation did not often fall under that classification.

The smooth, subtle bouquet caught his attention. A sip told him that it did not belie the taste, and his eyes flickered to the label on the remaining bottle. A Hedonite vintage.

By that time, their host had seated himself once more and filled his own glass. He raised it. "We've waited a long time to open these," he told them. "See that ye don't stay away this long again, Islaen."

"We'll try to get back more frequently," she promised. "This is really excellent, Father."

"It meets your approval as well, Captain?"

"Aye, of course. You could not have chosen better."

"I'm glad to hear it. Ye did say ye liked Hedonite wines, especially the whites, but that covers a lot of ground."

Islaen felt her husband's question. *I don't remember it, either, but one or the other of us must have mentioned it.* Her eyes sparkled, though she carefully kept her expression unaltered. *You certainly did not approve of our local hill mist.*

Varn did not respond in kind. Hedon's exports were expensive luxuries in the inner-systems and rare enough on most of those. Out here on the rim, they were almost unknown. These bottles must have been ordered through the merchants picking up the gemstones. *Your people are not wealthy, Islaen . . .*

We're not paupers, either!—They want you to feel welcome, Varn. You don't give them much other chance to do that.

Bandit's mind touched theirs. She was sitting dejectedly on the sideboard behind them, where she had been ordered to remain for the duration of the meal, but now her curiosity was aroused. *Varn doesn't like the wine?*

I do, small one. It is very good.

Good for gurries? she asked hopefully.

No. He smiled at the obvious hint; the Jadite knew full well that such products were forbidden to her. *It is not good for humans, either, if they take too much of it.*

Bandit settled down once more, folding herself into a ball as if she were going to sleep. Her movement caught Sinéad Murchu's eyes, and she studied the little creature for a couple of seconds. "Islaen, that pet of yours looks as if she's been exiled from her heart's home. You really can't expect any of us to believe ye feed her on the floor in your galley."

The younger woman flushed and then laughed. "No. She eats at the table with us. On it, actually. I didn't think you'd approve."

This business of having to pretend their odd comrade was an

animal had its disadvantages. One could look like a fool for according her what was only her right.

"We'll make an exception in this case," Sinéad replied dryly. "After all, you claim she's part of your team."

Yes!

Quiet, Bandit! the guerilla leader commanded, trying to hold her laughter in check. "A full member," she affirmed aloud.

"Aunt Islaen?" Will's son, Mic, interrupted the adults' erstwhile serious conversation for the first time. "Can Bandit really fight?"

"No. She's too small. Besides, gurries don't like to hurt things, even to protect their people. Despite that, though, she's managed to save every one of us at some time or another."

The Colonel described Bandit's more outstanding exploits, always making sure to intimate that she was acting under human direction where her power of reason would otherwise be betrayed.

Even so, her father shook his head. "It's hard to imagine that degree of intelligence in something so small."

"She's smart, all right."

"What does she eat, Aunt Islaen?" Kata, Mic's sister, asked.

"Anything she can get her bill around," Karmikel muttered.

"Jake!—Just about anything we can, but she'll only take meat if there's a true need and no other choice."

"A natural vegetarian?" Will cut in.

"Aye. That very nearly describes it.—She'd better go easy on these vegetables now, though," she added in warning both to the Jadite and to the humans around the table. "If not, she'll be very sorry. If I'm not badly off course, I think I smelled an amberberry tart when I went by the kitchen before."

"You did," Sinéad affirmed.

"Wonderful! They're almost good enough to tempt me to become a full-time planet hugger again just to be near a constant source of supply."

"You wouldn't like the hard work involved at all, little sister. Ye Commandos have had it too good."

Sogan's eyes darkened. "What do you mean?"

The other looked quickly at him. His voice had not risen, but it had gone cold. "Your schedule mostly. Granted, ye face a lot of danger when ye do fight, but that's only for an hour or so at a stretch now that the War's over. Then it's off on furlough for fortnight or a month. There's no break like that on a Noreenan farm, or on a civilian freighter, either, I'll warrant."

Bethe Danlo's laughter cut off any response the former Admiral might have made.

"Sorry," she apologized after a moment. "I was just thinking of myself up to my chin in an Amazoonan river, hauling a heavy boat and with a host of unpleasant wriggly things all around just drooling for a taste of my blood."

"That's a reasonably accurate description of a guerrilla's life," Jake told his hosts. "The fights may not last long, but we usually have to expend a galaxy of effort getting to a target and then away again. Very often, we encounter the bulk and the worst of our peril en route as well." His mouth tightened momentarily. "If Varnt weren't half-fish in the water, I wouldn't have a slightly undersized wife to be showing off tonight."

"I sense a good story there," Jeanie said eagerly.

Jake responded with a full account of the rescue to which he had referred. It lost nothing in the telling, although neither did it exceed the actual event.

Varn saw that the on-worlders were primed for more and quickly recounted several incidents in which Islaen or one of the others had figured prominently. Unlike the redhead, however, he did not spare them either the grimmer details or the extent of the peril involved, and a tight silence gripped those seated at the table when he was finished.

"I wouldn't like your work, lass," her father said in the end. "Caring for my family and land and the animals depending on me is one thing. Ye have to answer for whole cities, for entire planets sometimes. That's more responsibility than any man needs to carry."

"It can be bad," Karmikel agreed. "I tried to get out of the military altogether because of it." He shook his head in disgust. "I got involved in all of Islaen's missions anyway, and so I came back in again. Luckily, Ram Sithe had called my absence a long furlough and kept my rank and seniority privileges intact."

"He just knew you," Islaen said with a smile.

Jeanie bit down on her lip. "I wouldn't be able to do anything at all knowing so much was depending on me."

"You're short-selling yourself there, girl," Paud told her. "You'd force the thought out of your mind and get on with it.—Am I right, Islaen?"

"Aye. In a mission of that magnitude, there's no there way. You'd be paralyzed otherwise, and that, no team can afford."

"I don't envy ye any of it," Will said slowly, echoing his father's sentiment of a few moments before. A shudder went through him. "The price of failure is so high. Still, any man can only do his best . . ."

"That is a given," Varn agreed slowly, "and yet, for a Commando, it is meaningless. In work such as ours, there is only either total success or stark failure."

"There have to be times when victory isn't possible!"

"Too many of them."

"Then to say the effort expended is worthless . . ."

The war prince prince shrugged. "When the life and death of a person or a world or a cause hangs in the balance, there are no mitigating circumstances or excuses. The final outcome alone has consequence."

Will frowned. "You're saying any means are all right as long as you reach a satisfactory conclusion?"

"Hardly. That would excuse nearly every black deed done by either side during the War." And his own performance on Amazoon. "We are not discussing that, only the ultimate value of a soldier's efforts."

The coldness of his manner rasped on the other. "So a man should just sit back when faced with a major challenge affecting more than himself, accept defeat, and not try to avert it at all?"

"No! That would be criminal." Sogan recognized his mistake, but he was in it now and had to make some attempt to clarify his position. "There is little or no intermediate zone in most of the missions a team like ours is given. You keep the planetbuster out of the hands of the pirates also trying to claim it, and then you disarm it, or a lot of people die. That you were burned down or blown to atoms trying to prevent the disaster will not comfort the victims if you or your unit fail to do it."

Will's eyes dropped. "That's a pretty severe way of looking at it."

"What other way is possible if the responsibility is on your shoulders?" Varn countered quietly.

The Noreenan remained silent for several seconds. "In a sense, that narrow sense, you may be right," Will conceded slowly, "but it brings my other question into even stronger focus. How far can a company like yours actually go to fulfill its missions? There have to be some brakes on ye."

"I do not follow . . ."

"Well, you couldn't purposely set Visnu's ravagers or those leeches on Amazoon loose on an enemy party, could you, no matter who they were or what they were about?"

"Can it, Will!" Islaen snapped. "You're not that innocent!"

The Arcturian stiffened, but there was no sharpness in his voice. "Let him be, Colonel. It is never pleasant or easy to consider potential atrocity by one's own forces, but his question is sound and merits a response."

His dark eyes flickered back to Will Connor. "There is no fixed answer. That lies entirely with the circumstances. Many things are never done lightly or willingly, but only those actually involved can know whether there is no other option to prevent far greater evil or if they are but yielding to the temptation to seize the quickest and safest course for themselves. In some cases, that might never be resolved even in their own minds. . . ."

Sinéad looked from one to the other of them. She shivered inside but kept her voice and expression light. "This is getting too grim," she declared flatly. "Continue the discussion if ye want at some other time and someplace other than the family dinner table, but tonight, especially, we're supposed to be celebrating."

No one said anything for several heavy seconds, then Jeanie lifted her eyes from her plate and made herself smile. "I was half afraid Islaen wouldn't want any part of a humble farm family now that she's a real princess."

Paud Connor cleared his throat. "Now that the subject's been raised, daughter, I'm not at all sure I approve of that business. Most people content themselves with one set of parents."

She smiled. "You'd like Harlran Lanree and his lady a whole lot."

"The Doge of Thorne and his consort are worthy of your respect, Mr. Connor," Varn agreed, "and they are worthy of Islaen. They came to know her intimately under very hard and perilous conditions. Their naming her their daughter is not only a great honor but a natural extension of their relationship. I myself can attest to the fact that one cannot serve with Islaen Connor without very quickly coming to love her."

Jeanie laughed. "Well answered, Captain! You'll make a Noreenan yet!"

"It was only a statement of fact," he responded, smiling faintly.

Islaen's inner sigh of relief was echoed by her mother's. The Noreenan matriarch drew her chair back a little. "Ye all seem to have finished eating. Paud and I'll clear off the table and bring out the tart. There's always room for that, I've noticed."

Islaen and Jeanie started to rise as well, but the older woman waved them back. "Sit, both of ye. I'm not putting my daughter to work her first night back on-world, and I need you right here, Jeanie, to make sure Will and our guests don't draw down all the troubles of the ultrasystem and get so worked up solving them that they ruin the rest of the evening for all of us."

The demolitions expert looked doubtfully after the pair. "Maybe we should help them anyway," she ventured. "There's a lot of ware . . ."

Jeanie's brows raised. "They only have to load the cleaner cabinet.—This is a low-tech planet, chiefly in the sense of low-impact. We're not no-tech by any means, especially in our homes, since the bulk of our time has to be spent in our gardens, fields, and with our animals—not fixing up our houses. As long as Noreen and her life forms don't have to suffer for our comfort, we see no reason to live primitively."

Bethe felt relieved to hear that. There were a handful of worlds in the ultrasystem whose charters fixed their societies at or near pre-space levels. Courtesy would have forbidden her to mention what she thought of the sanity of their first ship authors in front of their descendents. Although she should have known it after having been with them this long, it was still good to confirm that Jake and their commander had been formed in a more reasonable environment.

Paud set the glasses he was holding in their cradles. "How did our daughter come to marry that man?" he demanded sourly.

"Very likely she married him because she loves him almost as much as he loves her."

"Maybe, but he's as grim . . ."

His wife sighed. "The War used Varnt hard, I think.—We figured that out on his first visit."

"Well, he's worse this time!" He restrained himself in tim from jamming a plate into the cabinet with shattering force.

"Physically, too," she pointed out. She shook her head. "I ha half thought that Islaen was lying when she pleaded the aftereffects of their missions as an excuse for not coming back. I'd feared that Varnt either did not like us or was too uncomfortable with us to want to venture a second visit. Now, I see she was right. He's had a rough time of it."

"They had to put their affairs on Thorne in order anyway," her husband said. "That alone would've held them all this time." His eyes shadowed. "Islaen's had her share as well. She looks tired." He sighed. "Not that either of them'd agree to it, but I'd like to have Tam give them both a good going over. The Navy may have fine physicians, but I still trust my own best in looking after my own."

"They're worried . . ."

That caught his ear. "Worried?"

"So am I." She gave him a sharp look. "And you, too, I think. Those four are never here on furlough, or not entirely for that reason."

"You figured that out as well?" Real anger touched his voice for the first time. "We've got two other offspring and four grandchildren, not to mention our stock. We've got a right to know."

"Not if they're working under tight security wrap, we don't," Sinéad said mildly. "Bring that pot of jakek. If we delay any longer, everyone'll be wondering what's keeping us."

She carefully lifted the platter holding the amberberry tart, moving slowly to avoid any chance of cracking its delicate top crust. "Wait until Will and his family leave. We'll see what they can or will tell us then."

SIX

ISLAEN CONNOR SETTLED back in the large, comfortably stuffed chair that had been her favorite seat from the time she was big enough to clamber into it and closed her eyes. She was tired after the long journey and busy day, but it was a pleasant weariness enhanced by the meal she had just finished, and she was content to drift with it.

She looked up in the next moment and sipped the steaming jakek from the cup she was holding. She set it down on the small table beside her until it could cool a bit more. "That's grand, Mother. No one else can make it the way you do."

Sinéad sipped her own before setting it aside as well. "Every mother since our species began must have heard that compliment in one form or another," she replied with a smile. Her eyes darkened then, and she nodded almost imperceptibly to her husband.

Paud Connor looked from one to the other of his guests. "If you can't tell us," he said bluntly, "say so, and we'll back off, but Sinéad and I would like to know why ye have actually come to Noreen."

The four Commandos straightened.

"Father . . ." Islaen began.

He silenced her with a quick wave of his hand. "We know Jake's fond of us, but if this were only a furlough, he'd have taken Bethe home to meet his own family first. That means ye're on assignment, and your kind of work's likely to affect everyone around ye."

The Commando-Colonel's eyes met each of her companions',

returning at last to her father. "What can you tell us about your tenants?" she asked.

He was silent a moment. "So that's it," he hissed. The Noreenan man collected his thoughts. "L. George Thatcher rented the place about four years ago, the house and barn and one hundred yards in every direction around them, when I was finalizing my purchase of it.

"I didn't care for leasing to off-worlders, mind you, but expenses were high, and I didn't want to let the chance to secure Dunbrityne go. My children are settled, but I have four grandchildren. That farm means yet another of them is assured a place on-world." His face hardened. "I thought the good gods were smiling on me, but it seems that a demon sneered instead."

He drew himself back to his daughter's question. "I can't tell you all that much, unfortunately. Thatcher and his friends don't socialize with the like of us. He pays his bills promptly, both his rates and our charges for the supplies we sell to him or order for him. It's mostly the last. Our homegrown goods aren't nearly fine enough to suit his tastes."

"One of his underlings brings the payments?"

"Yes."

"How many of them are there?"

"I can't say. He's got an energy picket around the whole place. It's high and strong enough that you can't see much through it. I think he has a good number with him. At least, he's ordered a lot of food, and a clutch of different faces show up on his various errands around here.—Maybe they think we're too provincial to see beyond their racial similarities."

"It's a common error, and one that's worked to a Commando unit's advantage before now.—They behave themselves?"

Paud nodded. "We've had no significant trouble. They're surly at best, and a couple of them have given Jeanie a hard time."

"Quite a hard time," Sinéad stressed, taking up that part of the tale. "They didn't actually try anything, but their advances were the unpleasant kind, not half-complimentary probes to see if she might be willing."

"Will doesn't know about it," the farmer said. "He'd go after the sons if he did."

"That wouldn't be wise," Islaen told them gravely. "Will would be in big trouble if he tried to tackle that lot alone. Thatcher hired the dregs of Albion for his private army, and they take care of such challenges in their own way. It isn't an honorable one.—Any increase or change in their activities of late?"

"A lot of fliers and transports moving back and forth, but I really didn't pay them much heed."

"You've had no reason to be watching them."

"Why your interest? What's he done?"

"We're more worried at this point about what he might still do." The Commando outlined Thatcher's recent history and her unit's mission.

All were quiet for some time after she had finished.

"So ye think Thatcher still has the fangs to inject his venom?" her father asked at last.

"Ingelligence does."

Sinéad Murchu frowned. "Could he be going after Albion? Such a man would want his vengeance."

Islaen gave her a quick look. "It would fit his character and past performance, right enough." She shook her head then. "No, not unless he's got far more than we suspect. Albion of Scotia's too strong. He'll have to satisfy himself with paying off his thugs and securing a fortune large enough to let him live in his definition of comfort, probably in the inner-systems. L. George Thatcher most assuredly won't want to pass the remainder of his life in the middle of Noreen's farmlands."

"You could find yourself in a hard position in your efforts to make an end of him," Paud said after yet another long silence. "What are the chances of trouble spreading to Kinkora?"

"Slight, we believe and hope, but they exist. That's why I wan the animals moved. They could never be shifted on shor notice.—It might not be a bad idea if you all went with them."

"Where would that leave your cover?"

"I'd like Uncle Angus to take the children anyway."

He nodded slowly. "All right. I'll ask him when I call abou transferring the stock."

"No," Islaen said thoughtfully. "Don't call. Send Will ove tomorrow. You can use the time until he returns to start gatherin the cattle still in the fields. Don't use the transceiver for any of th unless you absolutely must."

Jake frowned. "Monitoring?"

"It wouldn't be hard. These farms have only civilian sets wi an open frequency. Thatcher may not have the necessary equi ment, much less be using it—but then again, he might."

"How much should we tell Angus? And Will?"

"Will, everything. He's got a right to decide whether he wants to stay here or not. Just tell Uncle Angus that it's important and that I'm asking it officially. He won't refuse, and he'll keep his mouth shut."

"He will." The farmer nodded to himself, then centered his mind on his own role. "When do you want me to call Thatcher, and what shall I say to him?"

"As soon as you'd think it decent if you'd heard none of this. Act precisely as you would've done as well, except, as I said, only threaten the eviction. Ream him proper. Your animals were hurt, and it was his underlings who did it. Let him know gut level that you're mad enough to forego the credits he's giving you. That'll flush him out if anything will."

"You're sure, lass? He may just ignore us."

She shook her head. "No. He can't afford that. His plans have to be close to completion, and he doesn't dare chance losing his base now, not yet. That would just about finish him. He won't be able to hold his thugs if he doesn't come through soon.

"The way I see it, he'll do one of two things. What he should do is apologize immediately, offer to pay for veterinary bills or other damage, and promise to leash his staff in the future. In that case, we'll have to accept it, and I'll be forced into making some kind of courtesy call or breaking in cold. What I think will happen though, given the arrogance he's shown thus far, is that he'll apologize verbally, probably through a couple of bully boys who will then proceed to 'suggest' that you lay off their employer. That'll give me a chance to feel them out and if I can manage it, introduce myself to their attention rather dramatically."

"Is that wise, Daughter?"

"It's a gamble," she admitted, "but it's probably our best course. Having Commandos next door on a seemingly legitimate visit's one thing—unsettling and sowing doubt, but that's all. If we tried to conceal our presence or our affiliation, and the ruse were discovered, then he'd know we were on to him and would cover himself to the point that we'd never get anything on him; that, or strike at once and escape out of our hands."

"Maybe he's still waiting for those arms," Sinéad suggested.

"No, Mother. The Navy was careful to give a properly edited version of the seizure good publicity."

"I remember," she said tightly, barely repressing a shudder. "Those awful animals . . ."

"Aye. The official version said none of the bodies were identifiable, but that the arms were all accounted for and that the buyer had doubtless perished with the rest. Thatcher would feel free to thank whatever demons to whom he owes allegiance for yet another escape and revamp his plans for this final raid."

"There are a lot of ifs and possibilities in all that, Islaen," Paud Connor observed gravely.

"Aye, Father. That's another reason our team was sent in. We're good. One way or another, we'll get the answers the Navy needs, and if it proves too late for others to act on them, well, we've managed tight situations with high stakes before now."

He sighed. "All right, lass. This is your run. We'll do what we can to help ye."

"Thanks, Father. None of you asked for any of this."

"No. No, we didn't, but every planet out here on the rim's more or less the same—a lot of people working and hoping, trying to build a future for themselves and their children, many of them struggling to put their lives back in order after the War. They haven't asked for it, either. Sinéad and I, well, we're willing to lay ourselves out to see that those Albionan maggot's spawn don't pull that raid ye believe they're plotting."

Bethe Danlo gave a gasp of delight as she sank into the mattress of the wide bed on which she had just seated herself. "It's soft as a cloud!" she exclaimed. "You could just disappear into it."

"If that's a hint . . ." Jake suggested as he sat down beside her.

"You can wait a few minutes longer, you big ape!"

She started freeing her hair of its braid. The redhead watched her. "It's beautiful," he said. "Too bad you can't wear it loose sometimes."

"It would be real nice stuck in the drive controls." Her face grew somber. "I thought the Admiral had blown it tonight."

He sighed. "So did I. Once he got into it, there was no withdrawing again. He was just lucky the discussion turned out as it did."

"I've never known Varn to make a blunder like that before."

"It's the way the man thinks, Bethe. He's an Arcturian. There's no getting around that. He can't just chuck what he is, like he did his scarlet uniform—and it's going to come out now and then. That's why he keeps mostly to himself when not in our company, and maybe why he likes Thorne so much. He's got nothing to hide there." Jake shook his head. "Sogan wasn't entirely off the charts, either. We may not be accustomed to viewing life or our work so grimly, but it's that weight which drove me out of the Navy, however temporarily."

He shrugged off the gloomy mood settling over him. "Just be glad you married a simple former farm boy who gives you none of these problems, Sergeant."

"I am," she replied gravely.

Jake looked at her. "I'm glad you did, too, Bethe Danlo," he said as he folded her in his arms.

The war prince strode rapidly across the close-cut grass beside the farmhouse. Although it was not yet quite full, the moon was high and bright enough that he felt no need to slow his pace, not on the even land this near to the old dwelling.

He did keep a wary eye out for clumps of slightly taller vegetation. Herb nettles provided excellent food for both the cattle and the ever-present fowl, and so were permitted to grow more or less unmolested even close to human habitations. Only the lawns and flower beds adjoining a house were guaranteed to be completely free of the stinging plants. Beneficial as they might be to Noreen's animals, he had no desire to encounter them. They were not as incapacitating as their namesakes on Amazoon, but for the short while it lasted, the pain they generated was reputed to be equally intense.

Varn came to a stop at last in the shadow of the big stone barn. The air was heavy with the scent of the grain the Connor men and their neighbors had carried into it earlier in the day, before his party's arrival, and he breathed deeply. This was one of the better memories he would carry away with him from Noreen of Tara. . . .

He glanced skyward. Tomorrow would not be as fine, he thought, not to judge by those clouds scudding across the moon. The night had gotten very cold and damp, and he would not be surprised if it did not rain before morning.

No matter, the former Admiral thought, stifling a yawn. For once, he would be warm and dry, in a soft bed, and not trying to keep watch with a freezing cloudburst pouring down the back of his neck.

"Captain?"

He turned quickly. Paud had rounded the corner of the barn, coming from its entrance. "Good evening, Mr. Connor.—You were checking on your injured animal?"

"Yes. She's content enough now, praise the kind gods and your renewer."

"Good. I am no stock man, but I did not like seeing her hurt, particularly since the damage had been purposely inflicted."

"Her fear was worse," the farmer said grimly. "I'm glad that passed off so quickly." The Noreenan studied his guest. "You're up late yourself," he observed.

"I often like to take the air before knocking out." He smiled. "Tonight, I had the added need to walk off some of that fine dinner a bit. I had forgotten that aspect of life on Noreen."

"There's little that can beat fresh-grown produce."

"No." Sogan's eyes dropped momentarily. "I owe both you and your wife an apology," he said. "I should not have let my tongue run in there. You did not need to hear Islaen's perils described quite so graphically."

"You do tell a tale remarkably well," the older man conceded noncommittally.

"I do not enjoy seeing her in danger myself," he said very softly, almost to himself, "though I have to accept that I cannot shield her entirely, no more than she can shield me."

"Someone has to tackle the job ye're doing. From all that I hear, ye're about the best fitted in the ultrasystem to take it on." He paused. "We're damn proud of Islaen, all of us, even if it's only natural that we'd rather have her safe here at home with us. Will's just as proud of her as the rest of us," he added. "Don't misunderstand what he was doing tonight."

"I did not, really. I guess I just felt compelled to defend her military honor, and the unit's in general, of course."

"I, for one, think better of a man who'll stand up for his wife." Especially when he did not use the occasion to wind his own trumpet. Sogan had made almost no mention of his own part in the events he had described. They might have thought him no more than a minor observer had they not been well aware of his record. "I suppose I'd be asking a deal if I said Mr. Connor was my father," the Noreenan continued a bit gruffly, "and that he died thirty-four years ago last winter. My name's Paud."

Varn smiled again. "I thought it best to err on the side of formality. You and Mrs. Murchu might not have been particularly happy with your daughter's choice for a husband."

"Sinéad. Her mother's dead, too.—We're pleased enough, Captain. Islaen could've done considerably worse." He straightened. "It's been a long day. Are you ready to go back now?"

"Aye. I had just wanted to see what the night was like. I could use some sleep before we start trying to ferret out information about your unsavory neighbors."

SEVEN

A SHARP, PERSISTENT yanking of their hair roused Islaen and Varn out of a deep sleep.

The Commando-Colonel's eyes opened. "Bandit," she grumbled, "I know you have a reason for this. I just hope I think it's a good one."

The Jadite's feathers were extended. *Bandit's a gurry! Ugly birds not gurries! Islaen, Varn, tell Mother she's wrong!*

Sogan lay back again with a groan. *Space!* he muttered. *What next? I though the planet was under full attack the way she charged in here!*

"Bandit, of course they're not Jadite gurries," Islaen explained patiently, "but that's what Noreenans call brooding fowl. It's one of those linguistic coincidences with which the universe abounds, to the constant grief of hidebound philologists and their theories."

The hen's mood brightened. *Mother doesn't think Bandit's like them?*

"No, love, naturally not. You don't even look like one, and she can see that you're a whole lot smarter."

Good! She peered at the humans. *Breakfast's nice!* she ventured hopefully.

The woman glanced at her timer. "Not as nice as it would've been earlier. I'll be the one programming the range." Between her duties in the kitchen garden and dairy, her mother would hardly have the leisure to wait around to cater to late-rising off-world visitors.

She shivered as she put her feet on the cold floor. *I wonder what the day's doing?*

She went to the window. The sky was dark with a full cloud

cover, but it was dry. *The rain's stopped, at least,* she said. *Did you hear it lashing just before dawn?*

Not me, Varn replied lazily. *I was out solid by then.*

The Noreenan smiled. *I always loved to lie here and listen to it hammering away at the roof. House and bed seem twice as comfortable under those conditions. —Up and out, Admiral! An irate Noreenan farmer wouldn't wait long before lodging a strong complaint over injury to his animals. We should be getting a response pretty shortly.*

Islaen Connor's head raised as she sent her mind out yet again in search of approaching strangers. It had been two hours now since she had come downstairs, and she was beginning to wonder if she had not misread the situation completely. She had expected to hear something well before this.

A cold smile touched her lips. This time, her hunting was successful. They were coming, two of them. Underlings, she decided even in that moment of initial contact. Neither of the minds she touched possessed the brand of intelligence she expected to find in the former Minister. It was as she had predicted, then.

The Commando concentrated, trying to pick up what she could before their meeting.

The pair were not worried. They were annoyed and maybe a bit pleased despite their annoyance at having a chance to use some of their supposed strength again. Men of this type usually resented the tight rein needed to control them and keep them usable.

Varn, she called. *They're on their way. A brace of them.*

Shall I join you?

No, she said after a brief hesitation, *Keep close, though. I may need you to back me. Get to Jake and Bethe as well. Bandit, you stay out of it.*

She retained her link with Sogan's mind so that he could share her impressions during the interview and opened the transmit button on the tiny communicator strapped to her left wrist. Their comrades would be able to hear what was said as well, even if they could not see what was going on or receive the mental transmissions of their visitors.

The wait was not long. A transport lumbered into sight. It was a big four-wheel luxury-class passenger vehicle rather than one of the all-purpose work machines used by most Noreenans. She had not expected a flier, although her father had mentioned them.

Thatcher might have rented a couple at the spaceport to carry his increased staff to him quickly, but if he had one or more of his own stashed away, he would not be fool enough to betray the fact for so little cause. They were forbidden to long-term visitors and to residents except for the Garda, physicians and veterinarians, and priests—those who regularly had to respond to emergencies over considerable distances.

The two inside, both men, were about what she had expected—Albionans, of course, strongly built with their kind's heavy features. They were average looking, neither attractive nor exceptionally plain, but they were a hard crew, and there was that in their expressions which promised ill to anyone who crossed them or to whom they happened to take a dislike.

The guerrilla walked toward them. Their eyes fixed on her, first in surprise at finding a stranger here, then with interest.

Islaen Connor was a beautiful woman, and her work took her to all sections of the ultrasystem. She had felt men appraise her before, and she did not like the way these two did it. She did not envy Jeanie her earlier encounters with them or others of their ilk.

She did not have to pretend to be ignorant of their thoughts, which they made no effort to conceal, and raised her head in a purely Noreenan pride. "Can I help you?" she asked with cool courtesy.

"We're looking for Connor," the drive said.

"Which one? There's a whole family of us here."

"The old man. The head cow comber. Just run and get him for us."

"I'm his daughter. Why don't you tell me what you want?"

"Look, babe, we've got a message to deliver, and it's for your da, not for some little farm toy." His voice hardened into half-threat, half-leer. "Though we might just come back . . ."

"I am Commando-Colonel Islaen Connor," the woman snapped. "My father is a busy man and has no time to be leaving his work to meet the whim of a couple of micro-brained port rats. Tell me what you want—now—or clear."

Both stared at her, their expressions and their humor very different than they had been moments before. The Noreenan might be standing before them in a shirt worn loose over a nondescript pair of spacer's trousers, not in a uniform, but neither of them thought to doubt her statement. She had the look of the Navy about her, the look of an officer, and she was deadly. These men were well able to recognize that in an opponent.

"Look, Colonel," the driver said in an altered tone, "we really do have a message from Mr. Thatcher for your father."

"I'm aware of what sparked it," she replied. "If L. George Thatcher sees fit to send intermediaries to the master of Kinkora, they can jolly well say their piece to a representative of his."

Islaen could guess the thoughts going through the Albionans' minds almost as certainly as if she could read them. They had been sent over to subtly, or not so subtly, lean on a farmer and maybe his family. Instead of a supposedly easily cowed on-worlder, they found themselves facing one of the Federation's famed guerrillas. Had they been men of another sort, she might almost have pitied their dilemma. They did not want to pull their boss' anger down on them by failing to complete their assignment, but they also had no intention of putting her prowess to the test.

In the end, they resolved the matter precisely as she anticipated they would by delivering an apology and an offer of payment for the damage done, and giving an assurance that there would be no repetition of the incident. When they got back to their own base, they would no doubt report her presence and tell Thatcher that they thought it best to act innocent until he had time to decide if the guerrilla might mean trouble for their own plans and what, if anything, to do about her. The former Minister was a cautious man and would appreciate that kind of reasoning.

She accepted the apology and promise in her father's name and said that he would be in touch with Thatcher himself regarding any damages.

Her mind sought her consort's. Sogan was standing by the corner of the house where he had a good view of the Albionans' transport without betraying his own presence. *Cover me, Varn. I'm going to turn my back on them.*

I have my blaster on them now.

The war prince was a deadly shot, with reflexes sharp as laser fire, but still the Commando-Colonel intensified her monitoring of her opponents' transmissions as she turned away from the two, haughtily and unequivocally dismissing them. She had little doubt that these port rats had done their share of back-alley work. Burning her down might be a stupid move, but it would be no violation of their natures to do it.

The warning change came suddenly as fear abruptly turned to

petty rage. The woman cast herself to one side, rolling as she hit the ground. Even as she went down, a blaster appeared as if by magic in her hand. She fired at broad beam set to slay, but aimed at the front wheels of the vehicle bearing down on her rather than at its occupants.

Sogan's shot sounded almost simultaneously with it, searing the rear wheels and drive even as hers took out the front. A second bolt followed immediately upon it and ripped into the driver.

The machine spun wildly, fighting the inertia that would still keep it moving forward despite the loss of its wheels, then it ground to a stop.

Islaen Connor leaped to her feet and sprang for the transport. It was sturdy but only a civilian vehicle, not designed to withstand the shocks of battle. There could be an explosion, and two men remained inside, at least one and probably both of them still living.

Her mind sought and found the driver's. As she had expected, Varn had switched his weapon to stun before firing the second time.

Wrenching the door open, she pulled the unconscious Albionan out, then switched the engine off.

The second man had apparently been shaken and dazed but was now recovering himself. "Move!" she ordered.

"I will take care of him," Sogan told her as he came up on the other side of the vehicle.

She nodded curtly and withdrew. Their comrades had reached the scene by that time. Jake had already pulled the driver out of potential danger and was bent over the engine, whipping out the fuel disk to eliminate the chance of explosion and most of the likelihood of fire. Bethe Danlo was standing close by, her blaster drawn and at ready.

The man the Arcturian had hauled from the disabled transport aimed a sudden, vicious short blow at him in an effort to break free. Varn avoided it and slammed the side of his hand into his captive's belly.

The Albionan crumpled. Sogan yanked him to his feet and half-jerked, half-carried him to where his companion lay. There, he flung him contemptuously to the ground. "What do you want done with the vermin, Colonel?"

"Father has wire in the barn. Jake, go get some and tie them up.

Don't make a tourniquet out of it, but they don't have to be terribly comfortable, either. We're not the Stellar Patrol."

"Aye, Colonel."

"Varnt, get on the transceiver and put a call in to my brother Tam. His frequency's listed with the other emergency codes. I want to make sure this scum didn't suffer any real damage." That last was not just cover. Unlike her scanning of mental transmissions, the process of physical examination was not unobtrusive. She could not use it on a conscious person without betraying that something incredibly unique was going on. "After that, tell the Garda to come out here, collect this garbage, and hold them for either the Navy or the Patrol, whichever comes first." *—Use our transceiver for that. It's more than well enough shielded to block any spy gear Thatcher's likely to have.*

Will do, Colonel.

She saw and felt the conscious Albionan start. "What did you expect?" she demanded curtly. "Attempting to assault military personnel is a serious offense."

"We only meant to scare you, make you jump a little . . ."

"Tell it to the tribunal. You might escape an attempted murder charge, but rest assured that you'll have no worry about finding berths for yourselves for a good few years. Even a civilian court wouldn't let you off much more lightly."

The Noreenan's attention returned to her husband. "Get in touch with Thatcher as well. Inform him what's happened here and tell him to remove that wreck. I'm too furious to deal with him myself at the moment."

"No problem, Colonel." *—Though I am angry enough myself.* He hesitated. *Will an attempted murder charge take?*

No, she said flatly. *He was telling the truth. They only wanted to humiliate, not kill, me. I can't send men to the executioner for that.*

You are sure? They were following fast on you.

She nodded. *You were aware of their transmissions as well. I've felt blood lust too often in the past not to recognize it, and it just wasn't present here.*

She went on smoothly. "Bethe, stay with Jake and keep the prisoners covered for him. If this one moves, stun him down."

"It'd be the greatest pleasure, Colonel."

EIGHT

DOCTOR TAM CONNOR joined the silent assembly consisting of his family and their off-world visitors. "The prisoners are sound enough," he told them, then glanced at his brother-in-law. "That was some blow you gave him, Captain. A little more force, and we'd be rushing to get him under regrowth treatment."

The former Admiral shrugged. "It was not my intention to kill or maim him."

Jeanie shivered in her heart. "You can just-choose that?" she asked. "So easily?"

"Of course, though it is more difficult to check a strike than it is to use full force."

"Well, we can all thank the Spirit ruling space that nothing serious did happen to anyone," Will said fervently. "How did you know they were coming at you in time to get out of the way, much less be able to shoot so quickly, Islaen?"

"If they were going to try anything, it would have to be then. I was braced for it. As for firing fast, if you can't do that, you don't survive too long in my business."

Will's eyes fell. Anger coursed suddenly over his features, and even more strongly through him. "Your business! The Navy comes before everything else with you now! —How could you do it to us, betray our love and trust and friendship like this, use us . . ."

"What in space do you mean?" Bethe Danlo asked, surprised and hurt although she was no part of this family.

"She made Kinkora her base, knowing it could become a battleground, and she did not even have the basic courtesy to warn any of us until trouble became accomplished fact. She knew ye wouldn't be thrown out then!"

"No!" Islaen exclaimed in protest.

Her mother silenced her. "What else could they have done?" Sinéad Murchu asked quietly. "Some young colony will have to suffer all the horror of what amounts to a pirate raid if Islaen and her comrades can't stop Thatcher. Are you telling us they should just let it all happen because you don't want to be involved in what it might take to prevent it?"

"I'd go down to the great demons first! Now that my babies are safe, I'm in it as far as they'll let me go." Will scowled. "It's our farm and maybe our lives. They should've told us sooner, that's all."

"When?" the Commando-Colonel demanded. "I could hardly broadcast it before we planeted. Your transceiver isn't safeguarded at all. Even the Garda haven't been informed."

"That's what I mean! This damned secrecy, as if we lowly planet huggers aren't worthy of trust . . ."

Karmikel scowled. "What kind of game do you think we're playing, man? Tight security's essential to the success of most of our missions, and to the minor goal of keeping our own skins more or less intact as well."

"Easy, Jake," Tam told him. "I don't think that's what's actually goading Will. It's . . ." His eyes fell, and he lapsed into silence.

"Go on," the redheaded guerrilla told him coldly.

The physician sighed. "It's hard to see that our little sister has grown up into a very efficient killing machine."

"What?" Varn Tarl Sogan hissed. He had held his temper thus far, but this was an attack on Islaen herself, and that he would not tolerate.

"One more word," Karmikel growled furiously, "and you'll be swallowing those white teeth of yours, that and going under a renewer to repair what's left of your jaw."

"Let me finish this, Jake!" The war prince's eyes bore into the physician's. "Aye," he said contemptuously, "Islaen Connor can defend herself well, but, then, she went off to battle the Empire while her valiant brothers continued the peaceful course of their lives, safe from the War and all its perils."

"She won the draw deciding who would go for the family!"

"Won or lost, she fought to protect you all from the Arcturians.

They are 'killing machines' as well, and I assure you, you would not have enjoyed their attentions." Disgust almost overrode the contempt in his voice. "She is still fighting for you against slime like this Thatcher and others of his ilk. Apparently, this new war is a thankless one, at least on Noreen of Tara, where there is no threat to give the fighting importance."

Tam battled down his own anger. "That's not true, here or anywhere else on the rim. You know that yourself." He glanced at his sister. "I'm sorry, Islaen. What I said, I put badly, and I should have kept my big mouth shut in the first place."

She shook her head sadly. "I know what you meant, Tam. You and Will remember carting your pesky younger sister around on your backs, and we've been apart so much and so long now, that you never really got to know me as an adult. Seeing me actually function as a Commando officer has to be a shock." She sighed. "It's growing up at Kinkora that I remember about Noreen, too."

Sogan held his peace. He was nowhere near satisfied himself, and it tore him to see what this exchange was doing to Islaen. Even through her shields, he could feel something of her sorrow. She did not want to pursue it further, however, and he lowered his still angry eyes.

Much of his ire was turned against himself, at this latest failure of his. Bandit was perched on the Colonel's lap and was nuzzling her hand, trying to give her comfort. Maybe she would succeed, he thought with great bitterness. He could do nothing. He could not even comprehend the attitudes that had invoked all this.

Islaen Connor leaned against the fence overlooking the empty calf field. The Garda had just left, taking the two prisoners with them. They had already reported the incident to the Stellar Patrol, who had promised to send in a ship to collect the Albionans and see that they were delivered to Horus for trial. There was nothing more to be done for the next few hours except sit back and let matters hatch. Thatcher's entourage had not allowed Varn to speak directly with the former Minister, and they would have to give him some time in which to respond. Thatcher's reaction, even no reaction at all, would give them at least an idea of the time frame in which they had to work. That would in itself be a help, and with luck, they could learn a lot more besides.

She felt her father's familiar thought pattern and turned quickly as soon as his footfall supplied a more conventional announcement of his presence. He looked tired, she thought, but he should be. Every head of stock had been moved to Planet's Glory before Tara had set.

Paud came up beside her and gazed somberly over the fence. "It doesn't look natural empty, does it?"

"Not at this time of year," she agreed. "I miss them already."

"Don't think too badly of your brothers," Paud said, knowing full well that the earlier clash was preying on her. "They were a couple of asses tonight, but like you said, accepting you as more than their little sister isn't easy for either of them."

"I know," she said ruefully. "They'd cherished the image of me playing soldier. I wish they didn't have to see the reality of it. The old gods know, I surely don't want to carry the Navy here. I have my fill of war and its works everywhere else."

"There's a bit more to it than that," he continued bluntly.

"Aye. Fighting's man's business on Noreen. I'm an anomaly here—to my own as well as to the planet at large."

The farmer did not contradict her. "You've made such a success of it, lass. First off, you got into the Commandos, which was the dream of every lad on Noreen, and then you started gaining rank. Even after the War, when nearly everyone else was sent home, you kept your commission and proceeded to prove the wisdom of the Navy's choice by winning that string of first-class citations. It seems like every other week, your name's on the newstapes."

Her name only. Ram Sithe would not allow his best team's ability to handle undercover work to be impaired, or risk betraying Varn's antecedents to give him his full due, by permitting their images to be broadcast to the ultrasystem at large. "Not quite," she responded with a faint smile. "Even my unit can't perform miracles that quickly."

There had been a question in his statement, and the guerrilla went on more gravely. "The Navy's pushed the publicity as a message to the subbiotics crawling around the ultrasystem. It's a warning that there are people who'll take them down, no matter who they are or how seemingly carefully they plan their schemes." Her head lifted in pride. "We got nearly the whole government, top military brass, and chief industrialists of the Britynon planets tossed into the galactic pen for what they tried to do to Anath of Algola, not to mention annihilating their invasion fleet."

"That was a good piece of work," he agreed.

"Too bad it didn't have a salutary effect on Thatcher," she said with a sigh.

"Some tyrants never learn, not until they've been crushed themselves."

She studied him. "This can't be any easier for you and Mother."

Paud shrugged. "The hardest part for us is realizing you won't be coming back home, not permanently. We'd known it for a long time, I suppose, but meeting the man you married made it a certainty. Your Varnt Sogan could not settle on Noreen."

"Varnt could make himself adapt, but he'd be very unhappy here," she agreed. "He needs the stars."

"He's also no more a farmer than L. George Thatcher is," the older man said dryly.

"I couldn't come back anyway," she told him sadly. "A furlough's one thing, but I really am too much an oddity now to settle in permanently again. Time and life can't be undone."

"No, unfortunately, that they cannot."

He glanced back at the house and chuckled suddenly. "One thing for sure, farmer or not, that husband of yours will back you the full season. For a few moments there, I thought I was about to lose a brace of sons."

The Colonel laughed. "No fear of that! Varnt's temper might get stellar hot, but he usually keeps himself under pretty tight control. He wouldn't actually break someone's neck for a word." A physical assault was another matter. Sogan had come within millimeters of killing their guide on Hades of Persephone for that and would have done it had Jake Karmikel not slugged him.

"Controlled? He's more like an Arcturian officer commanding his troops than anybody . . ."

"Don't say that again! Don't even think it!"

Paud stared at her. "It was only a comparison, Daughter, not an accusation."

Islaen gripped herself. "I know, Father, but he is a dead image for one of the Empire's soldiers. We've run into trouble in plenty because of that resemblance."

"The same thing could be said about a good third of the Federation's citizens to a greater or lesser extent, the populations of whole planets, even."

"Aye, and a lot of them run into the same problems we do if they wander into the wrong place at a bad time. There's no one in all the ultrasystem who didn't lose in the War, and feelings are going to run high for a very long time. Even here, Uncle Angus saw his only son, his only child, go off to fight and die." Her eyes closed. "I have to accept the dangers inherent in our profession, but to have Varnt cut down by some mob or hate-maddened assassin . . ."

"All right, lass," her father said quietly. "I'll watch what I say. Noreen's a peaceful planet, but our people are no less susceptible than anyone else to passion and the stupidity it can spark. I won't have your Captain suffer because of my loose tongue."

Varn Tarl Sogan sat on the edge of the wide, soft bed. He was still in a foul temper, although he had been careful to conceal his ill humor when Islaen had separated from him following the removal of the prisoners.

A lottery to decide who would have to fight for their Federation's life! Among his people, every man of the warrior caste fought and was honored to fight. The women did not, but it was they who governed the planets of the Arcturian Empire and supervised the smooth continuation of the activities that kept the great ultrasystem a viable whole despite the eternal warring in which it was engaged. Their work was of no less significance than that taking place on the Emperor's battlecraft, and it was no less valued.

He gave a mental shrug. Were these people not menials, in point of fact, farmers and other tradesmen, little different from those who existed to serve his caste?

The former Admiral stopped himself. A Navy comprised of that seemingly wretched raw material had driven back and finally defeated the supposedly invincible Arcturian armadas. With the aid of a single team of professional guerrillas, an unofficial army of merchants had fought his own fleet to a near standstill on Thorne of Brandine. He was in no position to despise any of them.

He was also a totally insensitive bastard. He might not understand, much less accept, what had happened tonight, but Islaen did. She had been hurt, not angry. Deeply hurt.

Sogan rose to his feet. His consort was out there somewhere in Noreen's damp night, standing alone because the one who owed her comfort and support had not come to her. That neglect could not be permitted to go on any longer.

Varn's mind reached out and quickly located Islaen's. Her thoughts were tightly shielded, as he had anticipated they would be, but she was not otherwise trying to conceal herself from him. His mouth tightened. Maybe she simply did not think he would bother looking for her.

Perhaps she welcomed the idea that he might come to her, even while she doubted that he would make the effort. She had come to him often enough when he struggled under some cloud.

The Arcturian found his commander by the calf pasture, where reason alone would have brought him had he no other information but his knowledge of the woman to guide him.

She was clearly visible as the moon pulled free for a moment from the clouds and cast its light on her. Her head was lowered to meet Bandit's caress as the gurry alternately rubbed her face against the human's and licked her, trying to raise the heaviness smothering her spirit.

Islaen? he said softly, not wanting to startle her.

He wondered for an instant if she would be able to hear him behind those carefully sealed shields, but she turned at once. *Varn! I was about to come up to you.*

At least, she had the grace to reveal no surprise, he thought, but he quickly put that out of his mind. There was misery beneath her guards; had she been less strong, he would have found tears in the eyes she raised to meet his.

Sogan went to her. He put his arm around her and drew her close.

She rested her head against him, infinitely glad of his strength and more so of the love he was so freely giving her. *I can't say my own reason and my comrades didn't warn me that this would be no easy slide.*

I wish I could take it for you, my Islaen.

It's my charter all the way.

Aye, but you can have help carrying it. His lips brushed her hair. He could bear anything himself, but to see this woman so burdened . . . *The fact that L. George Thatcher forced me to dishonor myself is shrinking in significance among my reasons for wanting him dead,* he said savagely.

Islaen pulled away from him. *I don't want to hear any more of that from you! You are not dishonored. Renegades who deserved death died hard by repulsive means, but that part of it was not accomplished by your will. This is the Federation, Varn Tarl*

Sogan. The intention accompanying the deed decides guilt or innocence here.

The Commando-Captain smiled. *I prefer seeing you angry to upset,* he told her. Seeing what had happened, he resolved to go on in a lighter vein. *All the same, you may have to restrain me when we finally meet the former Minister of Justice, if we ever do. The urge to throttle him where he stands is growing stronger with every passing hour.*

We'll see him, all right, she assured her comrade. *It would be politic for him to contact us given the seriousness of the charge against his henchmen, but if he doesn't, we now have every reason to pay him an incensed call. We'll let him have until noon to decide. After that, some move will be expected from us.*

Sogan slipped his arm around her once more. *In the meantime, it will be pouring in another few minutes to judge by the way those clouds are filling in, and the night has turned plaguy cold. I suggest we avail ourselves of your father's fine, warm house while we can. We may well be lying up to our necks in a pool of rainwater trying to spy out Dunbrityne house this time tomorrow night.*

NINE

ALL FOUR COMMANDOS remained close to the farmhouse the next morning. An hour before the noon deadline, Islaen Connor was summoned to the transceiver. When she returned some ten minutes later, there was a cold, humorless smile on her lips.

"You spoke to the great man?" Jake inquired.

"Hardly! To one of his minions, but Varn and I have an invitation to take supper with him tonight so that he can 'apologize personally and properly' for this terrible incident, and also hear about it first-hand from us. We are informed that Mr. Thatcher dines formally himself, but we're not to concern ourselves about that. He appreciates the fact that we're only on furlough in this rustic place."

"The son of a Scythian ape!" Bethe Danlo snarled. "What's he doing? Trying to humiliate you before you ever get there?"

"Oh, his game's more subtle than a bit of petty fun. He knows we're holding the blaster in this and wants to unsettle us as much as he can psychologically and also to establish his essential superiority over his employees as much as over us. He doesn't seem to want to get booted out of Dunbrityne at this point in time. That, at least, is to our advantage."

"Are you going to let him play his game?"

Her brown eyes sparkled. "You know me a lot better than that, my friend. A Noreenan and a Federation Commando is the equal of anyone in this ultrasystem or any other, and I'm not minded to leave L. George Thatcher in doubt of that for too very long."

Jake Karmikel's eyes rested on Varn Tarl Sogan. No other man he had ever seen could wear the stark black Commando dress uniform as did this former enemy of theirs. He looked as if he had been born in it. The row of stars gleaming on his breast, each signifying a class-one heroism citation, did not diminish the dramatic effect, either.

"What's keeping Bethe and the Colonel, anyway?" the redhead grumbled aloud.

"Son," Paud Connor told him calmly, "when you've been married as long as I have, you'll realize there's no point in getting worked up over time when women are preparing themselves for some event. Just sit back and relax."

"What will she wear?" Jeanie asked curiously. "Her dress uniform as well?"

"I am not sure," Sogan told her carefully, concealing the sudden unease stirring inside him. "She had mentioned bringing one of her gowns to show off, chiefly to her mother, but I do not know if she did. She could not have expected to have any real use for it."

"You mean you Commandos do wear something besides spacer togs and your uniforms now and then?" Will inquired innocently.

"On occasion," Varn replied, refusing to satisfy the Noreenan's good-humored desire to spark a rise in him. For one thing, Will already knew the answer. Islaen usually adopted the surplanetary costume of high-necked, ruffled blouse and tight-waisted kilt when she visited here. None of her kin had seen her in Thornen garb, however . . .

His companions straightened suddenly—even Jake, who had been with them at the feast celebrating Islaen Connor's formal adoption as daughter to the Doge of Thorne.

The Commando-Colonel stood at the top of the stairs. Her eyes sparkled as she observed their reaction, and Sogan heard her soft laughter sounding in his mind. For his part, the former Admiral was filled with a fierce pride. It was freely acknowledged that his consort was capable and courageous, but he was always pleased in the rarer moments when this other aspect of her received its due homage as well. It was not often that others saw the beautiful woman as well as the much-decorated soldier.

She certainly merited that attention now. Her pale aquamarine gown was fashioned of the finest Thornen silk, light and soft with the faintest trace of a shimmer when struck by any movement or breeze. It followed the line of her slim body to midthigh like a second skin and flowed gracefully from there to a point just above the flat, intricately gold-embroidered slippers of the same fabric.

The sleeves were skintight as well, ending an inch below the elbow. At each wrist was clasped a narrow band of pale yellow Lir gold, not costly in itself but an ideal complement to the dress.

The back was high but the front dropped in a deep, sharp plunge, framing perfectly the pendant she wore there—a single breathtaking stone, thirty carats in weight and of flawless clarity. Its color was an intense blue-green, and the shape, which was naturally formed, was like that of a drop of water frozen even as it fell. Clasped within it at its very heart was a second equally perfect droplet, this of a slightly deeper shade than the jewel surrounding it.

Islaen's kin could see and appreciate the beauty of the gem, but he doubted any of them would recognize it for what it was or realize that it would buy Kinkora, aye, and most of the neighboring farms as well. River tears were the rarest of the major gemstones. Only three deposits existed in all the ultrasystem—in either ultrasystem—two known supplies and the rich loads on Bandit's homeworld whose presence there the settlers were determined to hold secret until their colony was well enough established that they would be able to guard and exploit them effectively. They had presented him with this one following his work to save the colony, knowing that he and his comrades would respect their confidence, and he had given it to his consort—the first gift of real value he had been able to offer her.

She wore no ornament on her head, nothing but her hair itself, nor was there need for anything more. She had, with Bethe's help, dressed it a very formal Thornen style—a complex network of interwoven locks, at once striking and soft.

"You look like a princess," Will gasped, breaking the silence.

"That was the gown she wore the night she was made one," Sogan told him, giving his pride full play in his voice.

I was made a princess the morning I married a prince. Varn looked up, surprised at the vehemence in her tone. She smiled and made herself continue more lightly. *Unless I've failed to fill the position, and he prefers to forget that part of it*.

I have not felt the need to search for a replacement.

The Commando leader came down to them. "All set?" she asked.

"Aye," Sogan replied.

"I'll get the flier," Jake offered.

"No," Islaen told him. "I'd rather our Albionan friends didn't learn about our having that at this point in time. We'll make do with one of the transports. That's what they'll be expecting to see."

"Good," the demolitions expert agreed. "Jake and I can put it to better use. The transports would be too noisy."

The other woman frowned. She glanced at the on-worlders.

Sinéad came to her feet. "This is Commando business. We civilians will go on out to the kitchen for a cup of jakek and leave ye in peace."

"Thanks, Mother."

The commander waited until they were alone before turning to Bethe. "What do you mean?"

"You're riding a comet's tail if you think we're going to let you two drive into that Thugee's lair without a backup."

"Forget it."

"No way, Colonel Connor. You may look fabulous in that dress, but it doesn't offer a whole lot of hiding places for a spring knife, much less a blaster. We can't do much for you inside that house, but we can make damn sure that nothing happens to you between here and there."

"She's right, Islaen," Karmikel interjected. "If they do try anything, it'll likely be while you're en route. They won't be wanting any extraneous bodies or bloodstains around their own lair. —The flier's dead quiet, and we won't let it be seen or reveal ourselves unless they try something."

"We could be glad of their presence," the former Admiral said quietly.

Islaen glanced at him, then at the other two. She nodded slowly. "Very well. Varn will keep his communicator open, and Bandit will stay in contact with us . . ."

The gurry's claws closed on Sogan's shoulder, penetrating the tunic to pinch the flesh beneath. *Nooo! Bandit protect Islaen and Varn!*

Blast you, let go! he hissed. "If Islaen tells you to remain with our friends, you obey her."

"I need to get normal readings, love. You'd soften them if you were there. Besides, you'll know if we get into trouble inside and may be able to lead Jake and Bethe to us."

Bandit will stay, the Jadite agreed reluctantly. She transferred herself to the Sergeant's arm.

Bethe stroked her. "Never mind, pet. You could do them a lot more good this way than if you went with them, and we really will feel better for knowing you're in contact with them."

Varn Tarl Sogan's eyes flickered to his wife's face. He said nothing, not wanting to break her concentration as she scanned the night for any indication of an ambush.

She was afraid. There was no need to question that or to conceal it. Only a rank fool would drive into an enemy stronghold without feeling fear. He was no less uneasy himself.

His dark eyes glittered with a hard, cold light. Scared or not, he was eager for this meeting. Only the Spirit ruling space could fathom how eager. Although they would take no physical action this night, their visit seemed to him to be their first direct blow at the man who had caused such ill.

The Arcturian's hands tightened on the controls. The man who had brought him to such ill. He had forgotten none of it. He could still taste the anguish he had known as he recognized with ever-growing certainty the course he would be forced to follow, given the loss of their assault weapons and the very little time left in which they could act. Sogan remembered vividly his bitter loathing of the thing he had done and of himself, the fear and numb acceptance of the revulsion with which his comrades and the woman he so loved could only hold him in its aftermath.

He had been spared that last, but how that could be, he could not comprehend. His victims had been pirates, aye, or something nearly as bad, but they had been human beings, and he had delivered them up to one of several very horrible deaths. That had to stand poorly against the Federation ethic.

He could accept none of the escape routes offered him by his teammates, not in his own heart. He had detested Amazoon's leeches intensely, yet he had loosed what he cringed from facing himself on others. He might not have actually summoned the blood suckers, but he had known they would follow the wasps, and he had known the fierce hunger that was on them. He could not deny that knowledge or the responsibility put on him because of it.

He had fought to restrain the crawling horde, using all the strong control he had over the jungle planet's wildlife, nearly stripping his own life in the effort—but what did that matter? He had failed. He should have known it would be impossible to hold so many that aroused, especially after some of their number had begun to feed.

He was equally responsible for the disaster in the river, which he had thought would be a safe refuge for the spacers. His party had encountered that sawmill school; and he should have taken its progress into consideration when he had plotted his assault.

The stolen arms had stayed on Amazoon of Indra, but his stupidity, his criminal carelessness, had cost the Navy the witnesses it had needed.

Now another darkness threatened not him, but his consort. She had been forced to bring the shadow of war with all its potential for death to her own closest kin, and if it struck, there would be little or nothing he could do to turn the blow or ease its effect on her.

Hate seared his mind and heart. All the dying on Amazoon, the spacers and the poor Amazoonans who had perished in the crash, all his unit's suffering and all the suffering planned for the target colony, the suffering that might fall on the fine people of Kinkora and their neighbors, everything lay with the greed and lust for power of one individual. The desire, the need, to destroy that man was a consuming hunger within him, feeding upon itself like the furnace that was a star's heart . . .

The Commando-Colonel stirred. She felt her husband's rage and turned to look thoughtfully at him. *I trust you were not serious about throttling our host,* she said gravely.

Varn took hold of himself. *I left my garotte at home,* he assured her with a forced lightness that failed to relieve her concern.

Your have your hands, friend. They can do quite as much.

I shall do nothing, he told her sharply, annoyed that she should feel it necessary to press the issue. *Unless we must defend ourselves, you may depend upon my control.*

I hope there won't be any need to fight, Islaen said, turning the subject. *At best, the odds will be very bad in there.*

Aye.

The woman glanced at him again, a touch of mischief rising in her. She ran her hand over the exquisite material of her gown. *I'd hate for anything to happen to this dress.*

Space! Sogan swore in his own language, but the smile she expected to follow did not come.

You're worried, Varn?

If you are not, we are both in bigger trouble than I had believed, he countered.

I am, but there's more on your mind, I think.

The former Admiral hesitated another moment. *That gown is not meant for this sort of work. Is it stung pride that made you wear it?*

No! Do you take me for such an irresponsible, egotistical mental defective as all that? Islaen stopped herself. She might be furious with him, but if he had doubts, it was his duty to question her. *We'll beat Thatcher at his own game and at the same time allay his fears. He'll be certain now that our arrival on Noreen was purely coincidental, that we suspect him of nothing beyond the two incidents at Kinkora. He'll never imagine Commandos would walk into his clutches like this if we had any idea at all of what he was actually doing.*

Sogan just shook his head. *Jake and Bethe are right. You are good, Islaen, with or without weapons, but you could not fight dressed like this, not well enough.* Thornen silk followed the body's movements extraordinarily well, and the flat slippers would not throw her balance off, but still, she would not be able to manage an extended battle tonight for all her skill at unarmed combat.

The Commando-Colonel seemed to read his thoughts, although she did not actually enter his mind. *Armed or not, we're on our last voyage if we're faced with a major engagement in Dunbrityne house tonight. As for me, I'm not quite as defenseless as I look.* While she was speaking, she unclasped the gold band on her left wrist. Beneath it lay a second bracelet fashioned of what appeared to be several tightly wound strands of thread or hair that glittered even under the dim light thrown off by the dashboard of the transport.

The man smiled, though without humor. Diamond wire. In skilled hands, it could slice the head off an opponent or pierce him through the heart. *My apologies for doubting you, Colonel Connor.*

Accepted, Admiral. —Why didn't you say something back at the house if you were afraid I'd wear this dress? she asked curiously.

I never thought of it. The possibility did not even cross my mind until I was talking with your kin a few moments before you came downstairs. It was too late by then.

They both fell quiet. While they were speaking, they had

penetrated the outskirts of the wood separating Kinkora from Dunbrityne, which comprised a sizable portion of the latter holding's lands.

Forests did not make up any significant portion of this region's floral profile, although it was trees that were farmed and harvested in other regions in place of grain or the soft, long hair of cattle. Lesser woodlands did abound and were cherished for the nuts, berries, and larger fruits they supplied, for the shelter they provided against the sometimes violent winds plaguing the planet, and for their beauty. Trees also formed the border between many fields, and one or more always grew within pastures, where they provided a quick escape should a bull or steer's temper suddenly turn foul, as all too often happened. A row, usually a double row, stood to the north of every dwelling and barn, a final break against the banshee's fury.

The growth was not impressive in itself, particularly after the magnificence of Amazoon's jungle. The trees were only twelve to fourteen feet tall, relatively slender of trunk, and widely enough spread to encourage thriving understory and ground-level communities, including the prized amberberry bushes and several species of viciously potent herb nettles.

It also afforded many excellent ambush sites. Fear tightened the Arcturian's stomach. His every nerve quivered with it. This was too much like Thorne of Brandine had been, when every building potentially screened a sniper and every scarlet uniform was a target.

He raised his communicator to his lips. "We are in the woods. Keep your eyes open."

"We'll be watching," Jake promised. "Just let us know if you plan any sudden changes in course or if the good Colonel picks up anything interesting."

"Will do."

Islaen's hand sought and slipped into Sogan's for a brief moment before allowing him to return it to the controls. At first, he believed he had broadcast his fear but quickly realized she was asking for comfort. Whatever the forewarning she could expect from her gift, the guerrilla commander, too, was afraid.

Jake Karmikel glared at his communicator. "I don't like any of this. I'd be a lot happier attacking that house outright than letting those two march into it."

"Let's just concentrate on seeing to it that they reach it in one piece," Bethe told him in a voice as tight as his own. "It's these blasted trees that I don't like. If we're going to have trouble, I'm nearly certain it'll be in the wood, not in the house itself—and," she added shrewdly, "I'll put credits down that it'll be on the return. Thatcher will want to get a look at them and hear what they've got to say before eliminating them."

"And if you're wrong?"

The Commando-Sergeant shrugged. "Bandit will tell us that. Then we'll have to burn our way in with the laser and hope we can get them out in time."

TEN

THE COMMANDOS' TRANSPORT came to a stop before the brilliantly glowing energy picket surrounding the old farmhouse and its barn.

Big, Islaen Conner commented. *Almost overextended, but not quite.*

It is strong, her husband agreed. *If your Navy had done as well in securing its supplies on Alpha Gary, we would not be sitting here now.*

I hope we won't be kept sitting too long. The Albionan thugs might decide to let them cool their fins for a while before admitting them, although she could not believe they would receive orders to do so. Thatcher should want to be conciliatory, at least at first. Unless he was so close to making his move that he did not care.

A part of the picket shielding the door went down almost the moment they stopped, however, and the pair went forward again. At the entrance, they stopped once more. Sogan came out and, crossing around the vehicle, gave his arm to his consort.

Her laughter sounded in his mind. The roughs admitting them did not leer. They gawked. No fictitious farm boy on his first visit to the inner-systems could have looked more ridiculous. *I guess this isn't quite what they expected of guerrilla officers,* she observed.

No.—Thatcher has a sizable force here, and I would say he is not revealing his full strength to us.

He's not. There are about ten in evidence, and I'm picking up readings from a good thirty more and perhaps a few beyond that.

Their mood?

They're not happy about our being here, but they're not overly nervous, either. She linked her mind with his so that the Arcturian would be able to share directly in the information she was receiving.

The Albionans were all uniformed in the costume of the disbanded Auxiliaries. They were a hard-looking lot, of one type with those the Commandos had encountered at Kinkora, an unpleasant and potentially treacherous company in any setting and particularly so in number in their own stronghold.

Dunbrityne house was unremarkable in itself. It was about the size of Kinkora and of nearly identical design, although it was of a considerably later date. It was bleaker, well-maintained, but these tenants did not impart to it the warmth and personality of a legitimate family. Indeed, L. George Thatcher and his cohorts had made little change in the place at all, using the Spartan furnishings that had come with it and adding almost nothing of their own—an obvious sign that the former Minister had no intention of staying permanently or long-term in it.

He did keep it warmer than the usual on-world custom—not a great deal more, but enough to be perceptible to those accustomed to the lower temperatures prevailing elsewhere.

Islaen's eyes lowered. This was an unfortunate holding, she thought. The farm had been the headquarters of the Britynons during their attempted take-over of the planet generations ago, hence its name. Now again, a dark, vicious crew was based within the buildings raised upon the ruins of the structures those old enemies had put up.

Her head lifted suddenly in pride. Her forebears had been instrumental in halting that first threat, and they had come out of it all sound and clothed in their people's honor, in the honor of the entire Federation. She offered a quick, fervent prayer that this, too, might prove the case in her own time.

They paused before the chamber that was the equivalent of Kinkora's sitting room while their escort knocked respectfully on the door. A muffled voice answered, and they were ushered inside.

L. George Thatcher looked even as the tapes they had studied portrayed him. He was not quite as tall as the war prince and was compactly built in proportion, with classic north Terran features that would be considered quite handsome on the Federation's mother planet, although they had a slightly overrefined cast for rim world tastes. His skin was fair and smooth, his hair a fine dark brown, his eyes gray. Although long since past the flush of late adolescence, he had availed himself to the full of science's discoveries, and age had not ravaged his appearance. His body was slim and sound but obviously unworked, its softness particularly noticeable in this part of the ultrasystem where the muscles of spacers and on-worlders alike were hardened by considerable physical labor.

His voice, when he gave them greeting, was well modulated. He spoke Basic with a carefully cultured Terran accent unmarked by any trace of the speech patterns of the planet on which he had been raised.

His dress was indeed formal, suited to a major banquet in the inner-systems, not a quiet dinner on the rim. Anger flickered through Islaen Connor's thoughts. *He's gone all out to overawe us, hasn't he?*

Her comrade shrugged in mind. *He does not know what is appropriate despite all his supposed high culture,* Sogan judged contemptuously.

The Noreenan looked sharply at him. This was not the man who had lived and served beside her since their meeting on Visnu. This was the Varn Tarl Sogan she had first known—war prince and Admiral of the Arcturian Empire. In a sense, she had never seen him precisely like this before. He had ever been courteous even in anger, and the contempt on him now was that of a warrior for a menial who had done the unthinkable and tried to overstep his place only to fail miserably. *Be careful,* she warned sharply. He could destroy their hope of learning anything here, aye, and bring both of them into even greater peril than they already faced if he was too open in displaying what she was receiving so strongly from him.

Do not worry. I shall not betray us before this garbage.

See that you don't. L. George Thatcher didn't err through ignorance. He wants to overwhelm us.

Unless he is mad, Sogan said in a different tone.

Aye, she agreed grimly. If that were the case, most of their assumptions might prove false, including the belief that they would at least be allowed to leave the house unharmed. She was not likely to detect such derangement, either, no more than she had been able to read Thurston Sandstone's illness.

The Terran, in his turn, studied his guests intently. His eyes went first to the woman and riveted on her, or rather, on the gown she wore and the jewel glistening on her neck. He knew both for what they were and realized that the stories he had heard about the place to which she had been elevated on Thorne of Brandine, which he had previously discounted as peasants' wish tales, must be true after all. No Navy officer's salary, even when supplemented by the credits accompanying the citations she was reputed to have won could have supplied these extravagances. At least, he thought, her sojourn in Thorne's culture appeared to have benefited her. She knew enough not to surround that river tear with the diamonds she patently could have used to accompany it, but rather allowed it to shine alone in its glory.

The jewel and her beauty. Islaen Connor was stunningly lovely. Noreen's race was attractive by Terran standards, and displayed thus, this guerrilla equalled and surpassed their prototype ideal. She would be well worthy . . .

Only for a moment did he permit himself to dwell on that possibility. Hers was a perilous beauty for the like of him, and only a stark fool or a boy would allow his thoughts to be muddled by carnal considerations with his plans so near to completion.

Thatcher's eyes turned to her comrade, who was also her husband. He sighed to himself, admitting his folly and annoyed with himself because of it. A child would have recognized the stupidity of it. A Commando's uniform was appropriate for any social engagement. It was he, not this man, who appeared ignorant and out of place.

He put that regret out of his thoughts. It had been a fool's game, unworthy of him from the start, and inevitably, it had backfired on him. There was nothing for it now but to make the best of it and salvage what he could of the situation. Perhaps he could still turn the evening to his advantage if he handled himself and his supposed guests well.

He concentrated on the man, trying to assess him quickly. It was no easy task. Such a one, accustomed to fighting a semi-clandestine war as he was, would almost habitually screen more of himself than he revealed and would be a challenge to read accurately in a lot longer time and under less tense conditions than prevailed here. The Commando-Captain's face was certainly impassive—even chilling, with those dark, cold eyes ever-boring into one's own.

Sogan was a different physical type from his commander, definitely of another root stock, perhaps some mongrel bred from a long-term Navy family. He carried himself as a soldier and with the air of a person well accustomed to command.

More than command. Thatcher's eyes narrowed. He had misjudged the Captain. This was no mere space or Navy mixed breed. The man held himself as one who ruled by natural right. He had seen that air before, a faint shadow of it, back in his days at the university, in the daughter of one of Terra's ancient kings. She and many generations of her ancestors before her were figureheads with little real authority. That might not be the case with the off-worlder before him.

Here was the secret of the Connor woman's acceptance into the ruling house on Thorne, he thought. The planet, though quite as old as Terra, had progressed on different social and economic lines. The various sectors of the world were controlled by the hereditary princes of the ancient merchant houses, all of whom owed allegiance to the Doge. Islaen Conner must either have married into one of those ruling families or perhaps even a younger son of the Doge himself and, given the debt the populace owed her, had been granted this adoption in order to legitimize the union. It was known that the Thornens did not encourage close contact with off-worlders as a rule.

Sogan was aware of Thatcher's scrutiny but was not troubled by it. Nothing else was to be expected under these circumstances. Its absence would have been unnatural and no small cause for concern.

The Arcturian's expression remained cold, impassive, but the hatred inside him swelled until he could all but taste the bitter sourness of it. This was the source of the shame he had called down on himself. Because of this accursed banker, this soft-bodied, arrogant glorified menial, the single illusion he had held to him in all the grief of his life was now shattered—the belief that his honor was proof against butcher work, against the ordering or committing of what both ultrasystems labeled atrocity, whatever the provocation, military or personal. Thatcher's stolen arms had provided the challenge, and he had folded under it, as so many had before him in humankind's stained history. That loss he would never forget and never be able to forgive.

L. George Thatcher stiffened under that fixed, chilling gaze. The bastard was looking at him as if he were less than some crawling thing, unworthy even of notice . . .

He gripped himself. The guerrilla's lovely and probably much-loved wife had very nearly been run down by those Albionan oxen. This was precisely the reaction such a man would display when denied the right to vent his anger, at least temporarily. Their visit was not a social one, after all, but a meeting to discuss in a civilized manner a very serious infraction. Not for the first time, he roundly cursed his two employees in mind and heart even as he exchanged preliminary courtesies with the pair.

The time was come to touch upon the subject of the incidents which had brought the Commandos. "Needless to say, I thank you for coming, Colonel Connor, Captain Sogan," he said with practiced warmth. "I know anything I tell you has to sound trite, but I am truly dreadfully sorry for what's happened, for both incidents. I am involved myself to the extent that the perpetrators are my employees.—But come inside now. Dinner is ready to be served."

Smooth, Varn commented.

Too smooth, the Colonel replied grimly. *We're not going to learn as much as I'd hoped to get out of this.*

He is also a liar.

Through his teeth, she agreed.

I do not suppose he will try to poison or drug us?

He'd be broadcasting something of that intention, or his minions would. I'd pick it up.

Thatcher had shepherded them out of the sparsely furnished sitting room to the rather larger eating chamber, giving them no opportunity to observe anything more of the dwelling. This, too, contained basic heavy Noreenan farm furniture, old and much used, not approaching that which graced her parent's house. In contrast, the service on the board was of fine quality, and the food even then being brought in looked and smelled wonderful.

That last observation gave the Noreenan little pleasure. She was not going to enjoy it or anything else this long evening, not with the level and nature of the emotions whipping into her from the two men. Violent passion of any sort was never pleasant to receive, and she dared shut none of it out lest she miss some detail or clue about the former Minister of Justice or his intentions. Islaen sighed to herself. Already her head was pounding, and she wished heartily that Bandit were here. She would welcome the Jadite's soothing influence at the moment to cool her companion down and give her a few minutes' relief.

This is hard on you, the war prince said sympathetically as hi mind brushed hers. *I can sever contact and raise my shields. That would relieve you of my part of the transmissions.*

No, she replied, rallying and once more setting herself to the task at hand. *What I learn, you learn. I may need your input.*

She sampled the wine in her glass. "This is excellent, Mr. Thatcher. You lay a commendable table."

"I feel that is a necessity both for myself and for my guests. It's one aspect of civilization available even here on the rim for those willing to exert themselves to find an importer."

They spoke in general terms for a few minutes, then the Terran brought the conversation around to the trouble his party had caused, this time for in-depth discussion. "I have your father's report of the problem with his animals, Colonel, and believe it readily enough," he said gravely. "Most of my people here are urban bred and not of the highest social or educational levels. They tend to find life on Noreen very tedious. I don't doubt that they might try to relieve their boredom in unacceptable ways without even realizing they could be causing damage. The second matter is of a totally different nature, however, and Captain Sogan gave no details when he reported it."

"I was very angry at the time," Varn told him, "as you can well imagine. I still am."

"You can't be blamed for that. I'm angry myself. Those were my men, and they'd gone to your father-in-law's farm on an errand from me. Please. Just what did happen?"

Islaen described the encounter.

Thatcher shook his head. "A terrible thing," he said. "You are certain that is what really occurred? You say your back was turned when the transport started moving."

"What she did not see, I did." The Arcturian's cool voice belied the fury inside him, that and his certainty that Islaen was right, that they were going to learn very little by these means. Their opponent was too good. Every gesture and expression, every word, every intonation was correct. Had he not been linked with Islaen Connor's mind and privy to their host's mental transmissions, he might have believed the Terran was indeed innocent. Thatcher would give them no opening, make no slip for them to seize upon.

His hate waxed stronger. There was no concrete proof of it, but he was convinced in his heart of their host's sanity now, even as the nature of those radiations, the unclean triumph and duplicity in them, convinced him of L. George Thatcher's guilt. He had once faced another man who was also plotting the destruction of those dependent upon him, those he was bound to aid, but Thurston Sandstone had been sick, his mind tragically shattered. Once his designs had been thwarted and he himself placed where he could do no one harm again, the guerrilla team who had fought to bring him down could only pity him, pity and grieve for the destruction of what had once been a fine intellect and sensitive spirit. The man before them now was evil, a traitor to his ultrasystem and oaths, a renegade willing to plunder lives and the hopes of generations to gain his desired measure of power and wealth beyond his already great store.

Thatcher gave an impatient shake of his head. "The fools!" he exclaimed. "Yet I can't just abandon them. I took them from among the dregs of their society, you see, like many of their associates in the Auxiliary Police, and gave them trust and authority. They're loyal to me as a result, and I suppose they reverted to their old methods of handling trouble when they felt I was threatened with still more difficulty. —Fortune has gone hard with me of late, as you may know."

Islaen nodded. She would naturally have requested a check on his background after the supposed attempt on her life by his hirelings. He would expect that she would be aware of his recent history. "I'm sorry for that. Many a good man has been caught up in a similar political sweep."

"I'm glad you can see it that way, Colonel Connor. Few enough do, official or civilian." He leaned forward. "Please don't misconstrue what I'm about to say. I'm not trying to offer anyone a bribe. I shouldn't dare with everything else that the Patrol is probably still trying to lay against me. —Nothing I have to offer could compensate you for what happened, Colonel, but would you tell your father that I am willing to make him any reasonable restitution for the damage to his stock and for the inconvenience he suffered as a result."

"I'll tell him," she replied noncommittally.

I should like to hear his definition of an attempted bribe if that is not one, her husband remarked dryly. *He cannot pay you off, but he could do well by our kin.*

"Mr. Connor mentioned the possibility of an eviction," the Terran said. "I should like to have a little more time. I have not only to settle myself someplace but my poor companions as well

Albion was their homeworld, after all, and they are not wealthy people able to pick up and drop stakes at a whim."

"That decision is his. He can't be blamed for wanting you all out of here, but I'll speak with him. He's neither heartless nor unreasonable."

"I appreciate that, Colonel." Thatcher pursed his lips and looked down at his emptied plate. "I'd like you to release my employees into my custody if that's possible."

"That's something entirely different."

"I understand the seriousness of what they've done, but I truly do not want them to suffer too heavily for their loyalty to me, for their own sakes and for the rest of us. My party's having a bad enough time of it without more bad publicity reaching the Stellar Patrol. I can guarantee that they'll be heavily disciplined."

"You are better off not having men of their sort around you," Varn Tarl Sogan told him. "They have already brought trouble on you, and with tempers like theirs, coupled with the lack of judgment they have displayed, they would almost certainly do so again."

"I realize that, Captain, and they'll be given no more assignments by me, but I do owe them all the help I can give them."

Aye, especially when he's eager to keep their mouths shut, the woman muttered in her mind. "It'll have to take the form of getting them a good lawyer, then, one well versed in military law."

"Military law!"

"Aye. They attacked a Navy officer, and it's a military tribunal that they'll have to face, not a civilian court." Her manner seemed to soften. "I have little choice in the matter, Mr. Thatcher. The Navy insists on full prosecution and maximum sentences in cases of assaults on their personnel. They don't want the slime infesting the starlanes and planets of the Federation to get the idea that it's safe to do that. Ever."

"Where are they now? Can I see them?" Thatcher asked after a brief pause.

"You can see them, but I'm afraid you'll have to travel to do it. The local Garda has picked them up and brought them to the spaceport to await the Patrol, who'll take them to Horus for trial."

"But will you two be able to spare time for that?"

"A tribunal doesn't take long to reach a verdict. The trial will start as soon as we return from furlough. We'll transmit formal depositions tomorrow morning. That'll cover us for testimony even if we're pulled into another mission at once or are delayed en route going back. There will be a formal session taped with questioning by both lawyers once we do reach base, of course."

Islaen! Sogan warned sharply.

I know. It's a gamble, but I want to provoke . . .

The reaction came even as she was speaking, so suddenly and of such a nature that she was hard pressed not to stare openly at the Terran.

The tension, even the hostility, left Thatcher—simply vanished from him entirely. There was no change in his expression or posture or behavior toward them, but he had eliminated the Commandos as a source of concern, as objects worthy of his attention at all, as completely as if they had ceased to exist.

For one instant, Islaen was tempted to smile. Varn Tarl Sogan was not accustomed to receiving such a dismissal, and he did not like it.

Anger overwhelmed her amusement, and the former Admiral's answered and reinforced it. This, then, was how L. George Thatcher had been able to plot and work as he had. He viewed the people of Albion whom he had been about to betray as well as those whose colony he was preparing to rape for his enrichment as creatures without value, whose rights and hopes, whose lives, merited no concern on his part and received none.

Sogan wondered momentarily at the strength of his reaction against that and at his arrant hypocrisy in condemning the Terran for it at all. Was that same attitude not his own and that of his own people? Had a few years in the Federation altered his thoughtways so greatly, or was this indignation stemming from less creditable roots, merely serving as further justification for acting against the man responsible for the great injury he had taken?

He checked himself. For now, at least, the forces spurring his hate had no relevance. It was the time for action, or the preparation for action, not for reflection. Both he and his Colonel were certain in their hearts that L. George Thatcher had violated the oaths he had taken with respect to Albion of Scotia and was a traitor to the Federation ethic to which he was sworn. With that knowledge came the ever-stronger determination to stop this renegade, to pull him down before he could reap the bloody fruit of his plot.

I wish he would give us the excuse to send a bolt through that void he calls a heart, the war prince snarled, sharing the anger he must otherwise control.

I know. He won't, though, not here. Once we leave, it'll be another story. She gave a bitter laugh *It may not be easy to incriminate him even then, assuming we're still around to try.*

You believe our deaths are determined?

You're sharing what I'm getting. He's come to his decision about us. That much is certain. It's likely that he'll have us ambushed on the way home to keep us from making that deposition tomorrow. She gave a mental grimace. *I blew that one.* She sighed. *Maybe he's just decided that we're not important enough to bother himself any further, but I doubt it. —Our host serves a fine meal, Admiral. I hope you're enjoying it more than I am.*

Colonel, he replied, *L. George Thatcher may set an elegant table, but trust that I would much prefer to be sitting at your father's board right now, or just about anywhere else in this vast galaxy, not excluding Amazoon's jungles—blood suckers and all.*

ELEVEN

THATCHER ESCORTED THE pair to their transport and, in the manner proper to a host, remained outside to watch their departure until they had passed between the glowing bars of the energy picket guarding his stronghold.

It was only after she felt him withdraw inside once more that Islaen Connor drew a deep breath, releasing the tension imprisoned within her. She closed her eyes. Noreen's night air was clear and clean, free of the human-induced foulness she had experienced in that house.

Her eyes opened again, and she stole a quick glance at her husband. He was himself once more. Or had he merely reassumed the mask circumstances forced him to throw over himself in order to survive, whether among the teammates with whom he was at ease or in the ever-perilous ultrasystem at large? That haughty master of menials she had seen in there was no stranger to her. She had seen him on Thorne of Brandine when Varn Tarl Sogan had functioned as a free, unshadowed man in his own place among the soldiers of his race. Yet even there, he had not shown himself in that aspect very often; only when compelled to assert his absolute authority had he conducted himself thus. When in battle or at administrative work with those comrades he loved, he had been different yet again. Which one was, in fact, the true man—or which combination made the truth?

Islaen shook her head. She would never know the answer to that. She feared it too much to ask.

The Arcturian shifted in the seat beside her. *Is your headache bad?* he asked sympathetically.

No. It's fading. It's hard probing continuously like that

particularly in so unpleasantly charged an atmosphere, but the effects wear off quickly.

I was not much help, he said ruefully.

No, she admitted, since he knew that full well already, *but my transmissions can't have been very comfortable for you, either.*

You were better controlled.

Sogan shifted again, uneasily. They were back in the shadow of the trees, and his fear had returned. Returned and doubled. They had more or less expected to be allowed to reach Thatcher's lair unmolested. Neither of them anticipated getting home again without interference. *Anything yet?* he asked, since the Colonel had broken her link with him save for surface communication when they had left the perimeter, giving the full of her concentration to the task of scanning their surroundings for the enemies they expected to find waiting somewhere out there.

Not yet, but they'll be stationed farther in the wood if they're here, not at their boss' doorstep.

Several more minutes passed. Islaen's eyes narrowed. *There they are. I'm picking up two, and they're primed to kill.* There was no mistaking that. She had encountered radiations like these all too often before.

Where?

Some distance yet. Probably at the outer edge of the wood on the Kinkora side. —Give our comrades a call. From the readings I'm getting from Jake and Bethe, they already know we've got company. Just tell them their intentions are something less than honorable. Ask them to keep the flier out of sight if they can.

Aye, Colonel, he said as he brought his communicator to his lips.

Jake Karmikel lowered his communicator. "Here goes, Sergeant Danlo."

In answer, Bethe checked her blaster once again and set it back in its holster. They had seen the two Albionans leave Dunbrityne house minutes after their comrades had entered and had followed them back here, where they had settled down to await the Commandos' return. That they had finally gotten their orders to kill them came as no surprise to her, no more than it must have to the assassins themselves.

"Bandit, you stay here, pet," she whispered to the gurry as she slipped out of the flier. "Human warfare's no place for you."

The spacer crouched low and followed after Jake. Her heart beat fast, and she prayed that she would do nothing, make no sound or other error, to betray their approach. Intellectually, she recognized that she had more training, aye, and more experience now than many a Commando who had been sent out to fight the forces of the Arcturian Empire and who had returned to tell of his success, but she could never hope to match Karmikel and Islaen Conner with their years of guerrilla service to back them. In moments like this, she was acutely conscious of that disparity.

There was no trouble. The pair moved like a couple of ghosts through the deeply shadowed woods until they came upon the Albionans. The assassins were concealed in the brush between two trees, straining to catch the first sound of the approaching transport. They had rightly assumed their targets would be coming this way, it being the only satisfactory road through the wood. Their weapons were drawn and held at ready.

"Drop the blasters, you sons, and grab the moon!"

One snapped her weapon up at the sound of Jake's voice, only to have it shot out of her hand by a pencil-slender beam from Bethe's blaster. The second dropped his without protest. "Freeze," he snarled in a whisper to his comrade. "They're Commandos. They'd fry us six times each before we could even start to fire."

"Sound advice," the Captain agreed. "Just keep real quiet, and you'll stay alive. For the time being, at least."

"We haven't done anything, and you don't got proof . . ."

"Can it. We're not the Patrol. We obey the commands of good, old-fashioned military expediency, not a slate of rules laid out by a pack of inner-system bleeding hearts. We may not be the type to burn you down outright, but none of us care much for back-alley work, even when our own friends aren't involved."

That, the renegades believed, and neither showed any inclination to cause trouble when Bethe collected their weapons and frisked them while Jake kept them covered.

"Safety's off both," she remarked when she finished, "and they're set to slay."

"What're you going to do with us?" the Albionan woman asked sullenly.

"You'll be going before a military tribunal, I suppose, like your other two friends. Whether it'll be individually or as part of a conspiracy or both, I couldn't venture to say at this point. It'll turn out the same in the end anyway, as far as your ultimate fate is concerned."

That silenced the prisoners. The charge they faced was a capital one, and the chance was good that they would be found guilty. Unless Thatcher could buy them free, they could well be looking at an executioner before the year was out. Perhaps even before the next couple of months were out. The Navy wasted no time in such matters.

The purring roar of an approaching transport dispelled the stillness that had fallen over the night, and minutes later, Varn Tarl Sogan brought his vehicle to a stop before the group.

"What is going on?" he asked the other Captain. "A welcoming committee?"

"These folk must have some important information to impart. Sensitive, too, or they wouldn't have felt it necessary to meet you here in the dark with weapons ready to fire and set to kill."

"That had better prove the case," Islaen remarked coldly. "The Navy knows how to handle back-alley thugs. —Use their belts to bind them, and toss them in the back. You ride with them, Jake. Bethe, stick around a while and see if any more company follows up on these two." Her voice dropped. "Bring the flier in once you think we're back home and inside."

"Aye, Colonel."

"We'll call the Garda to come and collect them once we reach home."

Jake chuckled. "Keep this up, and they'll be putting Kinkora on their regular patrol route, sort of like a mail stop where they pick up a new lot of prisoners each morning. —You two look beat. Go on up to bed when we get home. I'll take care of the transmission and put this scum to sleep."

"Thanks, friend. We are tired."

"Roust Thatcher out now or wait until morning?"

She thought for a moment. "Neither," she said in the end. "I think we'll just let L. George Thatcher wonder what did happen for a while. It might help unsettle him a bit."

Islaen paused at her parents' room to inform them about the two prisoners they would find tied and stunned in the hallway and then went to her own chamber.

Sogan joined her several minutes later. *It is good to have that over,* he said with real relief.

Our guests are secure? she asked. He would have passed them after putting the transport away.

Peacefully sleeping, he replied, touching the hand grip of his blaster as he carefully unfastened his utility belt and lay it aside. *Jake made a thorough job of it. They will not be rousing before morning.*

Good. That's one less worry for us.

The Noreenan had not begun to undress. She gazed into the mirror surmounting the well-used and well-remembered dresser and sighed. Despite all the tension of the evening, she still looked good . . .

What is wrong? Varn asked, puzzled by her delay. He knew how tired she was.

Stark idiocy, she replied with a rueful smile. *I'm reluctant to take this outfit off and go back to being a soldier again.*

The war prince came over to her and slipped his arms around her. His fingers ran gently across her back, then found and began to loosen the fastenings of her gown. *Perhaps we could discover a way to make the disrobing a little less painful, my Islaen,* he whispered as his lips found hers.

TWELVE

ISLAEN CONNOR SLIPPED from beneath the covers, moving carefully so as not to disturb her companion.

Varn was still asleep. She looked down at him, smiling tenderly. He still seemed tired and drawn, but there was a peace on him that she had not seen in a long while. The meeting with Thatcher, the stark evil of him, had settled a great deal for the war prince. He accepted at last in his own heart the absolute necessity of stopping those arms from reaching their destination, even if the means of that stopping remained a shadow over him.

She smiled again. She supposed she even owed Thatcher, though he would get no payment from her. She had disliked the magnitude of the hatred she had felt in her husband in their enemy's house, but it was preferable to the shame and self-loathing which had gone before it.

The woman glanced at her timer. It was morning but not yet dawn, too early for any of the household to be up as yet.

She shivered. The chill of Noreen's predawn had not diminished over the years. She thrust her feet into the heavy slippers waiting by the bed and drew on her fleecy robe, pulling it tightly around herself.

Islaen stole from the room. No sooner had she reached the stairs than Bandit hurtled from out of the shadows and landed softly on her shoulder. *Robe nice! Warm!*

It is, love. It's needed here. She spoke in thought, fearing she would disturb the rest of the house if she answered aloud.

Yes!—Breakfast now?

Not quite. I just wanted to get a cup of jakek and bring one back to Varn.

Varn's sleeping!

I know, but the Garda will be coming early. Besides, she added, recalling her brother's comments regarding the ease of a Commando's daily life, *I don't want us in bed too long after my family gets up.*

Why? the gurry inquired curiously.

Human illogic, my little friend.

By then they had reached the kitchen, and the Colonel hastily cautioned her companion to remain silent even as Bandit prepared to let loose the pleased whistle that announced the close proximity of food.

Now, I told you this isn't breakfast, the human said as she programmed the range. Glancing over her shoulder as if she were afraid to be caught in some slightly shady activity, she broke off a few pieces of sugarloaf bread. *Here, nibble on this, but you'll have to wait until everyone's really up for a proper meal.*

Islaen downed her own portion and filled Sogan's cup. Bandit quickly coiled her tongue around the last of the crumbs and hopped to the guerrilla's shoulder once more.

Stay here for a bit longer, Islaen told her.

Does Islaen want Varn to love her again?

She turned scarlet. *I want Varn to have his jakek in peace! Now stay put a while, you little minx!*

Islaen's face was still flushed when she woke her husband and handed him the dark, richly flavored liquid.

This is service, he approved. He took a long drink. *It is good. Thanks.*

He looked at her then and smiled, half-puzzled and half-amused. *What in space has happened now?* he asked. It was obviously nothing serious, but she was quite discomforted.

Bandit. The little witch caught me off balance. She told him what the gurry had said.

Sogan laughed. He finished the jakek and set the cup aside, then propped himself up on the pillows, studying her speculatively. *Our Jadite friend may have come up with a rather good suggestion,* he told her as he reached up to draw her close.

The elder Connors were at the table when the Commando leaders came into the kitchen. Bandit was with them, perched beside Paud's plate.

He raised his hand in greeting to the pair before dropping it again to continue stroking the gurry. "She can eat for something her size!" he enthused.

"Aye," Islaen agreed dryly. "Unfortunately, she's not the member of my household that I'd like to fatten up a bit."

She settled into her own chair and helped herself to a poached egg, a real one and no synthetic. "Any sign of my other comrades?"

"They're probably still asleep."

"Bandit," she commanded. "Wake Bethe. Wake Jake." *If you can get airborne after that meal.*

Bandit can fly! In proof, she rose from the table, circled the Colonel's head, and streaked out of the kitchen.

"How will she get into their room?" her father asked.

"They leave the door open a crack for her when we're quartered near one another."

"We saw our guests," the farmer said.

"Still out, I take it?"

"Yes. —What happened this time?"

"They were waiting to back-alley us on this end of the wood when we left Dunbrityne."

The two on-worlders fell into a grim silence.

"Well, lass," Paud said after a moment, "trying to run you down with the transport might have been spur-of-the-moment planning, but this sounds like something more serious."

"It was. I don't think we made ourselves too popular with L. George Thatcher."

"That's putting it mildly," Jake said from the doorway. "Did you send that little feathered demon to roust us out, Colonel?"

"Aye, but since both of you're fully dressed, I can see it wasn't necessary."

"That's immaterial. The cruel intent was there."

Sinéad Murchu laughed. "Sit down and eat. Life always seems brighter after a good breakfast. In the meantime, ye'll have to xcuse us. The harvest's on, ye know, and we don't want to keep 'ill and Jeanie waiting. We'd like to get a good start cutting efore the others arrive to help us draw in and store."

The Commandos ate quickly and in silence, following the habit f those accustomed to space and the speed with which emergenies could arise to terminate a meal there. When they had finished, ey settled back, taking their ease for a few minutes.

"That was marvelous!" Bethe exclaimed. "Bandit's not the only one in dire danger of losing her figure in this place."

"No one's ever starved to death under a Connor roof," Islaen agreed, smiling.

Jake nodded, but his eyes were dark. "What now, Comrades? Did you get what we wanted out of last night? It all sounded terribly civilized over our communicators."

"Including one attempted bribe?" Sogan asked, indignation rising in him as it had on the previous evening.

"Aye, naturally."

The former Admiral shook his head. "I do not believe the result was worth the risk," he told them. "We are now convinced in our own minds that Thatcher's guilty, if not of the crime we seek to solve, then of something equally grave, but we gained no concrete evidence. He guarded his speech too well, and he gave us no real look at the house or any hiding places it might contain. We did provoke him into openly acting against us in the end, but that will probably work more to our disadvantage than our good, unless his would-be killers lose heart and start talking a lot faster than I believe they will."

"I'm afraid I must agree," Islaen Connor said a trace dejectedly, "though we did pick up some information."

"Such as?" the redhead asked. "I heard nothing significant."

"No, but by having us attacked, or allowing it, Thatcher's told us our time's almost out. He still wants to delay eviction a short while longer, maybe a couple of weeks or so, but he doesn't care about a much longer stay. That's why he wasn't afraid to have us removed. He's too cautious a man to take the chance otherwise. He would probably have destroyed our bodies back at the house or had us buried somewhere so we wouldn't be found too quickly. What might happen long-term doesn't trouble him since he'll be well away."

"Why attack you in the first place?" the demolitions exper asked. "I can't fathom that one at all."

"He'd decided we were no threat, or no immediate threat, bu he still didn't like the idea of our being so near. If nothing else, w might follow after him too quickly and compromise his escape Besides, he owed us a burning for thwarting him on Amazoon. H lost all hope of making a really big haul when we took back thos arms."

"You think he knew about that?"

Jake answered for his commander with a cold laugh. "With the publicity the Navy gave that story—'A Second Tatarina Averted,' and all the rest of it? It would've gotten double exposure here, too. Our unit's always news on Noreen of Tara."

"I think I discovered something else as well," the Commando-Colonel continued slowly. "All the houses in this area are laid out on the same plan. Three of the downstairs rooms at Dunbrityne are used for the usual purposes—kitchen, dining room, and sitting room. The door of the fourth was closed, and I'd put a lot of credits down that there was a strong antipersonnel seal on it."

"The entrance and windows had them," Varn affirmed, "and they appeared to be alarmed as well. I imagine we can assume the same for upstairs and the rear, and for the roof door if there is one."

"There is. —Stout guards for innocent visitors, my friends, especially those who've made no other improvements or alterations in the house."

"Sensitive supplies or records?" Jake suggested.

"The latter, I think. Thatcher's hands would have their arms with them in their own barracks, and any big matériel would be with his fleet, not here."

Karmikel frowned. "You think he's keeping some sort of journal or diary?"

Islaen shook her head. "He's no madman, and even if he were, I doubt his insanity would manifest itself that way. He's after profit and maybe a measure of power, if only the power to crush, not an energy shot for his ego."

"Records are equally dangerous," Bethe reminded her.

"They're also necessary to a large, complex effort like this. Thatcher's had to assemble and then support his miniature navy, not to mention the staff he has with him, long-term. He has to have notes or ledgers of some sort, though maybe coded in some manner to conceal their true nature from casual scrutiny. That'll depend on his confidence in his power to protect them."

"Aye," her fellow Noreenan agreed, "and he would've begun keeping them long before Marta Florr planeted on Albion and disrupted Thatcher's supposedly secure life. If he didn't have them coded before then, he sure as space didn't have time to do it at that stage. He would just have to keep them hidden among his other, legitimate private papers and run with them."

"Granting all that," the Sergeant said, "what are we going to do about it?"

"Pick them up tonight," Islaen Connor replied. "If we can find them, that is."

The Arcturian's brows raised, but he was hardly surprised. That was their logical move. "Your plan, Colonel?"

"It's simple enough. We'll wait until dark, take the flier as far as the end of the wood, and Jake and I'll work our way in from there. You and Bethe will have to stick with the flier and cover us."

"What will the Albionans be doing while you two are burglarizing their headquarters?" the spacer demanded.

"Sleeping, I'd say. Their mechanical defenses are fairly strong, and Noreen's always been a peaceful world as far as they're concerned. They won't be feeling too nervous."

"What do we do until then?"

Islaen came to her feet and started removing the empty ware from the table. "I, for one, shall turn farmer. My family can use the additional help with the harvest."

"Count me in," Jake Karmikel declared. "It's been a long time since I've had a pike in my hand. It'll be interesting to see if I've still got the knack of wielding one."

"I guess that means I'd better volunteer as well," his wife said cheerfully. "It wouldn't do to make a bad impression."

Varn Tarl Sogan said nothing. Islaen's mind swiftly touched with his. *You'd best stay here,* she told him casually. *I want our gear checked thoroughly, and someone should really stick around to watch the fort, not to mention to greet the Garda.*

I shall take advantage of that escape this time. I would be as out of place as the Fairest Maid *would be in the center of a camp of pre-mechanical hunter-gatherers.*

That's not entirely true, Varn, not unless you made it so.

He swept up the remaining dishes and stacked them in the cleaner cabinet. *I want a few hours to really go over our notes and the material Ram Sithe gave us.* He frowned. *There is something pricking at me, Islaen. I cannot shake the feeling that some answer we need is right before me, if only I had the wit to grasp it.*

Take whatever time you need, she told him gravely. *Call us in if we can be of any help. An extra head can be useful at times.*

Mine has not been doing us much good this morning, he said ruefully. Varn gave her a quick smile. *Do not kill yourselves today. Remember that we have a night of clandestine labor ahead of us while Noreen's honest farmers will be blissfully sunk in the sleep of the just.*

The former Admiral pressed his fingers to his eyes in an attempt to ease the ache forming behind them.

It was no use. He had examined every shred of information they had and then gone back over it all yet again, to no avail. Several times, something had teased at the outer fringes of his consciousness, but no matter how he had encouraged it, the embryonic idea had always faded again before he could grasp it.

He was frustrated and angry. It might be nothing, but if there was some fact he should know and the mission failed because he could not call the information to mind, then a great part of the responsibility for whatever happened would be his.

He came to his feet abruptly and strode away from the small table where he had been working. Going on like this would accomplish nothing.

Sogan's mind reached out. Communication over distance was more difficult than face-to-face conversation, but he knew his consort was not very far. *Islaen?* he called.

Varn! Any luck?

No. I have brought up a blank screen. I still feel there is something . . .

The Colonel was disappointed as well, and concerned. She put a great deal of trust in her husband's ability to sense danger and in his power to analyze a situation. She would very much have preferred knowing precisely what was troubling him.

She took care that none of that entered her words or the open thoughts behind them. *You won't learn it by pushing any further, then, at least not at this time. Break it off completely for now. Go for a walk and then fix yourself something to eat. Your mind will be fresher after that.*

That was my intention. I just wanted to check in with you first.

Shall I send Bandit back to keep you company? He could feel her smile. *You'll be doing me a favor. The work's going so well that we're not likely to be stopping for a while yet. She's already swooping around the lunch baskets, and she'll be embarrassing me before much longer.*

The man laughed. *Aye, give me a few minutes to tidy up here and then send her to me. It may be still another proof that my mind is slipping, but I miss having the little rogue around.*

THIRTEEN

VARN SWEPT THE material he had been reviewing back into the safe-lock portfolio and left the room, first setting devices similar to those he used on the *Fairest Maid* to alert him to any attempted tampering during his absence. The distance between Kinkora and Dunbrityne was not so great as to preclude the possibility of spying, particularly with the Connor house empty for large portions of the day during the harvest.

He closed the outer door as well, satisfying himself with just pulling it shut, and drew a deep breath of the sweet air. It was a bit heavier than usual, he noted, but not enough to be uncomfortable. The temperature was high for the time of year as well, and the sky was nearly clear. Tara's light flooded the farmyard. Her heat felt wonderful beating down on his head and shoulders, and he was glad he had chanced leaving his jacket inside. He would have no need of it.

Sogan strode away from the house, feeling more himself than he had all morning. He had been right to take this break and probably should have done it a lot sooner. Besides, he was getting hungry. That did not help concentration, either.

Nooo! Varn jump! Bad man!

Even as Bandit's warning screamed in his mind, the Arcturian threw himself to the ground. His blaster flashed into his hand, but fast as he moved, he was given no chance to fire. His body jerked as a vicious bolt seared into him. He was conscious of the agony burning his left shoulder and chest, then a merciful darkness closed in, and all awareness of himself and the world around him was gone.

* * *

Grief and rage exploded in Bandit's heart, but she did not delay even to look at her fallen comrade. She dove for the assailant in a desperate drive to reach him before he could strike again and assure the end of his dying or already dead victim.

The renegade was confident of his victory. He smiled coldly and raised his weapon, steadying it to make certain of the Commando-Captain's death.

The gurry had recognized Sogan's danger from the moment she spotted the intruder poised to fire and had made no audible sound to betray either her presence or her too-late warning. She was so small and so fast in her approach that he did not become aware of her until she was upon him.

The man's shot went wild as he instinctively raised his hand to ward off the brown fury ripping suddenly out of the sky, straight into his face.

The Jadite deftly avoided his blows and went straight for her target. The human screamed and screamed again as merciless claws drove into his eyes, shredding them. His world was black now, but still the pain continued.

Bandit retreated from his hands as they frantically lashed the air in front of him. He would not escape, but he had retained his weapon through it all, and he knew where the Arcturian lay. If he calmed himself and thought, he could still fire and finish what he had begun.

She had to protect Varn!

She flew to him. Sogan's blaster was in his hand as well, an it was pointed in the right direction. If she could manage it . .

The firing mechanism was simple to understand, only a littl more complicated than that of the renewer, which she had worke on a number of occasions.

She knew the control that would make the blaster bring force sleep instead of pain and death, but human implements were larg and heavy for a gurry to manage. The switch controlling th blaster was impossibly stiff. Bandit fought with it, tugging an pushing it with her supple toes, but she could not so much a budge it.

Suddenly, her grasp slipped. She stumbled forward, strikin Sogan's hand where it closed over the trigger. There was a flas of light and a sharp report, a truncated scream, and finally silenc

* * *

Islaen Connor's hands closed and whitened on her pike. The Jadite's fear slammed into her mind, then Varn's, followed too quickly by agony and a terrible, abrupt severing of contact.

She dropped the implement to the ground. Fortunately, both her comrades were working nearby. "Jake, Bethe, come with me!"

Even as she spoke, she was racing for the transport that had brought them down to the field.

She paused before whipping open the door. "Father, there's trouble at the house. Get back up there and send for Tam. We may be too busy outside to make the call ourselves." If there was anything that a physician could do.

She saw the off-worlders stare at her, and she raised her left wrist in explanation. Better reveal this tool than her true source of information. "Communicator. —Hurry! Varnt's hurt!"

The other two guerrillas pushed in beside her. "What's going on?" the Captain demanded, steadying himself against the instrument panel as she threw the machine into high gear.

"An attack on Varn. He's down—maybe unconscious, maybe dead."

For a few minutes, Islaen's attention had to stay with the transport. She was taking it straight through the fields, and though it was designed for use on rugged ground, she still had to guide it carefully over the roughest places. Any accident could be serious at the speed at which they were moving.

Her years of hard experience stood by her. The Commando-Colonel gripped her fear tightly, knowing she must function despite it. Her mind went out. Still nothing from the Arcturian, but she found Bandit readily. *Love, can you hear me?*

Yes! —Islaen help!

I'll try. She was relieved by that response despite the burning terror in it. She had feared the Jadite would be too upset to answer or think coherently. She braced herself. *Varn?* she asked.

Hurt bad! Islaen come! Help Varn!

What about yourself?

Bandit's fine!

You probably can't do more for Varn, Little Bandit. Take wing now. See if there are any more attackers or others around the house, then check that no reinforcements are on the way. Examine the area near the field, too, in case that might be a target as well.

No one's here, Islaen! Bandit already looked!

Good thinking, love. Do the rest now.

Yes, Islaen!

The commander reported their conversation to her comrades.

Bethe Danlo's eyes closed. "Alive, praise the Spirit of Space. Even if he's hurt beyond the renewer's power to heal, it'll keep him going long enough for us to get him under regrowth."

Islaen shot her a quick, grateful look. "That's what I'm hoping as well." She had felt enough of the bolt's strike to know that the injuries it had left were not slight.

The transport rumbled into the farmyard and screeched to a halt as the Noreenan woman hit the break. Two dreadfully still figures were sprawled before them on the bloodied ground.

She leaped out, almost instinctively pulling her pack after her. It was light, for it held no rations or gear for an extended wilderness stay, but no guerrilla left it far from his hand while on a mission. She would have had it with her today even if that were not true. Minor accidents were not rare during harvest time, and she had wanted to keep the renewer close by on the chance that it should be needed. Her caution might now give her husband his life.

Islaen hurried to Varn and dropped to her knees beside him. He was lying on his back, his arms outstretched. The blaster remained grasped in his right hand.

Her throat closed to see the amount of blood on his singed clothing and on the path beside him, but she mastered herself and made herself look beyond that. The former Admiral's eyes were closed. His face was not white but a ghastly gray, and his breathing was labored. Not delaying any longer, she used her mind power to enter his body and study for herself the extent of his wound.

Immediately, she realized that the worst of her fears were unfounded. The lungs and heart were sound. Everything else, the renewer could handle.

That was more than damage enough. Sogan had only barely moved out of direct line with the assassin's bolt. It had missed the organs of his chest but had burned through the left shoulder. The beam had been broad, and the tissue damage was extensive probably fatally so had they lacked the renewer.

She frowned, and fear again surged through her. Fortune had deserted him in the site of the attack. He had fallen on the grave path rather than on the grass beside it. Her father kept it visually clean, but generations of animals had trodden it as they moved between pastures and barn, and a vast array of beings too minute for the human eye to detect lived on and beneath those small stones. The wound was dirty, and she was nearly certain it was infected. Fever was already building inside him, too much for the shock of the experience and the burn itself to explain away.

That was bad. Their immunization shots protected against most infectious diseases, but parasite-borne illnesses and those mechanically induced like this one sometimes got by them, and the microlife of one world could rapidly overwhelm the defenses of a body native to another.

The Noreenan glanced about her. Bethe was crouched next to her, her face grave. Jake was kneeling beside the attacker.

"Bethe, get me hot water, a lot of it. I can't turn the renewer on this until the wound's cleaned."

The spacer sprang to her feet and ran for the house. She needed no special gift to see that the war prince would not last much longer without treatment.

"Jake," she called. "Alive or dead?"

"Dead. Burned right through the head, whatever of it Bandit seems to have left intact. It's not a pretty sight."

"Drag him into the barn, then, and throw a sack over him. Come back fast. I'll need you here."

"Aye, Colonel."

A low moan brought her attention back to her patient. *Varn?*

"Accursed Resistance," he muttered. "I knew they would burn me eventually . . ."

She looked up in horror. The crowded transport carrying her kin and their neighbors was already coming to a stop in the yard. Few of them might speak Arcturian, but there was scarcely an individual on Noreen of Tara who would not recognize the language itself if he heard it spoken.

Admiral, she said in the precise tongue of his Empire, *be silent now, and use their Basic when you must speak, or you will betray our disguise*.

He moaned again, but he nodded faintly and seemed to set his lips against any further speech.

Paud Connor came up beside her. "Bad?"

"Bad enough. We'll need Tam. Tell him to bring every

antibiotic he's got and equipment for identifying infectious organisms."

"I'll send for him."

"Have someone give Bethe a hand with the water, and I may need you and Will to help bring him inside, but keep everyone else back. I want him to have air. Stay out of the barn as well. Jake's putting what's left of the back-alley man in there."

Once the water reached her, it did not take the Commando-Colonel long to wash out the wound and turn the renewer on it, working carefully so that the bleeding would not resume during the healing process. The hot energy of the blaster bolt had sealed many of the blood vessels it had severed. That had saved Sogan, but he had still bled heavily enough that she feared to see him lose any more blood.

Healing, once it began, progressed almost magically. Only a little better than ten minutes passed before Varn's skin was once more sound and the color returned to his face.

Too much color. The ray could not dispel illness as it did injury. Quickly, she administered a broad-spectrum antibiotic from her medical kit.

Sogan's eyes opened as she was sealing the needle in its presterilization bag. They were unfocused for a moment but cleared in the next instant. He smiled at her, then his face tightened as memory of the attack returned in full force.

"Easy," she said, aloud since the others were near. "It's over."

"Aye," he replied in a voice whose unsteadiness he himself could hear and disliked. "I appear to be sound again."

"You're anything but," she told him firmly. "You have a fever. Either the wound's infected, or something left over from our stay on Amazoon is breaking loose now. In any event, you're on the casualty list, my friend." It was only with difficulty that she kept the grim shadow darkening her thoughts out of her voice. If they could not track down and counter this infection fast, Varn Tarl Sogan might be out of the fight for a long time to come.

FOURTEEN

AS SOON AS Islaen Connor appeared at the head of the stairs, her comrades hastened up to join her.

"How's he doing?" Karmikel asked in a low voice so that their discussion would not carry to those waiting below.

"He's sick enough, but I think the antibiotic's working. Tam's concoctions are specific to Noreen's microbes and will probably speed up the job considerably." She glanced over her shoulder. "We'll have to wait until he comes out for his report."

Bethe's hand touched her commander's sympathetically. "That's better news than we might have expected." She eyed the other woman. "At least, it means you don't have another four-day vigil ahead of you."

"Maybe not alone, but the three of us are going to have to be on watch as long as he's like this. We can't allow anyone else to stay in there."

"You can trust your family, lass," Jake told her, a bit surprised.

"It's Varn that I can't trust at the moment. All we need is for him to call down the Arcturian equivalent of a murrain on Thorne and all her Resistance in front of them."

"Space!"

"It's only logical, Jake," his wife said after a moment's horrified silence. "He fought that Resistance for six years, and your team as well for four of them. Where else can you expect his mind to go after he's been burned down like this?"

The redhead made no answer. They had reached the bottom of the stairs, and the on-worlders were coming towards the Colonel for news. Islaen gave them the same report she had to her team and then sank into the chair Will had vacated for her. She had not realized how tired she was until that moment. Jeanie brought her a brimming cup of jakek and a sandwich, both of which she accepted gratefully.

A small whistle caused her to look up. Bandit flew in the window which had been left open a crack to admit her and perched on the arm of the woman's chair. She had cleaned the blood of the battle from herself, but her feathers were ruffled with the misery she was radiating. *Varn's still hurt?* she asked.

He'll be all right, I think. It'll just take time and some sleep. She stroked the hen. *What about you, Little Bandit?*

Bandit's fine! —No more renegades! Other guards good! Bandit could come in!

Islaen looked at her, puzzled, but then realized what she had meant. Their neighbors would not have abandoned the Connors in this trouble. Paud would have given them enough of the story to explain the attack—the incident here at Kinkora and their arrest of the perpetrators would be sufficient in themselves given the character of those involved—and some of the men would have gone to collect their weapons and the weapons of those remaining here. Noreenans loved peace and even more so liberty, enough to keep themselves prepared to fight for both. The house would not want for sentries, or defenders either, should that need arise.

She had her role to carry and glanced at her father. "We have a watch out, I take it?"

"We do," he replied grimly. "Relax on that score, lass. The locality's behind us. We'll not lack warning of any other attack or protection should one come."

The Colonel caught a movement out of the corner of her eye and turned her head in time to see her brother appear at the head of the stairs. His expression was set, hard, and she came to her feet, fear forming an icy knot within her.

In the same instant, she realized it was anger—stark fury—that was on him, not pity or grief, and her head lifted. Jake Karmikel and Bethe noticed the change in her. They had seen her like this often enough before, when she braced herself for battle, and both quietly rose and moved to stand on either side of her. If she was facing a fight for their comrade's sake, she was not going to wage it alone.

Tam said nothing until he had reached the group. He fixed his sister with blazing eyes. "What happened to that man, Islaen?"

She understood then. Noreen of Tara had been spared th

horrors of an invasion. Her brother, like all the planet's citizens who had remained on-world, had been spared the worst nightmares spawned by the cruelty of which some of their species were capable. He was a physician, dedicated to healing stricken bodies, and he could accept as part of the course of life the illnesses and accidents whose effects he fought. Conscious abuse of a man by other human beings was a different matter; Sogan's scarred back would have given Tam a nasty shock. "He ran afoul of the Arcturians," she answered quietly. Her eyes held his. "You said nothing to him?"

He shook his head. "No. The scars are obviously old, and I was afraid he might be sensitive about them." He had also not been entirely certain he would be able to completely conceal the strength of his own reaction if he pressed the matter.

"He is. —Don't say anything to him, any of you. Varnt lost a galaxy more than a lot of blood and skin, and he doesn't like being forced to relive those times."

"That's history anyway," Jake cut in. "How is he?"

The on-worlder instinctively glanced back over his shoulder, as if to look his patient over once more before responding. "It would've been close without that renewer, but he'll be fine. Your antibiotics would have taken care of the infection eventually, and mine will hasten the process immensely. I don't want him fighting any wars in the next twenty-four hours, and a couple of days' rest after that wouldn't be amiss, but you're quite safe in sending the doctor home right now."

"Praise the Spirit ruling space," Islaen Connor said in relief. "Can I go up?"

"No reason why you shouldn't." He smiled. "I doubt I could keep you away anyway."

"Not for long," she agreed even as she slipped by him to mount the stairs.

Varn closed his eyes against the light. It had been a long time since he had felt like this, not wounded or in pain but only ill. He found it difficult to adjust to it and wondered when the promised relief would become perceptible to him. His eyes opened again. By all the old gods, he hated to be felled like this and hoped the cure would come soon. He certainly was useless the way he was.

The war prince smiled in response to two familiar mind touches and turned as the door opened. *Welcome, Islaen, and my little Bandit.*

Islaen sat beside him. Her cool fingers brushed across his forehead. *The fever's dropping,* She shook her head. *You're going to have to stop scaring the starlight out of me like this, Varn Tarl Sogan. My nerves aren't spun out of titanone.*

I did not find the experience very pleasant myself, if that's any comfort to you.

Her hand covered his. *I know. Coming to Noreen hasn't worked out to your good this time, has it?*

Blame our profession and not your homeworld, Sogan told her mildly, but fire and hate rippled through him. Their profession, aye, and their thrice-accursed enemy.

The gurry fluttered from Islaen's shoulder to his pillow. *Varn's still wounded?* she asked in concern.

"No, small one. I shall be all right soon." He turned slightly so that he could stroke her more easily and frowned. He was not so ill that she should look this upset, nor did his assurances appear to ease her. *What is the matter with her?* he demanded sharply.

Nothing, Varn! the Jadite protested. *Bandit's not hurt!*

That's true, Islaen agreed, although her own eyes were dark as they fixed on their strange comrade. *I checked her out myself.* She reached over him to run a loving finger down the upturned head and neck. *She's the heroine of the day again,* the woman added. *She fought that son of a Scythian ape and stopped him from finishing you off. We're very lucky your bolt didn't clip her while she was at it.*

He looked up. *I never fired, Islaen, or I do not remember doing so.*

The gurry whimpered. *Bandit killed renegade!*

"You what?" the Colonel demanded. "How?"

Bandit wanted to stun him. Knew how, but blaster too stiff. Bandit's foot slipped, hit Varn's hand. She whimpered again. *Gurries don't kill! Bandit only wanted to protect Varn!*

"Blasters require strength even from humans, small one," the Arcturian said. "There would be too many accidents otherwise. They are not like renewers. No gurry could manage one."

Varn would say no matter! Renegade's dead! —Bandit's no different from Varn! Gurries know good and bad, too!

"By the Empire's gods!" Varn Tarl Sogan's head dropped back

on his pillow as if he had taken the edge of a stun bolt. "Because I am a fool, must you be as well?" he demanded in a voice hoarse and perilously close to breaking. "At least, I have a lifetime's unbreakable conditioning for my excuse, but you have always been the most sensible of beings . . ."

He turned away, flinging his arm over his eyes even as he slammed tight shields over his thoughts. What had he done? What infinite harm had he caused to this wonderful little creature, because he could not adapt to the ways of the ultrasystem which had given him refuge—he who should have died, would have done better to die, beneath the lashes of his people or cleanly by his own blaster?

Islaen's eyes filled, but she kept the tears out of both her voice and the open thoughts behind it. "Varn, stop this debris, and you too, Bandit!" she commanded sharply, aloud since his mind was closed to her. "I'm sick to the depths of my soul of everyone around me heaping guilt upon guilt on themselves. —Look, Varn, she's upset. Gurries don't like to hurt anything, and you were hit badly enough that she had every reason to believe you were dying. How completely rational do you expect her to be in the face of a double shock like that?" *—Don't make a liar of me, Bandit,* the woman warned in her closed thoughts. *Lie yourself if you must, but help him!*

Bandit will help! The reply echoed in her inner mind as the hen moved closer to Sogan. She timidly licked his cheek. *Bandit's sorry, Varn! Don't be angry. Bandit thought she was right.*

The former Admiral could not reject her plea. He cupped her in his hand and drew her closer to him. "I am not angry, small one. I was just afraid I had hurt you by teaching you to think there was blame where none should exist."

Varn wouldn't hurt Bandit! she responded. She began to purr loudly, as if she were wrapped within the heart of bliss.

Thank you, Little Bandit, Islaen Connor murmured silently.

The Colonel came to her feet and withdrew a bit, but she waited a few minutes before quitting the room. Varn was played out and should sleep again soon. It was what he most needed. She momentarily weighed giving him a light soporific but decided against it in the next instant, knowing she could depend on his body to claim the rest it required.

Several hours passed before the war prince woke again. When he did, he found the lamps lighted and the room oddly silent.

Islaen was there. He had felt her presence before he had opened his eyes, but she was keeping very quiet in mind and movement so as not to disturb him. She had changed her clothes and was now clad completely in black.

Time to go? he asked.

She turned quickly. *Almost.* She came over to him. *How are you feeling?*

Well enough to work.

Forget that one, Admiral. You're still grounded. Tam's orders.

He smiled. *How would a civilian know how tough we Commandos are?* he countered.

That argument won't compute, my friend! Besides, it's a horrible night. You'll be a lot better off staying nice and warm for yourself here.

Sogan sat up. The room was comfortable, almost hot. That meant the heating system was on in the house despite the season. There was little noise from the outside, and that was muted. A glance at the window supplied the explanation for the uncommon silence. The inner shutters were closed, and he supposed that was true of the outer pair as well.

He frowned. They were not only shut but tightly bolted. *What is happening out there?* he demanded harshly. He had been told on his first visit that this was only done during a major tempest. That could mean trouble. The banshee did not care when it struck or where, and from all he had heard, it would be death to venture out into it in a small vehicle like their flier.

A storm. A big one. We've been delaying in the hope that the rain, at least, will let up. We'll have a demon's own time trying to conceal a water trail going into Dunbrityne house.

Maybe you should abort altogether for the time being.

The Arcturian knew that was impossible, barring the arrival of the banshee itself. The Albionans were not fools. Their first set of assassins had vanished last night and now another one today. They would realize the Federation soldiers had stopped and probably captured them. That the guerrillas would be taking countermeasures, and soon, would have to be regarded as a given with only a presumed need to summon and await the arrival of reinforcements to hold them back.

How long has Thatcher's crew been on-world? he asked.

Long enough to have developed a respect for her weather. He'll believe himself safe tonight. —It's probably our last chance to get at any records he has, Varn.

I know, he agreed grimly. *He would destroy them at the first hint of an attack, if he has not already done so.*

I don't think he has much fear of that. He's almost ready to go. If he weren't, he'd never have moved so openly against us. He figures we're too few in number to retaliate directly and knows he'll have nothing to worry about by the time we can slip in the necessary aid. The tension she was fighting to control flared in her, and her hands balled tightly by her sides. *We have to discover his plans, and do it now!*

Easy, Islaen, Sogan told her quietly. *You have done as much before.* His eyes went to the shuttered window. *I would like to come with you.*

Islaen shook her head emphatically. *It's Jake and I who'll be going inside, anyway. Bethe will be able to guard the flier alone.*

Bandit will help, Varn! Take care of Islaen and Jake!

The Colonel looked at the gurry. "I'm having second thoughts about bringing you, love."

Nooo!

"This storm may be no banshee, but you still can't face wind like this. I'll have enough to concern me without having to worry about you, too. —It would be best all around if you remained with Varn."

Islaen doesn't trust Bandit anymore! she wailed. *Bandit did do bad . . .*

Varn Tarl Sogan laughed until tears came to his eyes. "You manipulative little micro-sized ball of feathers!" he managed at last. *Take her, Colonel, but only on condition that she stays in the flier. Bethe will need her company and maybe a warning if you two get into trouble.*

Bandit will help Bethe! the gurry promised eagerly.

The man's mood sobered abruptly. Islaen and Bandit. Bethe Danlo and Jake Karmikel. Those four formed the whole of his universe now, and he was letting them go off into Noreen's potentially treacherous weather to penetrate the camp of an enemy as vicious as any they had yet encountered.

The wind howled so loudly outside that he heard the gust plainly through the shutters. An icy chill spread through him. *Is this the only sealed window?* he made himself ask calmly.

No. It was closed early so your rest wouldn't be disturbed, but all Noreenan dwellings are battened down in this sort of weather as a precaution.

A precaution against the banshee. He had not feared wind as a force before tonight, but he was worried now. *Be careful, will you? I know you long-term Commandos are good, but do not get careless. Both L. George Thatcher and Noreen herself demand better than that.*

FIFTEEN

THE COMMANDO-COLONEL'S hands tightened on the flier's controls as she fought to hold their course against the buffeting of an exceptionally sharp gust of wind. There was almost no rain now, but a full gale was blowing, and it was giving no sign of losing force. Only a very little more, and it could switch into the screaming horror that was the dread of every dweller of Noreen's vast open lands.

"It's worse than when we started out," she said to her two comrades in the back without taking her eyes off the instruments.

"It's no better at any rate," Karmikel agreed dryly.

"What do you say, Jake? Abort or go on? We won't make it through a full-blown banshee. I'm having my troubles even as it is in this."

The redhead thought for several seconds. "It's hard to guess how far it'll go," he said in the end, "but I vote to finish what we've started. This bit of rough weather's providing us with the last good crack we're likely to get at Dunbrityne house and its occupants. Fail here, and we may well get our answers after the fact from a newstape. —Bethe?"

The demolitions expert shrugged delicately. "Noreen's your world. You two should know what to expect from her. I'll abide by your decision."

She would say nothing of it, but for her part, Bethe Danlo heartily wished to be back within Kinkora's thick stone walls, safely out of the madness whirling around them. She was space bred, and until she had joined the guerrilla unit, she had never needed to concern herself with the mighty, mindless forces scourging so many of the galaxy's planets. The starlanes had their own share of perils, but those were familiar threats, and they did not arouse in her the same intense dread she felt now at the prospect of continuing to battle the menacing storm.

She suddenly longed to have Varn Tarl Sogan beside her. The Arcturian was essentially a spacer himself, and they shared not so much a sympathy as a camaraderie that she could never find with either of their other companions. Many a time, he had given her the comfort of acknowledging in himself something of her uncertainty in the face of surplanetary challenge and had encouraged her to meet it well. Their exchanges had never been much in such moments—a smile, a touch of his hand, a few words if no one else was near enough to catch them, sometimes only a raised brow—but he had always given her spirit the lift she had needed to begin and keep going as she must. She hungered for something of the same now on this dismal, wild night.

Bethe flushed as she recognized the direction of her thoughts, and she glanced at her husband's set profile. Jake had shown considerable jealousy over the strength of her feeling for the former Admiral almost since their first meeting. That had always infuriated her. She loved the Noreenan Captain. She loved him in mind and heart, but she wondered now if there might not be some solid cause for his concern. It was to Varn that she wished to look for comfort . . .

Karmikel felt her gaze on him at that moment and turned. He found the Sergeant looking up at him, her eyes large and grave. Cursing himself for his lack of feeling, he put an arm around her and drew her close. With the other, he continued to grasp the back of the driver's seat, bracing himself against the occasional sharp jerks of the machine. Bethe rested against him, sure of herself once more if not about what the night might yet bring them.

The outer fringes of the woods made a fairly frightening sight with the treetops whipping and swaying in the fierce wind, but once they had passed into it and traveled beyond its edge, the force of the gale dropped drastically.

Islaen Connor drew a deep breath and flexed fingers cramped from struggling with the controls. The respite would be a long one and would hold, as far as the flier went, until they reached this place again upon their return. They would make their actual approach to the house on foot.

"This is a vast improvement," Jake said with strong feeling.

"Don't relax too much, friend," his commander replied. "Branches do fall in these storms, sometimes quite large ones."

"You're reassuring!"

They fell quiet after that. Islaen's mind fixed on their upcoming work, and in a few minutes, she spoke again. "We'll leave the flier well inside the wood," she said. "It'll be safer from a security standpoint and from the storm. Bethe, stay with it unless you're threatened. You'll have a hard time keeping watch yourself, but Bandit will warn you if anyone approaches. She'll also know when we're coming back or if we run into any problems. We'll keep our communicators activated too, of course."

"Any idea how long you'll be?" Bethe asked.

"As short a time as possible, you may be sure, but as to an actual estimate, that depends entirely on the kind of luck we have."

She lifted the gurry from her lap and reached over the seat back to deposit her in Bethe's. "Don't you leave the flier unless you absolutely must, love. One good blast of this wind would sweep you halfway around the planet. It could very nearly batter an unprotected human to death in its worse moments, never mind you."

Bandit'll be careful!

"Good. —Sergeant, shift into the front seat for now, in case you have to move fast." She touched the controls in an instinctive, concerned gesture. "Jake will be driving on the way home," she told them grimly. "I barely had the strength to hold our course on the way here, and I don't see this storm's lessening any in the next few hours."

The two Noreenans crept to the edge of the treelands and lay there a while studying their target.

There seemed to be no sentries out, as was only to be expected given the weather and the lack of difficulty the off-worlders had experienced thus far.

The mechanical guards were another matter. The yellow glow of the energy picket burned through the windswept night, lighting the target area for them but also threatening to expose them to any eye chancing to fall on the place where they were operating.

There was no help for it. Islaen signaled Karmikel to move out with a touch to his arm. They would be going straight in through the front door. The bedrooms most likely to have multiple occupants were in the rear, as was the barn serving as barracks for the bulk of the Albionans. There was a far greater chance that someone might peer out from that side than from this direction, though the tight storm bolts and shutters should discourage that.

The pair crept forward on their stomachs, snaking their way through the trampled, unkempt grass surrounding the house.

Islaen swerved to avoid a patch of vegetation. Her fingers struck her communicator sharply, tapping out a message in her unit's battle code. "Watch for nettles!"

"Aye." Karmikel's mouth hardened. The stinging plants were all over the area, invaders taking advantage of the lack of care Paud Connor's tenants had shown to the property at large. The younger, smaller plants were plaguy difficult to spot even in the picket's bright glow.

They jolly well would have to see—and avoid—them. He had been severely stung by a nettle tree on Amazoon, badly enough to have put him out of the mission had it not been for Bandit's heroism in extracting the embedded hairs from his arm despite the pain she had suffered in consequence. That would not happen here, of course. The effects of Noreen's herb nettles faded quickly, within a few minutes, but they were intense while they lasted; even a few moments' incapacitation could be too long under these circumstances. An emergency could arise with every passing second, and they had to be ready and able to respond to it.

Almost too quickly, they reached the energy picket. The Commando-Colonel slipped a miniature coil of wire from her belt pouch, then carefully examined the barrier. Blowing it would be easy, but that they could not do. They had the far more difficult task of briefly opening two bars while they slipped through and then closing them again before the breach in the house's prime defense was noticed by any of its occupants. That job was hers.

Working with infinite care, she attached first one end of the wire and then the other to the connecting base of the picket. A tiny switch protruded from the last. "Get ready!" she signaled. Her fingers pressed down on the mechanism, and the slender pillars of energy between the connections shimmered and went down.

Islaen shot through the clear space. She had no trouble, but her breath held as Jake made his move. It was a civilian picket, not military standard, and the space between its component bars appeared to be uncommonly short. Was there room enough to admit his broader shoulders?

The Commando-Captain made it through without difficulty. He dove directly for the house while she deftly drew the switch mechanism inside the barrier and depressed it once more, restoring the integrity of the fence.

Jake reached the door and began examining its guards. His eyes glittered with pale ice. There was more than one, and all of them were strong. One, at least, was dangerous as well, and he fought to hold his hand steady as he worked to deactivate it. One jerk, one tremor even, and he was fried meat.

When he had that and the others down, he studied the entryway again before signaling his commander to come ahead. Varn Tarl Sogan had taught him how effective a seemingly simple alarm or lock could be if subtly used.

There were none. The door opened noiselessly, praise Noreen's gods, and the pair slipped inside.

Karmikel spun around in a full circle as he came to his feet. No one was there, but he did not reholster his blaster. At any turn now, at any moment, they could find themselves facing one or more of the Albionans.

That would be a bad cast of chance, whatever the immediate outcome. They wanted to get their information and leave again undetected. That would hardly be possible if they were forced to leave the hall and rooms strewn with corpses.

Islaen made her way to the locked door she had spotted the previous evening. The seals were indeed impressive, as were all those they had encountered thus far, but they gave her no greater trouble than had any of the others. She and Jake Karmikel had honed their burglary skills against the defenses devised by the Arcturian Intelligence Service. The efforts of even a cautious civilian well able to pay for quality posed no major challenge after that schooling.

The Captain watched as she worked. It all seemed eerily familiar to him.

So it was familiar. They had found themselves in very nearly the same sort of situation on their very first active assignment. His memory rushed back through the years. They had been so young then, he thought, and so scared. They were still scared, maybe even more so. They had confidence now in their skills, but they knew too well what they faced in the event of foul fortune or failure.

The door swung open with a creak that stopped the breath of

both guerrillas. They released them in the next moment. Once again, Noreen was fighting on the side of her offspring. Every part of the ancient house was groaning in response to the tempest ravening outside.

Islaen slipped into the mysterious room. She stopped and looked about.

Her expression tightened. This chamber differed little in spirit from the others she had seen and illustrated well the transient nature of the residence. L. George Thatcher had done no more to personalize or improve it than he had with the rest of the floor. The furnishings were very sparse, just a few chairs and a couple of old tables pressed into service to hold the transceiver and to serve as a desk, respectively. The latter supported tape and graphics reader/writers and capsule cases as well as paper and writing materials. Notes and ledgers, perhaps, and some general correspondence, but everything inside her said that she would not find what she sought in this casually stored material.

All the same, she slipped the first capsule into her microcopier. The tiny device was one of the better espionage tools to come out of the War, and variations of it would find an excellent commercial market once the design was unclassified and released. Its almost literally microscopic internal spools could store a well-nigh inconceivable amount of data, not compressed but in readily accessible form easily displayed either on its own small screen, visible through the accompanying magnifier, or by attachment of the device to a conventionally sized reader.

It was fast as well, duplicating the contents of the Albionan's capsules very nearly as quickly as she could pop the old one out of the drive and insert the next.

Now and then, the Colonel slowed the process to scan the contents of the files being copied, each time concluding with a disgusted shake of her head.

"Not here," she signaled in the end.

"You're sure?"

"These contain only housekeeping records and some inconsequential private correspondence. There would have to be more even if he were dead honest."

"Destroyed to keep them away from his family?"

"Some maybe, but Thatcher is a wealthy man with many investments of his own. He must have records of those, at least and have them with him."

"His bedroom?"

"I'm afraid so." That was not a pleasant prospect. Her talent told her the Albionans were all sleeping soundly, probably buried to their chins in warm blankets and maybe some with pillows over their heads to shut out the roar of the storm, which was growing increasingly perceptible even through the tightly closed windows and the two sets of sturdy shutters. All the same, to have to locate the correct chamber and then search it with the occupant snoring only a few feet, or perhaps mere inches away . . .

It did not really strike her as the correct answer, anyway. L. George Thatcher maintained the proprieties as he saw them. —Guests were entertained in the sitting room. Meals were eaten off a proper service in the chamber reserved for that purpose. Machines such as transceivers and readers were confined to an office, even a most rudimentary one, and not permitted to intrude upon the remainder of a civilized house. He would not want to turn his sleeping quarters into a storage area, however important the materials, not if he could devise something more appropriate.

On the other hand, he was no fool. The data she sought was monstrously sensitive . . .

"Look for a hidden safe or catchall." Security was a whole other crew from mere redecoration. He would make changes for its sake, if not for mere comfort or appearance—witness the strength and variety of the guards on the house and on this particular room.

There was little place to conceal data spools or anything else in quantity, but the Federation guerrillas carefully went over the small room and its meager contents. Suddenly Jake stood back, his eyes narrowing. Islaen felt his triumph and caught the direction of his gaze. She nodded. Of course. It was well done, but the answer was quite obvious to any Noreenan bending a portion of his power of observation to the task.

All these houses were basically the same: simple, functional, and comfortable. Their lower story consisted of four rooms, two on either side of a central hall. Those rooms were inevitably square. This one was decidedly rectangular.

Islaen and the Captain spotted the camouflaged door in the new wall at the same moment. It was held closed by a simple drop lock, which gave before the woman's first attempt. Thatcher had shielded his stronghold and office well, and he simply would not believe that anyone coming this far could be other than a friend, admitted with his knowledge and by his will.

His reasoning was probably more subtle than that, too, the woman decided after a moment. If any extraneous visitor should happen to note the false wall, L. George Thatcher wanted to lend support to his explanation that it was merely an unsightly repository of records that he was, therefore, concealing, material valuable to him, certainly, but of no major significance otherwise.

The space inside was small, with scarcely room for a slender man to turn around. The wall opposite them supported a shelf so placed as to be convenient to hold a cartridge or spool storage box while someone went through its contents. Below this and along the full length of the opposite wall were enclosed shelves housing various kinds of data media. Each was locked, but again, simply. There were no destruct or other concealed safeguards, although the two Commandos checked each seal and each individual item for them.

Islaen pulled a second, slightly different microcopier from her utility belt. "Take the cartridges."

"Aye. —Just copy. There's no time to spot check," he signaled back.

Her eyes flickered to him. "They're asleep."

"Look at the window," Karmikel hissed in a barely audible whisper. It was the first time either of them had spoken since entering the house. "The treetops are kissing the ground out there."

The guerrilla leader stepped quickly from the hidden room and went to the window. The outer fringes of the wood were just visible beyond the glow of the picket. The trees were tossing as if they would wrench themselves free of the soil. Her eyes closed. Banshee. They would be fortunate indeed if they made it back to Kinkora before it broke on them in full force, and if they did not . . .

She returned to the records chamber, her face set and grim. There was a lot of material here, and they would have to take it all, maybe to no purpose in the end. They would not know until they reviewed it. If they lived to review it.

It took time—another full hour—but at last, the Federation guerrillas were ready to make their escape. Departing the house was as slow a process as entering it had been. The need for caution had not lifted, and every sign of their presence had to be removed.

There must be no indication that the security of the place had ever been violated. Should Thatcher receive sufficient forewarning, he might still be able to put his plan into operation or else to at least effect his own escape, negating all their efforts and risk.

Islaen tried the front door and then tried it again but could not push it outward against the hammering of the wind.

"Jake!"

Karmikel's strength was equal to the task, and the Commandos forced their way outside.

The woman gasped as the gale struck her, driving the breath from her body like the blow of some mighty fist. Even hugging the ground like this, she had to fight to advance against it, or across it, for it altered direction seemingly with the changing seconds. She could not have stayed erect at all; she doubted her companion could have managed that despite his greater weight and muscle.

They reached the picket. It's deadly beams rose unaltered through the chaos around them, unaffected by the wind's fury even as they represented no hindrance to it. Not to the tempest, maybe, but the barrier was a staunch defense against some of its by-products. Just as the pair reached the burning line, a great branch whirled into it almost directly above their heads. There was a crackling sound rendered nearly inaudible by the wail of the storm, a flaring of light and fire, and a carbonized cinder fell to the ground on the far side of the picket.

Islaen's lips tightened, but she made no delay in closing the switch on her jump wire and passing over the space it opened to the lands beyond the Albionans' territory. A few moments later, her companion was across as well. She removed the device and stowed it in the belt pouch whence it had come.

They faced greater peril from flying debris now, but the Commando-Colonel pushed her awareness of that aside and made herself press on toward the tossing trees. Speed was of the essence. The full banshee was not on them yet, but the great storm would not withhold its strength much longer. If they were not safely home before it struck, it was likely to prove their doom. Their flier was a sturdy vehicle designed to withstand violence and stress, but it could not battle a planet's unbridled rage with any hope of victory.

The pressure on them eased once they entered the wood. The Colonel drew her first uncontested breath since leaving Dunbrityne house and staggered unsteadily to her feet. She had no trouble keeping them. The wind was still powerful, but the trees broke enough of its force that it no longer blocked her movements or threatened her. The danger in this place came from branches and other missiles breaking loose and plummeting groundward from the tortured canopy.

"Bethe?" she called into her communicator. She felt secure enough to use speech at this point, although she still pitched her voice very low.

The reply came at once. "Islaen! Praise the Spirit of Space! Are you both all right?"

"We are. We'll be there in a couple of minutes."

The demolitions expert was sitting stiffly, tense and alert, when the Noreenans reached the flier.

"Move over, Sergeant," Jake told her. "It's freezing out here."

"You deserve to freeze," she told him tartly. "This is the last time I accompany you two shooting stars on a midnight jaunt."

He just laughed. "I'm glad to see you, too. —Was it bad out here?"

"The wind seemed to get stronger by the minute. I guess it was worse in the open."

"Worlds worse," he affirmed.

"You got what you wanted?" Her voice was deadly serious now. She had followed their communicator transmissions, but they had provided no final answer.

"We hope so," Islaen responded. "Let's go, Jake. We'll have to make all the time we can while we've got the trees to cover us."

Bandit shivered, and she stroked the gurry, who had flown to her as soon as she had taken her place in the rear seat. *Bandit's scared! Banshee wind bad!*

"I know it is, love, but Jake will get us through." She hoped that was not a false reassurance, but the redhead was a better pilot than she was, on-world as well as in space, and he was a lot stronger. Whether he or any other human could prove the equal of the challenge before them, that only time could tell.

Jake Karmikel kept the flier at the highest speed he dared use in the midst of the trees that were both their defense and an ever-present hazard. Nothing troubled them or delayed their progress, and all too soon, they found themselves approaching the end of the wood.

In the instant they put the trees behind them, the machine shuddered and reeled as if under a powerful blow. Another followed, and then another. A fourth struck seconds later from the opposite direction.

The man fought to hold the controls, to keep the vehicle under his command and moving toward Kinkora house.

It swerved and bucked like a wild thing eager for its freedom. His knuckles whitened under the tightness of his grip, and sweat dampened his clothes. No one spoke lest the intense concentration needed to meet the ever-altering and ever-growing challenges besetting him—besetting them all—be broken.

Somehow he did keep the flier on course in defiance of the tempest's rage, and after a seeming eternity of battle, the solid mass of the ancient Connor farmhouse loomed up before them, a deeper blackness against the dark sky.

Breathing a prayer of thanksgiving and also for continued favor, he turned the vehicle's nose upward.

It started to climb, then an awesome and eerie wail filled all that mattered to them of the world, a sound like the scream of the damned that stopped the very hearts in their breasts. The banshee was upon them at last in all its power and terror.

SIXTEEN

VARN TARL SOGAN's fingers closed over the blaster set close to his hand even as he came fully awake.

"Easy, son," Paud Connor's voice said quickly. "It's only the wind."

That terrible screaming? "The banshee?"

"It is."

The farmer lighted the lamp and came closer to the bed. "Sinéad was afraid it would disturb you and asked me to sit here a while." He smiled a trifle grimly. "I must confess. I was a bit concerned about startling you myself, especially when I saw that blaster."

Sogan put the weapon down with a half-embarrassed shake of his head. "No need. My senses are not that sharp yet." He saw the other's look. "It is no false modesty. I was a-spacer before meeting with your daughter and Jake on Visnu. They have spent years in this work, and it will take me a good while still to attain their level of skill, if I ever do."

The war prince realized Paud had been speaking in part to distract him, and an icy chill filled his heart. "They are not back?"

"Not yet."

Varn swung out of bed and caught up the clothes neatly folded on the chest at its foot.

The Noreenan took a quick step toward him. "You can't go after them," he said sharply. "That would only accomplish your death and be of no help to them." His voice gentled. "Jake and Islaen both know their way around Noreen, and neither of them have ever been fools. You can trust them to hide out in the woods until this blows over." Unless they were in the open when it struck in full force . . . "How about that communicator of yours? Can you try to raise them?"

Sogan switched it on. "Not actively. I might distract them at the wrong moment." He could not use his mind to call either Islaen or Bandit for the same reason. "We can keep it open to see if we can pick anything up, though."

His eyes went to the dial of his timer. Bad, he thought. Whether it was the Albionans' defenses or some difficulty they had met en route, this delay in their return meant trouble given the storm outside, maybe such trouble that they might never come back at all.

The Arcturian said nothing. Islaen Connor was this man's daughter. Paud loved her, and he knew all too well the power of his world's mightiest and most greatly dreaded natural force, yet he kept his fear to himself for the sake of his guest, tried to comfort him and give him hope . . . "It will not hurt to dress, at least. I have slept the day away."

The other frowned. "With good cause. Are you well enough to be up?"

"Aye. The antibiotics have done their work."

"Sinéad and I'll be in the kitchen."

Varn hesitated. "I would like to remain here for a while," he said after a moment. "Communicators are meant for short-range work, and their transmissions over a distance are faint."

"May Noreen's gods give you a quick answer, Captain." He turned to go but paused. "If you get chilled up here, there'll be plenty of jakek on the range."

"I should be down in a few minutes. Thanks."

Once the farmer had left him, Sogan sat on the single chair in the room, a simple, straight-backed, wooden affair, and closed his eyes. He dared not search for the patterns of those he loved more than his life, but he could hold himself open to receive anything, conscious or unconscious, that they might be broadcasting. He had sealed his mind for fear of troubling Islaen with his illness, but that was past, and it was safe to use at least his receptors again.

Varn sprang to his feet. Fear! Intense and near!

He flung open the door. "Paud! Sinéad! The roof! They are coming back, and they are in trouble!"

* * *

The flier fought, almost crawled, its way up along the side of the house, trying to utilize the protection the structure provided and at the same time avoid being slammed into it by the whirling gusts punctuating the storm. It gained the battlement, topped it, and dropped into the partial shelter of the sturdy stonework.

Jake's expression did not soften. There was some relief, but not a great deal. The wall was meant to shield a human, not a machine of this size, and then only at the tempest's beginning. It was not much use now. Nothing would be until they reached the vestibule. If they could reach it.

Sogan threw open the inner door. All was bitterly cold inside the outer shelter, cold and so filled with the shrieking madness of the storm that the sound of it was physically and psychologically painful.

He used more caution in sliding back the metal barrier, but even though he braced himself against it, the inrushing blast of wind nearly flung him to the ground. The noise was deafening and nearly unspeakably terrifying . . .

Gasping for breath, he clung to the side of the structure and peered into the wild fury of the night outside. Paud had been right, he thought numbly. The unprotected human body could not face this and live, not for long.

He gave an anxious look at the structure around him, fearing it might lift. There would be no saving the flier then.

It was a danger, he decided, but not imminent. The place had been designed to hold against pressure, though not of this brutal strength, long enough to give a trapped person refuge. If his comrades could get inside reasonably quickly, it would not give way.

He watched the machine crest the battlement. It was fighting for its life, struggling for every inch it gained.

He whirled for the inner door. "Get lights up here!" It was dark as Hades' caves out there. Even with the flier's own beams, a guide should be welcome.

Paud appeared at the top of the stairs. "We have them. Strong emergency torches."

He hoisted a cylinder about a foot in diameter and two feet long onto the floor. Sinéad brought a second up in the next moment.

"Set them by the outer door, one on each side," the Arcturian directed. "Aim along the roof, not high. We do not want to blind them."

The flier homed in on the beams. The wind was hammering it mercilessly, driving it to one side or the other, once flinging it back nearly the whole distance it had advanced, but always, it returned to the bright shafts of light beckoning it to safety like visual lifelines.

Fraction inch by fraction inch, it won its way. The entrance was scarcely five feet away . . .

The front passenger door flew open. Instantly, the banshee seized the advantage thus given it and struck as if with sentient and malignant force, literally whirling the vehicle around.

Sogan's throat closed in horror as he watched. Bethe struggled to pull the door closed. She could not get a proper grip on it, forced back on its hinges as it was. Even if she were able to claim a real hold on it, he doubted she had the strength to draw it shut.

She was leaning too far out!

A great fist of angry air struck her, and the Sergeant was on the roof. She clung desperately to the bottom of the door but could not hold against the pummeling of the gale. Her grip broke, and she was thrown back, beaten back, and sent rolling across the paved area like a twig carried on the crest of a flood.

Almost without thought, the war prince sprang after her. He tried to keep low, but even so, the gale flung him down. It was a bruising, irresistible punishment, a screaming fury that drove terror through heart and mind despite all the effort of his will to check it. There was no fighting this, no hope of fighting it . . .

Perhaps not, but he had won free of an angry river on Amazoon by working with rather than totally against it. That same tactic, or a variant of it, might be effective against Noreen's renegade wind as well. He squirmed on his belly, stopping when the storm swung against him, lying still, pressed against the roof and tense with the need to endure its battering, moving when it blew with him.

He neared the spacer at last. She looked to be unconscious, or barely conscious, and he sighed to himself. It all rested with him.

Sogan caught her wrist and held firm against a gust that sought to wrench her out of his grip once more. There was nothing for it but to drag her. He hoped he would not break or dislocate her arm, but the renewer could fix that later. Nothing mortal could repair death.

To his surprise, Bethe responded to his efforts. She was enough aware of what was happening to recognize his purpose, and she willed her failing body to aid him, to crawl with him, following his lead and using his strength but always working to win her own life. And his.

Several times, Varn feared they would be torn apart, but he compelled himself to hold on. An eternity passed while they struggled against what seemed to his desperate mind to be the conscious hate of the storm, then the lighted place that was their goal appeared larger and brighter. With one final surge of effort, the Arcturian pulled his companion inside and into Sinéad's waiting arms, then rolled into the safety of the vestibule himself.

It was not over, not yet. The former Admiral knew that and fought free of the waves of blackness rolling over him. The others were still outside.

Struggling to his knees, he crept to the entrance once more. The flier was tossing wildly, completely out of Jake's control. The force of the gale kept the door fully open, and if the guerrillas could not close it they were finished. The machine could not be managed like that, and very shortly it would be lifted and flung back over the battlement.

The trapped pair realized that as well. Islaen was trying desperately to slam the door shut, exposing herself again and again to the fate that had almost befallen Bethe Danlo, but to no avail. She could not grip it well enough.

He saw her hand jerk back, and when it extended again, the back and fingers were covered with a dark stain.

Varn Tarl Sogan steeled himself. He crouched by the entrance, shielded by it, and waited. The wind veered, blowing away from the shelter rather than into it as it had a moment before. Not permitting himself to hesitate or dwell on what he was about to do, he dove into the tortured night once more.

Trying to ignore its deafening wail, he lurched to his feet and let the gale carry him forward, running in an attempt to keep pace with it. If he went down prematurely, both he and his slender hope of a plan were doomed.

The banshee turned again as abruptly as it had when he had thrust himself into its power. He was thrown to the roof, but he forced himself to his knees. The flier should not be far . . .

There! The war prince gathered himself. His target was not three feet from him. He would have but one try, and his chances of success would grow no better.

He leaped for the machine. Sogan struck the door with a force that drove the breath from his body. It swung inward and slammed closed with a crash that reached him even over the storm's scream.

Varn dropped down, trying to make himself as small a target for the wind as he could.

Had he been in time? Would Karmikel be able to pull the vehicle out of its wild spinning and bring it through that entryway? Everything hinged on the Noreenan Captain now.

Jake fought the machine and the banshee, willing himself not to fail in the single opportunity given him to save them all. For several tense seconds, he did not know if he would be able to turn the situation around, but Sogan had provided the opening, maybe at the cost of his own life, and he battled to seize all that he could from it.

Gradually, the violence of the flier's movements eased, and it began inching its way in the direction he wished to go.

The Arcturian smiled as the vehicle moved back on course, then lowered his eyes to protect them from the lashing wind. His comrades had their chance. Now he must try to make his. It was a long crawl, too long, but he had realized that from the start. He could do no more than make the best attempt possible to reach shelter or to fall fighting, as befitted one of his race and caste.

Varn, we're coming back for you, but you'll have to help us pull you inside.

That pierced the mists already beginning to close in around him. *No way, Colonel. It would be death to give back any of the way you have gained, even so much as a few inches. Do not cast away what I have tried to win for you.*

He could feel her anger, but also her surrender. Islaen Connor was too much an officer not to recognize that he was right.

Her mind closed, and his head lowered in acknowledgment of the inevitability of his destruction.

The woman's thought slammed into him in the next moment, sharp as a force whip in its insistence and urgency. *Grab onto the tail fin. We'll try to haul you in. —Move, Admiral! Jake can't hold this thing in place forever!*

Sogan lurched to his feet. It was only a couple of yards that he had to go, a few steps under normal conditions. Now he wondered if he or any man could cross it. The strength of the invisible fury hammering him doubled, trebled, as soon as he raised himself off the surface. He could scarcely make headway against it when it blew counter to his course, and always, he faced the risk of being taken up and borne bodily off the roof. Many of the gusts were more than strong enough to do that now if they should hit from the right direction, and the tempest was worsening seemingly with each passing second. Soon, neither human nor machine would be able to withstand its assault at all.

He reached the waiting flier and fell against it. His arms closed over the slender, smooth spine of the tail fin with infinite relief. For the time being, at least, this was sturdy enough to anchor him, and it afforded some protection from the pummeling he was enduring—a beating as savage as the fists and boots of a mob would have given and whose eventual effect would be identical if he remained much longer at its mercy. *Ready, Colonel,* he announced calmly, carefully concealing his misgivings. The former Admiral clung to the shred of hope his consort's plan gave him, but he doubted in his own heart that it would be accomplished with any less difficulty than they had encountered during the rest of this nightmare. He could only pray he would not have to endure whatever was to come for long.

The flier moved, inching its way slowly toward the haven of the vestibule.

Varn's heart sank. His fears had been too well founded. The Noreenan Captain kept the vehicle on its wheels rather than taking to the air again to give him a more solid base, but there was no place to get a secure grip. The fin, while providing good support to lean upon, was deadly smooth. It would soon slide out of his grasp if too much pressure were put against it or on him.

That must not happen. His life depended on retaining that hold. His body no longer had the mass to fight the storm effectively. H could not make it back from here without the machine's help, an Varn Tarl Sogan did not want to die on this dark roof, pounded t death by the vicious madness screaming around him. He ha survived too much, conquered too many perils, to meet his en thus.

The banshee seemed to realize that its victims were on the poi of escaping and responded as a hate-filled, intelligent thing migl have done, seeming to concentrate the full of its strength on tl most vulnerable of them. The gale whirled about, well-nig ripping Sogan from his place by the very suddenness and she force of the change. The storm struck the flier head-on with a renewed strength that told it was at last at the peak of its power and rage. The vehicle could not have held against it, much less the man, but they were now close to their target, and the wind broke apart around the carefully designed mass of the vestibule structure. The flier was just enough in its lee to benefit.

Sogan lacked the machine's strength and weight. Despite the partial shielding, he was in trouble. With a sense of sick terror, he felt himself sliding inexorably back along the fin, an inch at a time. His grasp tightened until his nails were broken, his fingers white and bleeding, but he was powerless to keep himself in place.

He was waging his silent war for life blind. With the wind striking directly into his face, he dared not open his eyes even a slit lest he be blinded for a fact, lest the balls be gouged out of their sockets by the violence of the storm's lash.

Islaen was aware of his difficulty, but there was no aid she could give him, nothing she could do at all except tell him to hold on—that, and pray he would be able to do so.

The end came suddenly. A blast stronger than all the rest struck him squarely and struck low. His legs went from under him. For a fraction of a second, his hands maintained their hold, but inevitably, they slipped, slid back, and with a sickening finality, e tip of the flier's tail fin pulled loose from his clutching fingers. The man fell heavily, striking the side of his head and face on ie rough surface of the roof.

He had set his will as he felt himself go, and he managed to hold nto consciousness against the darkness summoned by the blow to is head.

The storm seemed less violent at this level, and was to a slight xtent. The greater part of its force went over his prone body, and oth the battlement and the vestibule offered him some actual otection. He could lie here a while, rest . . .

Sogan roused himself. He chanced one quick glance in the ier's direction, and exultation filled his spirit. It was passing ough the door, safe at last from the banshee's anger. Whatever own fate, he had helped his comrades, his consort, win their es.

His mind reached for and found Islaen's. He wanted her to ow that it was enough, that he regretted no part of this ending ept having to leave her so soon, that for him, the gain was well rth the price. Her thoughts melded with his for a moment in pride and in love, but anger followed fast that he should yield his life before his power to fight for it was spent. That, and even more powerfully the anguish and grief lying behind it, spurred the former Admiral's will. There was such a short distance to go. Even a lone man might attempt to defy Noreen's banshee over so insignificant a space of ground.

He started to wriggle forward, painfully, ever against the wind which strove to drive him back, away from the haven of the lighted door. Four feet. Three. They were so close now, Islaen and safety, but his strength was nearly gone.

Hands seized one wrist, then the other. He was drawn forward. Varn was conscious of a rush of warmth, the sudden muffling of the wind's scream, and a freedom from its abuse that was almost unbearable in itself. The lifting of his torment released him from the need to battle against it, and as his defenses lowered, the darkness his will had been holding at bay rushed in over him.

SEVENTEEN

THERE WAS A piercing in his temple and left cheek, and the war prince jerked his head away from the irritant provoking it.

"Hold still," Jake's voice commanded. "You've got a couple of nasty gashes here. Islaen told me to take care of the preliminary first aid while she was finishing up with Bethe. —How do you feel?"

"Too sore to be dead." He struggled to sit up and finally succeeded with his companion's help. He was on his bed, he saw. The coverlet over the pillow was stained with blood, enough to surprise him. "I seem to have lost some skin," he commented.

"A bit," the other said. "You'd be an interesting sight for a while if it weren't for the renewer, that's for sure." He would also have been facing some reconstructive surgery, the redhead thought, though he kept quiet about that.

"What about Bethe?" He knew the spacer had been hurt. She had spent less time in the banshee's grip, but she was so much lighter that it had been able to work on her with greater effect.

"Better looking than you by half a light year." He smiled. "She's fine now. Apart from a bad crack to the back of her head, she took about the same degree of punishment as you did. Our Colonel just ordered me to stop pacing and see to you while she gave her the full treatment with the renewer."

"That is a relief," Sogan said gravely. "I was afraid she had taken some heavy damage."

"The bang on the head could've finished her. We were lucky here."

"Islaen herself? I saw blood . . ."

"Debris of some sort raked her hand. It was nothing. She

could've done without the ray altogether, but she didn't want to risk stiff fingers with the possibility of a fight still in front of us. Bandit and I escaped unscathed," he added, forestalling the questions certain to follow. "So did Paud Connor. He helped me haul you in."

"I figured as much, though I couldn't see either of you. I owe you both for that one."

"You owe me considerably more, friend. Had I not intervened, he would've poured a good jigger of his best hill mist down your throat to help bring you around."

Sogan winced. "The banshee fails to kill me, so the locals try poison instead!—You bravely disposed of it yourself, I suppose?"

"No, I'm ashamed to confess. I was too worried about Bethe at that point to bother with it."

The other chuckled, then winced. He wondered if there was a square inch left unbruised anywhere on his body.

Varn swung his legs off the bed. The room remained reasonably stable, and he came to his feet. He was well enough to find Islaen and get treatment from her instead of making her come here to administer it.

Karmikel had started toward him but stepped back again once he saw the Arcturian was having no trouble. Sogan looked at him a moment. "Thanks, Jake," he said softly. "I know what it cost you to stay with that flier."

"Ah, I knew you were waiting in reserve."

Jake's eyes fell as soon as Varn turned away. How long could he expect Bethe Danlo to continue to respect him, he wondered bleakly, if some other had to come to her aid in her every major need?

Islaen Connor's eyes lowered from the screen of her tape reader to rest on the table below it. Still nothing. She had taken an enormous gamble to get this material, a gamble they had very nearly lost, and it was beginning to look as if it was all to no purpose. They were no closer now to the answers they sought than they had been three hours ago when they had begun this study.

Her eyes closed. The records were unquestionably valuable, especially those Sogan was studying, but important as they were, they would still only assure payment for past deeds. She had learned a little about the former Minister's present situation that would prove useful to her—chiefly that he had forty of his ex-Auxies with him, all but their sergeants being housed in the barn, which he had furnished to serve as their barracks without altering it structurally—but nothing had surfaced to help her alter the future L. George Thatcher had devised for some hapless colony.

The bulk of the material on her microcopier consisted of highly detailed records of his personal finances, extensive and complex to a degree that she found difficult to follow. Another man would have left all this to an accountant, or a team of them, but Thatcher seemed to enjoy handling this aspect of his life personally, or he had accepted the need to do so; anyone capable of managing his extensive legitimate business affairs would also quickly come to know about the rest as well.

There was no time to read all of it. She had to content herself with quick-scanning the seemingly endless screens of data, hoping to spot the details she sought.

Varn Tarl Sogan worked closely beside her on another reader. The Commando-Colonel had given him the second microcopier, the one Jake had used. His luck had been no better than hers, although the information he scanned was potentially of greater interest to Albion of Scotia and to the Stellar Patrol. These were the records Thatcher had concealed when Marta Florr's investigation had torn his life and plans for Albion apart, and the data in them would set him before the executioner or, failing that, send him to the galactic pen for the rest of his life—a fate which would probably prove even more repugnant to him. The most consisted of files on his Auxiliaries, those with him or presumed to be still in his service, and those who had definitely remained on Albion.

Two other lists of names and addresses accompanied them, mostly Albionan on one, entirely Albionan on the other. Neither was labeled, but they could represent potential or actual suppliers—or potential victims. Not dead victims, both Sogan and the Noreenan decided at once. L. George Thatcher was not such a fool as to maintain even privately a tally of those eliminated by his order.

None of this was any good to them in their present need, Sogan thought in disgust. Jailing Thatcher for some of his past crimes or slaughtering him after the fact would not help his intended victims, not unless they could be identified in time to shield them from the small but deadly fleet even now preparing to sweep down on them.

He stifled a yawn. There was no longer any soreness or stiffness, but the renewer could not lift the weariness left by his battle of the previous night. He stole a glance at his consort. He had slept most of the day before. Islaen had been active for the whole of it, and she had taken even less than the four hours' rest he had stolen after their encounter with the banshee. Her eyes must feel like two burning coals by this time. His did.

Sighing inwardly, he forced his attention back to the viewer and brought up yet another of the interminable screens. Almost automatically, his eyes flowed down the length of it.

The former Admiral paused and read it more carefully. It was another listing, untitled like its predecessors, but all it contained was the names of four planets repeated in various configurations with a date beside each entry. The whole was arranged chronologically. Kimberly, Motherload, Goddess, Hedon—the latter appearing less frequently than the rest . . .

He stiffened. Bandit, who had been sleeping on his lap after having shifted from the more restless Islaen, muttered in protest at the unanticipated motion. She started to settle herself again but felt the change in him and flitted to his shoulder.

His commander read the new mood on him as well and looked sharply at him. *You've found something?* she demanded.

The war prince's dark eyes glared at the screen as if he would blast what it contained by will alone. *Islaen Connor, you and I should both be stood before a wall and burned down.* There was no trace whatsoever of humor on him. *Look at this.*

The woman came over to him and bent to peer at the screen. Her eyes narrowed into two slits of hate-filled fire. Her lips drew back in an unconscious, silent snarl, and she spat out one biting oath in her own ancient tongue. *Of course. We've been blind, arrant fools not to have seen it. Thatcher's target is Noreen herself.*

EIGHTEEN

"THE GEMS STORED here for Hedon," Jake Karmikel said bitterly. "You're not to blame, Sogan, and neither is Bethe, but Islaen and I should be invalided out by reason of senility. This is our homeworld. We knew about that arrangement and should've guessed right from the start."

"We know the where. We still need the when," the demolitions expert cut in, "and what's actually coming against us. All we have so far are estimates and guesswork." She was fed up with her comrades' self-recriminations, and she was gripped by the strong fear that their time was almost gone. She did not want to see these kindly people decimated because her team could not move quickly enough to defend them.

The Commando leaders had shared their discovery with the on-world family as well as with their own comrades. Noreen of Tara was the Connors' planet. It was their right to know the danger threatening her, and there was no reason why they should not be informed. Now, Sinéad Murchu shook her head. "We always believed that stockpile to be too small and of too little value to tempt a pirate raid. It's to keep it that way that our government insists on such frequent pickups."

"It would be too small for a wolf pack," her daughter agreed, "and it would take a miniature fleet to do the job, as is indeed coming against us. Pirates wouldn't spend the fuel, much less take the kind of risk involved in hitting a planet for so little. However, for a single individual like Thatcher, those jewels represent a real prize. He could pay off his thugs with what he'd get for them black market and have plenty left over to set himself up as he wishes to live in the inner-systems, maybe with a residence on

Terra and a seasonal suite on Hedon, all without having to touch the core of his own wealth. He's too careful a man to dip into his mainstay merely for pleasure."

"I don't know," Jake said doubtfully. "The joys of the inner-system can be expensive. He might need a deal more than the raid will net him to see himself content. He's young enough to have a lifetime before him and not much chance of ever being able to pull off another coup like this."

"Thatcher's interested in upper-level society, not debauchery. Even in his university days, he never went in for that. He might even marry money if the opportunity arose. —That part of it's speculation and of no concern to us. We've hit the answer, I think, or part of it. Now we've got to get the rest. Fast."

Islaen glanced at the Commando-Sergeant. "Bethe, get on our transceiver and give Ram Sithe a full report—everything we've got or can surmise. Tell him to stop that Hedon freighter from coming here. By the look of the deliveries on that list, she should be arriving very soon. Jake, check the flier out. The banshee gave it a hammering."

"Aye, Colonel," he said, as both guerrillas saluted and left the room.

Paud Connor watched his daughter speculatively. He did not seem particularly surprised by the calm efficiency of her manner, this warrior's side of her which she had not before been forced to show on Noreen. "Will stopping the Hedonite starship help?" he asked.

"Perhaps. At least, the raiders won't find the jewels sitting out on the docks for their easy taking instead of having to blast them from their vaults." There was no question of the renegades' knowing where to find them in either event. Everyone on Noreen did, and Thatcher had been on-world long enough to have acquired that easily learned information.

"What'll that mean to us except more destruction?" the farmer inquired steadily.

"It'll buy the Navy and Patrol time in which to get here, even if it's only to avenge us."

Her eyes had the look of battle-tempered titanone. The devastation would be immense at that stage. In order to prevent that, the attackers would have to be kept away from the planet altogether.

There was much that could be done to minimize the slaughter i they did get through. "I want all but essential spaceport personnel evacuated and the inhabitants and stock of the farms in its immediate environs as well. Those sons will be coming in spitting fire, and they'll keep it up until they get what they're after. They'll want us to stay as disorganized as possible while they make good their escape."

In one fact, they were fortunate. There was but a single target, a single locality to feel the worst fury of the assault. This would not be a second Tatarina, even if the Albionan renegades possessed that sort of power, which they did not.

"What about Thatcher?" Will asked. "What will he be doing while all this is going on, and afterwards?"

"He'll just wait until the turmoil settles, then quietly take his leave of Noreen and pick up his loot."

"Unless the maggot's spawn working for him decide to blast him and keep the stones themselves."

"Not likely. They know they'll get more from their share of the sale he's lined up than they would trying to peddle the stones on their own. L. George Thatcher wouldn't be so stupid as to broadcast the identity of his buyer."

"Will he have the power to blow the vaults?" Jeanie inquired. "I've seen them. They're really strong."

"If he didn't, he wouldn't bother with the attempt." The Hedonite freighters followed no fixed schedule in coming for their gems. The Terran might like to pick the shipment off the dock, but he could not figure on being able to do so, and he knew full well that he had no chance whatsoever of seizing it in space. Hedon's merchant craft habitually carried high-value luxury products. They would scarcely be able to move outside the secure starlanes of the inner-systems at all had they not made their defense the fact that not only would they fight savagely if attacked but would inevitably blow both themselves and their cargoes to space dust if defeated. Pirates left them alone as a result; they had use only for sound, salable goods. Thatcher, or those working for him, would be no less aware of that than the rest of the ultrasystem and would not trouble the starship once she was spaceborne.

The Arcturian's dark eyes were somber. His thoughts were running somewhat ahead of his commander's. "Kinkora should be evacuated as well," he said quietly. "We have given Thatcher trouble and some cause for concern. He has shown himself to be one who will take vengeance for that."

"Not from space," Islaen responded. "We're too close to Dunbrityne, and he'd not care to find laser fire raining down on his own stronghold."

"We can handle anything else," Paud Connor interjected.

"He has some forty of those Auxies with him. They may not be worth much in terms of quality or courage, but they can use their weapons. Many, maybe most, of them are probably out-and-out killers as well."

"What can a handful of farmers expect to accomplish against them?" the older man inquired, lowering his eyes to conceal the laughter in them.

"You are peaceful people," Sogan responded evenly. "Numbers aside, those inured to violence usually have the edge in such a situation. Their familiarity with their arms alone would give them that—"

He stopped. The farmer was smiling openly, and he saw the same amusement on each of the other Noreenans.

Paud went to a locked cabinet set chest high on the wall beside the door. He opened it and took a gleaming pellet gun, one of two, from it. After removing the safety and activating the firing chamber, he casually opened the door. "See what the banshee left of my wind arrow there on the far end of the barn?"

The former Admiral nodded. The decorative, steer-shaped weather vane itself had been snapped off, leaving only the upright shaft that had supported it.

"Do you agree that it's within pellet range?"

"Aye, barely."

Without visibly sighting the weapon or seeming to study his target at all, the Noreenan let loose a shot. In the next instant, most of the narrow strip flew off the roof.

"Paud!" Sinéad exclaimed, claiming the gun from him. "A man of your age showing off like that! Besides, you left a good three inches of it sticking up there." Once again, the gun gave its characteristic soft hiss, and the profile of the barn roof was smooth.

Her husband took the weapon back and locked it away again. "You always were a better shot than me," he conceded gruffly.

He turned to Varn. "Well, Captain? Do you judge us familiar enough with a pellet gun? —Will and Jeanie are the good shots in the family, by the way. They met at an advanced sharpshooter class."

Paud laughed then. "I'm sorry, Captain. I figured you were grossly underestimating some of our talents and couldn't resist jinking you a bit, even under these circumstances."

Paud grew grave in the next moment. "You admire the Thornens, a peace-loving, pre-space people prior to the War who learned what invasion would mean, acquired Federation weapons, and forged themselves into a magnificent Resistance army. Noreen was spared that world's agony, praise the good Spirit ruling space, but don't imagine that our response would've been any less.

"You're right in saying this is a quiet planet. Violence isn't encouraged as an appropriate response to difficulty, and the few incidents that we do have are usually severely punished, but there's another side to us. We're a disciplined people—the Navy never had much trouble drilling that trait into our recruits—and we passionately love both our homeworld and freedom. Just check the War records for the history of Noreenan soldiers to see how much. To preserve them, we have our militia. Every man is an active member, trained to it since school age. Our women, too, since they might have had to fight as well had the worst befallen us. Noreen of Tara will never be helpless before a tyrant's heel and will never submit to such rule while one Noreenan remains alive anywhere in this ultrasystem, or beyond it for that matter.

"L. George Thatcher and the maggot's spawn serving him have attacked my stock and my family, and they've threatened Noreen with gross violence. Rest assured that we're prepared to meet his renegades with the same. I'm commander of this region's militia. In one hour, I can have a hundred men roused and assembled here. In three, I can bring you a thousand. We may not be Commandos, but we know this part of our world, and I don't think ye'll find us wanting as partisans."

"The hundred will suffice," Islaen Connor told him. "I was going to ask for a muster. —Have them gather at Planet's Glory, in the woods there. I don't want them spotted in case there are spies around here. We'll hit Dunbrityne as soon as I brief our party and can get them there."

None of her companions questioned that, nor would Jake or Bethe when they learned of it. Not only did the Albionans have the information they needed to defend the port, but it would hardly be sensible to leave so large a hostile force free on-world whether trouble struck from out of the stars or was averted.

"How will you summon your troops?" Sogan asked curiously. He knew the civilian transceivers used on Noreen were not safe enough for such work. They would not have sufficed for an army fighting the Empire's soldiers at all, and these Noreenans were not children playing at being warriors. They would have allowed for the security deficiencies of their normal communications system.

"I'll place a call to one of my neighbors. A 'static' whistle will precede it, sounding over all the local sets. Similar disturbances occur all the time, but there's a peculiar note to this one. We all use party frequencies since they're cheaper, and only courtesy keeps folks from listening in on others' affairs. I'll have a large audience this time and will just give the location and hour for assembly during our supposed conversation."

"Admirable."

"We find a simple system works best for us."

"Thorne's systems were simple as well. That did not hinder their effectiveness."

The necessary transmissions were soon made, and Varn Tarl Sogan found himself standing beside the elder Connors in the final minutes before setting out. Jake was bringing down the flier after giving it a final testing, the Colonel and Bethe were finishing setting the charges they would require under Bandit's ever-curious eyes, and Will had already gone to join the mustering militia. Jeanie had accompanied him and would remain at Planet's Glory with their children until the issue was decided; the fighting would be done by Noreen's men in accordance with the on-worlders' custom.

The former Admiral was silent and withdrawn, but his eyes glittered with cold fire. He had been waiting a long time for what was soon to come. L. George Thatcher had directly and indirectly caused his unit and himself personally a great deal of trouble and pain. The assassination attempts he could pass over as part of the war his unit now waged had there been nothing else, but not the diminution of his honor or the suffering that might soon fall on Noreen of Tara and on Islaen Connor herself. If any spark of justice remained in the universe or in those beings all believed controlled it, he would claim payment from that man in his life's blood.

Paud Connor glanced at the Arcturian. He sighed, misreading the cause of the frigid wall Sogan had raised around himself. "I should've thought that knowing how we Noreenans have trained ourselves would make you feel a bit better about the prospect of having a company of us beside you in a fight."

Varn looked quickly at him. The knowledge did increase his respect for Noreen's citizens despite all his previous appreciation of their worth in other areas. He was ashamed to confirm that before these people. Besides, their skill or lack of it was not the question here, apart from his hate. "Were you the finest soldiers in both ultrasystems, I should be no happier about your presence on this mission or on any other that Islaen Connor commands. I do not want to see her bear responsibility for the deaths of her dearest kin."

"As you do for yours?" Sinéad Murchu asked swiftly and softly.

"Aye."

The reply was curt, inviting no probing. Paud's eyes flickered to his wife, then back to the younger man, but he respected Sogan's will and did not press the subject. "Don't worry overly much on that score. A partisan who lives to strike and strike again is a lot more valuable than a hothead, however brave, who throws himself away on a fatal frontal assault. Noreen's militia are trained to the former goal, willing as we are to die if we must. We'll take care of ourselves, Captain, and take care of Thatcher's maggot's spawn as well."

One hundred and three men materialized from out of the trees at Paud Connor's signal. The war prince studied them carefully. He vaguely recalled having seen some of them at Kinkora during his first visit to Noreen, but they were very different now, grave and as silent as the wild things of the wood. They were also a force likely to compel the respect of any formal military unit unfortunate enough to draw blaster against them, or he had lost all ability to judge the quality of a fighting company, regular or guerrilla.

Islaen read her consort's reaction, and her head lifted. Her people were doing her proud, although she had never imagined that it would be otherwise when the time of need was upon them.

The Noreenan militia had conducted their muster with total professionalism, although they had not imagined it to be more than another of the many drills that drew them together like this even during the busy harvest season. The sight of the four Commandos with their commander gave them pause, however, and a cold feeling gripped the heart of each one as he realized there might be something more to this summons. No one broke the silence, but every eye fixed on the flier's occupants, waiting.

Paud did not hold them in suspense. "Islaen's not here as my daughter and your neighbor but as leader of a Commando unit on an active mission directly affecting Noreen. She requires our aid." He motioned for her to come forward. "It'll be better if ye get the details from her."

The Colonel described the arms theft on Alpha Gary and both the Navy's and her team's efforts to recover them, then told of the thwarted attempt against Albion of Scotia and the danger currently threatening Noreen. "We want the information those Albionans have," she concluded, "and I don't want them to slip away in the confusion of an attack or in its aftermath. For both those reasons, we plan to capture Dunbrityne house now."

Her eyes swept those gathered around her. "We outnumber them, and the most of them are pretty low-caliber fighters—port rats with small stomach for facing real opposition. Don't let any of that make you overconfident. They're well armed; the barn, particularly, affords good cover, and if cornered, even scum like that will fight. Firing from out of the shadows comes naturally to them, however little they relish the prospect of having their shots returned.

"They'll be shooting to kill, but if you feel uncomfortable about that, go for a major wound. Remember, in all but immediate or very quick death, the renewer will either heal or keep the victim going until we can get him to the hospital for regrowth treatment. None of you need feel ashamed because you hesitate to slay," she added. "It's not easy to do it the first time. For a person who respects life, it's never really easy. Don't be surprised if those of you who are veterans of the Navy find themselves in the same position. Killing an individual foe is mentally very different from blowing a starship."

She then described her plan for taking the renegades in detail and finally gave her party the order to move out.

Varn said nothing mentally or verbally during the briefing or afterwards. His hands gripped the controls of the flier as if he would crush them beneath his fingers, but that was the only outward indication he gave of the blow his commander's orders had been for him. It had been sharp, almost in the nature of a betrayal, and would have been a betrayal had the circumstances been different.

A vague resentment rather than real anger filled his heart and mind. How much more of importance, aye, and of need to him was he expected to surrender? Even this . . .

He tried to shrug it off. Islaen was not to blame. She had merely acted for what she believed was the good of the total mission, as he himself would have done in her place.

Silently cursing the course of his life and the gods whose cruelty had set him on it, the former Admiral compelled himself to concentrate on guiding the vehicle through Planet's Glory's heavy woods. They would keep as much as possible under cover during the approach to eliminate any possibility of their being spotted before they were ready to strike. The lay of the countryside was with them in that, and they would have to cross completely open ground for only a couple of short stretches. With care and Islaen's gift to give them warning of observers, they should be able to reach target without giving themselves away.

Islaen glanced at the Commando-Captain as his silence continued. She knew full well that he was displeased with the role she had assigned to him, although he would not protest against it. *There'll be no trouble outside, and Thatcher himself won't fight,* she said. *He'll realize that would be useless and surrender fast, trusting in bruised innocence and righteous anger plus Noreenan respect for the law to get him free. The battle, if there is any, will be in the barn. Our troops are green, Varn, whatever their basic skills. They could need us in there.*

Why me? he asked. *I should have thought you would prefer to have Jake with you in that kind of situation.*

The woman smiled. *You're the expert, Admiral.* His surprise rewarded her, and she laughed softly. *Don't always put yourself behind us, friend. Commandos are good at hiding in shadows. It's you Arcturians who have the experience in trying to flush the like of us out.*

With only passing success, he reminded her.

Your hunters found their quarry all too often for our comfort, and this slime isn't the Thornen Resistance.

He nodded, but his thoughts remained closed. Islaen sighed. *If you really want to take Thatcher yourself, this isn't essential. I can bring Jake with me,* she continued.

Give me credit for some sense of responsibility! the war prince snapped. He gripped his temper. *What I really want is to burn him down where he stands, and that you would not permit in any event short of legitimate self-defense, would you?*

No. The Navy wants a live prisoner to try and an example to display, not a corpse.

Then what is the difference who slaps the secure-cuffs on him?

Sogan retreated behind his shield after that. There was no point in continuing the discussion. An Arcturian warrior served where his talents would prove most useful. If that meant his foregoing the minor satisfaction of capturing his enemy himself, so be it. Whining or protest would only degrade him still further, and he would not even be able to claim need as a pitiful defense for that display of weakness.

NINETEEN

THE NOREENAN HOST lay at the edge of the trees surrounding the Dunbrityne farmhouse. Three of the Federation team waited with them, each holding a pellet gun mounted with a slender cylindrical projectile in place of its usual barrel. Bethe Danlo remained with the machine, her small fingers caressing the controls of the laser Varn had mounted there. Only Bandit was absent. The gurry had retreated to the crown branches at Islaen's order to wait out the battle.

There were only a few of the Albionans to be seen behind their glimmering picket. The rain that had been threatening all morning had begun falling as a heavy drizzle roughly half an hour previously, and most of the off-worlders were only too pleased to remain inside. That was a disappointment for the attackers, since they had hoped to take a good number of their enemies in the open, but there was no help for it. With any luck, it should make little difference to the difficulty of their endeavor or the speed with which it would be brought to a conclusion.

Islaen studied the energy picket, then raised her weapon. They would have no trouble with this, whatever was to come later. The barrier was a civilian protective device, one of the many on the market designed to hold back would-be intruders and animal life with varying degrees of force. This was a strong one set to deliver a fatal charge to anything human disturbing it, but it had never been designed to withstand a military assault. Her nail struck her communicator once, sharply. She counted off three seconds and eased her finger back on the trigger.

On either side of her, the soft hiss that was the only sound a pellet gun made echoed her own gun's discharge. The three miniature rockets flew simultaneously. They struck the base of the picket, detonated, and the glowing wall was gone.

That was Bethe's signal. She sent the flier forward, firing the laser mounted on its nose as she did. A streak of blue light struck the farmhouse door, played over it, literally burning it around so that it fell into the building, opening it to the attackers. Swivelling her weapon, she served the barn in the same manner.

The Albionans caught outside at the beginning of the totally unanticipated barrage had dropped to the ground. Now, at the Sergeant's command, they stood, their arms lifted. Only a fool would try to battle an artillery-class laser with a hand blaster.

Bethe ordered them to march into the wood, where the squads assigned to prisoner guard took charge of them. She quickly brought her attention back to the two buildings and loosed a burst of fire along the front of both to discourage defenders manning the shattered doors and the windows from trying to cut down the Noreenans rushing across the open place. Or herself. Her own position was not a secure one despite the power of her weapon and would quickly become perilous if the Albionans could concentrate their fire on it, particularly if they possessed arms stronger than the blasters that Islaen believed comprised their arsenal.

The attackers separated into three parties. One, the smallest, struck the farmhouse under Jake Karmikel's command. The second, led by Islaen and Varn, went for the barn. The third remained concealed, a reserve force to prevent the escape of any of the renegades and to come to the aid of the primary assault teams should either of them run into serious difficulty.

Jake crouched down as he cleared the door and tensed himself to leap aside from any stream of blaster fire that might be loosed to greet him. None came, and he tore down the hall, motioning to some of his companions to follow him and others to mount the stairs.

They found a man and a woman, who quickly surrendered, in the sitting room. L. George Thatcher himself was in his office. He was standing, his arms well away from his body, his expression dignified and angry.

Twice, the clap of discharging blasters sounded from the floor above. Silence followed lasting a few minutes, then the tramp of heavy boots sounded on the stairs.

"That's all of them up there, Captain," the on-worlder in charge of that phase of the assault called in to him.

"Good work. Bring our prisoners outside and stash them with the others. —Let's go, Thatcher. You can watch my comrades mop up the rest of your crew from the woods."

Islaen Connor's nerves felt raw as she darted through the huge doorway of the old barn. She knew the lay of it well, at least. Like her houses, Noreen's barns all followed a more or less identical floor plan, especially those of a particular region. Inside was one enormous space where a herd could be driven in quickly to wait out a storm. Roomy stalls lined either side where bulls, young calves, injured beasts, or others requiring separation from the rest could be kept. The rearmost quarter of the building was closed off to serve as a carriage house to store the family's transports and other large and smaller farm gear. The equally spacious second story was used chiefly for storing grain, hay, angora hair, and other produce as well as bulk supplies and goods.

This place, of course, had been serving as a temporary barracks for close to forty individuals and was furnished accordingly. In the front area just before her were four long tables with crude benches for seating plus an institutional-size range and food storer. In the rear, she could see two long rows of bunks and guessed that more must be in the carriage house beyond. There were no draperies separating one from the other; much less the cubicles the Navy or Patrol would have required, but they were at least well apart, and area heaters were placed between every other of them. Each had a space chest at its foot.

Navy Personnel might not have passed the Albionans' quarters, but the Commando-Colonel was well pleased with them. Properly divided sleeping spaces would have provided a myriad of sheltered niches for assassins to utilize.

All that raced through her awareness as her eyes skimmed the big room. "Grab the moon!" she ordered those assembled inside, firing off a quick bolt even as she spoke to knock the blaster out of a man's hand as he started to bring it to bear. "Drop the armor, or we'll fry the lot of you!"

There were too many too widely scattered within for all to be taken easily even had they no forewarning. Those by the door obeyed, for they were directly under the barrels of the invading party's weapons, but those farther inside, by far the greater number, were not so ready to yield themselves. Most dived for whatever cover was available. A few nearest the stairs fled to the second level to hide and prepare their defense up there.

Some of Islaen's company hastened the prisoners outside both to remove them from the firing zone and to ensure that they would not break loose to join the fray. The rest settled in to clear the barn of its defenders.

Islaen would have preferred that this had not occurred, but her inexperienced troops could not be blamed for that. Seasoned guerrillas would have taken a few more of the Albionans—and would be able to guard themselves more efficiently in the fight to come—but most of the off-worlders would have escaped to do battle in any event. The laser might have held them all, but Bethe could not have brought that to bear on the interior without abandoning the farmhouse for a time, and she dared not fire it at all now with their own party inside. An artillery-class laser designed for use in deep space could not be controlled finely enough in a planet's atmosphere to function under melee conditions.

She heard shooting, the ping of a ricocheting pellet and the answering roar of a blaster. The same sounds, or variations of them, were being repeated throughout the building. Her talent told her that better than half the renegades remained within and helped her place a few of them, but she had to raise her shields once the actual fighting began. The distraction of the powerful emotions being generated on all sides would otherwise perilously reduce her own efficiency. If a person were killed while their minds were in contact, she herself could be momentarily paralyzed by the horror of the severing of life and perhaps take real injury herself. Varn had suffered two extremely grave wounds of that nature on Omrai of Umbar . . .

Warrior's instinct made the Colonel whirl. She fired twice in quick succession, even as she moved, dropping two figures crouched behind the lowest slat of the fence forming the stall at her right.

Islaen moved closer to examine them, her face set and grim. That had been a close one. The bottom board of the barrier was wide, and she had very nearly missed the pair entirely. She would have gone to her death never knowing they were there had they not shifted slightly to keep her in their sights.

She moved closer to the stalls, signaling two of her companions to accompany her. They would have to give close attention to these deeply shadowed places if they were not to lose some of their comrades or see some of their enemies elude them. Her lips tightened. It would be the latter if the Albionans felt they had a chance, she judged. The off-worlders were obviously trying to delay capture until the anticipated assault on the port should come and they could hope to join forces with the attacking renegades. Otherwise, there would be no point in escaping into the wilds of a planet whose populace was suddenly totally hostile to them. They were urban-raised and could not readily manage to survive away from the haunts of their own species. That was yet another indication that the raid was scheduled to come very soon, maybe considerably sooner than the already short time she had been anticipating. Even now, it might still be too late to save the spaceport and its defenders and maybe a lot of other people and animals, depending upon how far afield the raiders would range.

Varn Tarl Sogan cautiously mounted the stairs. The upper level was his charge.

Only when he had reached the top and positioned himself to defend the entrance did he signal the squad under his command to come ahead. That narrow flight of steps could turn into a massacre site if it were not well guarded.

When the first of the on-worlders, Will Connor, joined him, Sogan turned that task over to him and gave his attention to the work that had brought him here. His mouth felt dry, and his pulse ran fast. Danger lurked in every shadow of this accursed place. Mind gift or none, he could all but taste it. He had lost a lot of good men on Thorne of Brandine under conditions not too very different from those reigning here.

The Arcturian wished heartily for his consort's talent, although he knew full well that she could not really use it during battle. Any help at all would be welcome at this stage.

He steeled himself to go on. His trust would have to lie in himself, in the skills honed in the long years of bitter war, and in the strong nerves and keen shooting of his Noreenan companions.

The militiamen were worthy of that. Even now, he could be certain of that. He had seen enough of how they handled themselves outside and below to confirm his initial impression of them. Their approach had been disciplined, their conduct professional. Had he not known this was their first action, at least as a guerrilla unit, he would not have realized it from observing them. Islaen's people were not blaster shy, nor were they cursed with the overconfidence too often found in green troops, and when they discharged a pellet it nearly invariable found its target. With a fleet, or even a single battlecraft, manned with such soldiers, he could—

The war prince cut off that thought. Let his mind wander again, and he would probably be carried down from here with a hole burned through his heart.

The fighting on the second level of the barn proved to be dirty, nerve-wrenching work, for those up here had been given time in which to conceal themselves, and most of them had no interest at all in being taken. These were for the most part the leaders in Thatcher's plot and formerly officers in the Albionan Auxiliaries. If everything had been uncovered, as the Commandos' attack testified to be the case, it was execution, not imprisonment, that they faced. If they could not elude capture and the fate that would follow it, then they might as well go quickly, and they were determined to a man to take at least one of their opponents out with them.

There were more hiding places up here to aid their cause than on the ground floor, and every one had to be checked out thoroughly.

The danger was greatest on the approach to a site. Anyone hidden there would realize the only hope of avoiding detection was to kill the searcher before he could shoot or sound the alarm, drag the body into his hole, then carefully move back to an already examined area himself. With luck, he might just be able to slip out before the hunter was missed and what remained of him was discovered. Three times, the Arcturian fired a scant moment before one of the renegades cut him down, and he began to wonder how much longer he would be able to elude the Grim Commandant's summons like this. On Thorne, a building would conceal one or perhaps two partisans. Here, there were many more, far too many . . .

A shadow, black among the grays to his right!

Once again, almost without conscious thought, his blaster discharged. This time, he had an extra second's warning, and so his peril had not been so extreme, but still, his heart hammered hard. He wished passionately that this business was over. If it did not end soon, he knew he would lose some of his companions even if he survived it himself. Two had been felled already. Their wounds had proven light thanks to the speed of their reflexes, but time and their exposed position were against them. It would not be much longer now before their luck turned.

There was not a great deal more of the barn to search, he saw with relief. A few minutes longer, and they would all be able to go down.

Sogan glanced to his left, to the great multitiered rack of bins where angora hair would be sorted by grade and color had this been a working barn. Will Connor had the unenviable task of searching them. It was a job the war prince was glad enough to forego, for the complex offered a honeycomb of bolt holes to desperate men and women.

His breath caught. One of their quarry, at least, had made it out. He was there, lying full length along the support beam of the uppermost bin. The Albionan knew Will would spot him and had taken aim. Even as Sogan saw him, he was tensing to fire.

Varn leaped for the Noreenan, letting loose a long, broad bolt as he moved. His body struck Will's, literally driving him into the rack, just under the bolt fired by muscular reflex from the blaster of the already dead assassin. So close did it come that he could feel the heat of it burning across his shoulders, although the absence of pain told that he had taken no damage from it.

Both men lay still an instant, the breath knocked out of them by the impact.

The Arcturian recovered himself first. Some of the other militiamen were starting toward them. "Cover us," he ordered the nearest. "The rest of you, go back to the hunt. They could flame the lot of us like a crippled freighter if we bunch up together." The former Admiral spoke rapidly, almost automatically, barely checking himself from using his own language. This was a familiar situation even for one of his former rank, and he slipped into it instinctively. He had commanded many such a hunt before . . .

Will groaned and struggled to sit up. Sogan gave him a hand. "Are you all right? I might have cracked a rib or two throwing you against the rack like that."

The Noreenan tried an experimental deep breath. "I'm sound out, I think, apart from a number of bruises. Thanks." He grimaced. "The furloughs ye people get don't make up for this sort of thing."

The dark-eyed man smiled. "I knew you would see the light eventually. —You are sure you are well enough to continue?"

"I am. I won't stiffen up until later, and I guess my sister will give me a turn under the renewer before that happens."

TWENTY

THE PAIR WORKED together to finish inspecting the rack. By the time they had completed that, the final portion of the building had been cleared, and they were able to go down and join the task force now assembled in the farmyard outside.

The Arcturian's mind touched Islaen's even before he left the barn to assure himself that she had taken no hurt. The fighting had been hard on the ground level as well, if not quite as bad as that which his squad had encountered, and he knew the Commando-Colonel would take no secondary role in it.

Her response was quick and a little sharp. *Varn! You had trouble up there?*

Some. We took care of it.—What about you? And the others?

We're all sound out. A few bumps in my case. Not even so much as that on Jake or Bethe.

How did we do?

A total success. We lost one man and had four wounded, none of them dangerously. Our opponents are out five slain and another two dozen wounded, most of them heavily.

Impressive statistics, the war prince said. Very impressive for a green company, particularly since theirs had been the more exposed party. He knew a moment's deep gratitude that his Empire's forces had not been compelled to fight this people during the War. They might have had even worse difficulty than they had faced on Thorne of Brandine. *What about the prisoners?*

I was just about to order them brought back in for questioning. The Colonel sighed. *I'm afraid we're not going to have as easy a victory in this as we did in taking them.*

Varn did not respond for a moment. *Tell Bandit to keep out of sight for a while,* he suggested then, although he kept his inner thoughts closed. The idea which had just come to him needed consideration before he either acted on it himself or laid it before his commander.

A good idea, the woman replied at once. *She doesn't like confrontations of this type, and those sons will be more likely to take us seriously without her flitting around our heads.*

Those prisoners able to face questioning were soon marched before the Commando-Colonel. The severely injured were under Tam's care and would not be troubled, at least not until their condition had been stabilized.

L. George Thatcher managed to hold himself apart even in that crush. Sogan, whose eyes bore into him from the moment he had been returned to the farmyard, had to admire the dignity and courage of the man. Both were part of him and no mere front.

Islaen watched her consort. She had been proud of Varn Tarl Sogan many times since she had first encountered him as the cheifmost of her enemies on Thorne of Brandine, but rarely was that pride stronger than in this moment. She knew or knew enough to imagine the intensity of his hate, of his desire to rend this treacherous-creature, yet he held himself quiet, his control so firm that no sign of his anger or bitter disappointment escaped him. There was no need to warn him to take care, nor would she insult him by doing so.

Her own fury was in greater danger of slipping its bonds, she thought as her attention turned to the Terran. This evil renegade was the cause of so much pain to the finest man in both ultrasystems, men and women had died trying to reclaim the arms he had stolen and others before that by his direct order, killers under his command were poised to ravage Noreen.

The former Minister met her gaze without wavering. "What is the meaning of this outrage, this murder of my employees, Colonel Connor?" he demanded with an icy fury.

"Put it on freeze, Thatcher," she snapped. "We have you for direct commission of and for conspiracy on multiple felonies up to and including murder, treason to Albion of Scotia, and your plotting against Noreen of Tara. The actual charges on the latter will depend upon the outcome.—I want to know where your ships are, their strength, and when they plan to strike."

"I know nothing about any of this, and even if I did, I should hardly compromise myself and my colleagues here with me by telling you anything. May I suggest, Colonel, that if you expect that some sort of violence will be launched against the planet, you would do better to see to her defense rather than go on brutalizing innocent residents."

"Ah, stretch the lot of them out on the planeting field," an angry voice called from somewhere on her right. "Let them be the first to meet their friends when they come in blasting."

The former Admiral stiffened. *One of our officers was tried and condemned as a war criminal by your Federation for doing that with prisoners.*

Islaen's anger flared, but she quelled it in the next moment. The temptation had been there, however short-lived. "That would put us on their level," she said aloud. "However, there's no reason why they shouldn't be stashed at the spaceport, on the top floor of one of the warehouses bordering the field."

Thatcher glared at her. "You have assumed responsibility for our safety, Colonel. If you believe some sort of attack to be imminent . . ."

"You needn't be housed any more securely than the innocent citizens whose duties demand that they remain at their posts," she replied coldly. "You called this down on them. You'll take some of the risk as well."

She turned from him to face his minions. The promise of a lesser sentence would eventually move a few of them to talk, but it would take time.

Before she could speak, Sogan's mind touched hers. *Give me leave to handle this.*

They're all yours, Admiral. It won't be easy, though. They all know their best move's to keep their mouths shut and disassociate themselves completely from those who'll be conducting the attack.

I can be persuasive, Colonel Connor.

The war prince eyed the captives contemptuously. "Take this back to the flier," he ordered, indicating the Terran with a sweep of his hand.

When Thatcher was gone, he turned to his own party. "There are plenty of herb nettles around. Gather a good supply and bring them here." The dark eyes flickered over the prisoners. "You three," he ordered, seemingly choosing his victims at random. "Drop your trousers."

The Albionans looked completely puzzled for an instant, then they blanched as they saw the on-worlders gingerly carrying the fiercely stinging plants and realized what he meant.

Sogan gave an inward sigh of relief. That had been his gamble. The renegades had gained enough hard experience with the nettles to recognize them. "Move," he commanded. "Now. Delay further, and we shall burn your clothing off you."

"You can't . . ." one of the three began.

The Arcturian's expression never altered. "Understand this. I ordered your people's energy picket blown on Amazoon of Indra, knowing it would be the wildlife and not my team that would make the assault. You are all aware of how they died.

"I had no particular feeling against that party, merely my orders to prevent the arms from escaping. Here, on the other hand, I find my family in direct danger, I have faced a brace of assassination attempts myself, and I have seen my commanding officer almost run down by one of your transports. How reluctant do you imagine I shall be to use whatever means I deem necessary to get the information I want out of you?"

The prisoner stared at him in agonized horror. To speak was to doom himself to a long imprisonment or, more probably, to death. He looked at the implacable face of the Commando-Captain. He would probably be convicted anyway . . . "Forty-nine fighters." The words spilled out in a rush. "Three ten-class, the rest five- and two-man. There used to be fifty, but you got the brig already."

"When do they move in?"

"They'll be here in about thirty-six hours, give or take some."

"Their coordinates?"

"I don't know!"

Sogan believed that. The man was a port rat, not a spacer. "Coming from where?"

"The Corlian Belt. I don't know where inside it."

The war prince nodded. The big asteroid field was a major feature of this part of the Sector. Centrally located and giving ready access to many of its major starlanes, it had provided a haven for many a wolf pack over the years. That Thatcher's thugs should have used it as their lair was only reasonable.

The size of the fleet, on the other hand, was a surprise, and an unpleasant one, as was the fact that it would be arriving so soon. They had been figuring on having several more days, worst case, and probably on two or three weeks in which to prepare an adequate reception.

"Start moving these vermin back toward the spaceport," Varn told those of his small army in charge of the prisoners. "We will contact the Garda and have them intercept you en route."

Before long, the Albionans had been tightly roped together for greater security and herded away into the treelands. No one else had moved in the farmyard, and Varn Tarl Sogan felt many eyes boring into him. He met them evenly. He knew what the Noreenans had to be thinking, but a stubborn pride would not allow him to defend himself.

"Would you have gone on with it?" a voice asked at last.

Varn recognized the speaker as Angus Connor, Paud's brother. There was anger in the man, but with the question open in front of him, the former Admiral found himself smiling. He shook his head. "There was never a question of having to do it," he told them all firmly. "They did not have the courage to face the prospect of torture."

"Why didn't you try it on Thatcher?"

"He is made of other stuff. Neither the threat nor the suffering would have broken him, not quickly enough to meet our needs."

Jake Karmikel pushed through the crowd. His face was angry, and so was his voice when he spoke. "Varnt Sogan never resorted to needless bloodshed in his life, much less to something like this." His look was no friendlier when he fixed it for a moment on his comrade. "As for that Amazoon business, none of us planned for it to turn out the way it did."

"The ruse worked anyway," Paud said as he hastened to stand beside the two Federation guerrillas.

To his surprise, Sogan smiled again, this time even more broadly. "Too well, it seems. There is that about me which makes it easy to believe me capable of many a hard deed."

"Maybe," the farmer admitted—the dark-haired man had sent a shiver through him for a fact. "We'd better remember, though, that those maggot's spawn also firmly believed we'd allow you do it, that we're some sort of savages not much bothered by human pain."

"That's the kind they are themselves," Karmikel informed him.

Islaen joined them. Bandit was riding her shoulder, sitting quietly. "Let's be moving out," the Colonel said. "I'll put a call through to Admiral Sithe and to the Garda, but I have a feeling that anything that's to be done to stop this business, or to delay it long enough for real help to arrive, is going to fall to us."

TWENTY-ONE

THE COMMANDOS SILENTLY awaited their leader's return in the sitting room of Kinkora house, which their hosts had left so that there would be no constraints on their discussion.

Islaen appeared at the top of the stairs in what seemed to be far too short a time. The heaviness of her step and the grim set of her face as she descended confirmed for her comrades that her news was not what they would have chosen to hear.

Bethe Danlo instinctively braced herself. They had not anticipated anything else, not with the time frame facing them, but fear still rippled inside her. Just how bad was it going to be?

The Colonel sat on the short couch beside her husband. Bandit perched on her knee. She looked up with bright, worried eyes and chirped in concern and question. Islean stroked her for a moment, rubbing the upturned head and softly feathered back with the tips of her fingers.

At last, she raised her head. "Both the Navy and the Stellar Patrol, represented by the *Free Comet*, are on their way."

"With what chance of getting here in time?" Karmikel asked bluntly.

"None for the Navy. Commander Florr might just make it, though I doubt it."

"So we're on our own?"

"We are. We might be able to pick up a little help at the spaceport, but Noreen is not Astarte. If there are ten ships on-world including ours and the Garda's two, it'll be a miracle."

It would be an even greater miracle if any of them apart from the Garda craft would give active aid. Freighters were armed to fight, but their masters were sane folk who preferred to run when they were vastly outmatched.

"Even with some help, we cannot expect to defeat so many," Varn Tarl Sogan said slowly. "We are to delay them, then, buy Noreen time until Commander Florr arrives?"

"Those are our orders, more or less." The *Free Comet* was a cruiser, one-hundred-class. She should be able to manage the renegade fleet, particularly if the *Maid* and the *Moon* managed to decimate it first.

The demolitions expert frowned. "I could see the reason for some of our other near suicides, but casualties could be knocked to a minimum here by evacuating the port and sending the populace into hiding. It's a completely rural society, and there are plenty of bolt holes."

"Those statistics will be small comfort to the families that are hit, as some inevitably will be," Islaen responded, "and there'll be no defense at all for the stock and crops, not to mention the wildlife caught in the strafing and resulting fires. The cost to Noreen will be enormous even if the human death toll is kept down.

"On top of that, once those Albionan sons take the stones an get off-world again, they're gone. We'll have lost the whole pack. Worse, there are other vulnerable colonies around. They may wel have made up their minds to pick up something extra fo themselves. In that event, the slaughter would be ghastly. Whil that potential exists, the Navy wants them stopped—and I don' mean Ram Sithe, either. He takes his orders, too."

Bethe nodded. The renegades had too much power to simpl stop. Either before delivering the stones or afterwards, they woul strike again. Drunk with victory or the hope of victory as the would be, that was well-nigh a certainty. Islaen was right abou the impact on Noreen as well. The havoc wrought on the herds crops, and buildings would be an economic disaster for this part the planet. It would also be an emotional disaster. Noreenar loved their animals, as evinced by the Connors' reaction to th battering of their heifer. Hell, that was apparent to anyor knowing Jake Karmikel or Islaen Connor at all. "Can we ho them off long enough?"

Her question was directed to Varn. The former Admiral w unquestionably their master when it came to war in space, and h had been the right of command in that element since he had joined the unit.

"I believe so." He had been giving a great deal of thought to the struggle ahead and was able to answer promptly and with assurance. "We should be able to take out a good part of the pack, too, if fortune fights with us.

"The vermin will probably be traveling massed and will not spread out and separate until they enter Tara's system. They may not do so until they reach Noreen's near-space. They will definitely be moving with either no screens or else screens set at very low power, since they will want to keep on-worlders lulled as to their intentions as long as they can. They know they will be spotted well before they reach their target. When they do attack, they will come in fast."

"Aye," Jake agreed. "All that's pretty obvious."

"If we are waiting in space ourselves, and conceal our presence well, we should be able to hit them before they ever guess they are in trouble. Both our ships are exceptionally fast and maneuverable, with weapons and screens powerful beyond anything they will expect from craft so small. If the pack is traveling in convoy formation, with the larger ships moving closely together escorted by the rest, the *Maid* could conceivably take out all the former, particularly if she utilizes her full battle potential. The *Jovian Moon* and the port gunners would have an easier time managing the lesser fighters with those gone."

"Full potential?" the redhead demanded. "You're not thinking of your pletzars?"

"The lasers may not be able to do it alone," the former Admiral responded reasonably.

"You've blow half your circuits, man! The *Fairest Maid*'s too small. You'd be able to hold the fire for only a few seconds, at the cost of deactivating all other systems, including your own screens. Keep it up a second or so too long, and the drain would be permanent, leaving you dead in space. The rest of the pack would have you—"

"Then or a few minutes later. What is the difference, Comrade, especially if by going sooner we would materially aid our cause, Noreen's cause?"

"Ease up on the drive, both of you," the Commando-Colonel told them sharply. "Go on, Admiral. I don't like the way you're reading this, but I haven't known you to be wrong yet about a space fight."

"I do not propose using the pletzars," he conceded gruffly. "We must merely keep their potential in mind."

"All right, we won't forget them," Karmikel said sourly. "How do you propose we fight the fleet, with or without their questionable aid?"

"That is fairly obvious. The *Jovian Moon* and my *Maid* are our strongest ships and will have to carry the brunt of it, taking out as many as we can and concentrating on the biggest of them in our first attack. Any help we manage to collect should go after the lesser fighters at the same time. That will reduce the odds against us all before it turns into a slugging match, which it will in very short order unless our opponents are incompetents altogether." There was no need to stress that they were not likely to get enough of the raiders to alter the outcome as far as their fate went, but every enemy starship they blew, every second they delayed the assault, increased Noreen of Tara's hope of escaping devastation. "We will have to stay in it long enough to make the effor worthwhile. It is chiefly that fact which makes me dismiss th pletzars as a practical option."

Jake scowled. He was no less aware than Sogan of what the were facing and what their too-early destruction would mean fc Noreen of Tara. "Bethe and I'll do what we can to keep the sor off you if you do try them. I just wish you'd shown the sense t follow my lead and told the Navy where they could attach thos blasted banks. If you didn't have them, you wouldn't be tempte to fire them."

The war prince smiled. "Supposedly, our power base has bee upgraded to better support them. I have been rather eager to try t banks again, but there has never been the excuse."

Bethe stared at him, then she saw the laughter in his eyes a laughed herself. "Ignore him, Jake! He's taking you over the j proper."

Immediately, she grew grave once more. She was glad th could still laugh, but this was a war council to plot what amount to a suicide mission. "Where do we intercept them?" she ask "The farther out, the better, I should think. If nothing else, would mean that much less distance for the *Free Comet* to tra to get to us."

"So it would, but without their precise location or any ot

detailed coordinates, we can only make a guess as to their approach route. Unless we stay near Tara's system, we run the danger of missing them. That, we dare not chance."

Varn had met his comrades' eyes steadily while he was speaking, but now his gaze wavered. There was no belief in his heart or his mind that any of them would live through the upcoming battle, nor did he think that any of the others cherished such a delusion. The sacrifice would be easier to accept if they could be certain of accomplishing their aim, but it was doubtful that they would be able to deflect all major damage from Noreen, especially if they were compelled to fight completely alone, as might well prove the case. The best they could hope to do in that event was to blunt the attack, to dilute the renegades' venom, before their two small ships were blown.

Bandit read her companions' gloom and whimpered. The Arcturian's vision misted. His face tightened as he struggled to keep down the grief that was welling up in him. It was the cruelest blow of all that this innocent little being must perish along with the rest of them.

He touched her once, then withdrew his hand. "She should stay with your parents, at least," he said to Islaen.

The gurry's demeanor altered instantly. Her feathers extended, fully doubling her apparent size, and she hissed in her outrage. *Nooo! Bandit not stay! Bandit part of company!*

The Colonel smoothed her plumage. "I wish we could leave her, too," she replied sadly, "but she's earned her place with us. We can't deny her the right to claim it."

"No," he agreed. His eyes were bleak as they rested on the two of them, woman and gurry. He would willingly have died for them. Instead, they would in all probability perish, following the only excuse of a plan he could devise to meet this emergency.

The Connor family gathered beside the flier as the Commandos prepared to leave. They knew what the four intended to do and that none of them was likely to return.

Varn checked the engine. He replaced the partly used fuel disk with a fresh one. They would be flying long and fast, and he did not want to delay for this en route,.

There was a movement at his side, and he glanced up to see Islaen's brother standing next to him. "Aye, Will?"

"Everything check out?"

"Everything," he responded, closing and sealing the nose chamber. "Jake is a very dependable mechanic."

The farmer hesitated. "I owe you an apology for a few of my remarks."

"Forget it. I provoke argument at times."

Paud joined the pair. "All right, Will. Don't embarrass him."

The younger man left them to bid his sister farewell.

"Ye'll be leaving in a few minutes," Kinkora's master said.

"Aye." Sogan's head lowered. He knew what this Noreenan must be suffering. They both loved Islaen Connor, and soon now, they would lose her. It was worse, if anything, for Paud. He would have to survive the loss. "I am sorry," Varn said softly, almost in a whisper. "I would save her out of it if I could."

"Don't give up yet, on any of ye. Ye've all faced nearly certain doom before and come back from it."

"We have also always gone into it accepting its inevitability. That does not mean any of us ever thought to surrender meekly to it."

"There's no more need to do it this time, then, is there?" Paud lay his hand on the Arcturian's shoulder. "We've never been able to make you feel a part of us, but you are one of this family all the same. We want you back, Captain, after this and as often as possible in the future."

Connor caught a movement out of the corner of his eye and saw that Islaen had already taken her place in the flier. "The Spirit of Space go with ye all," Paud whispered, then he stepped away from the machine and those it would carry to stand Noreen's defense.

TWENTY-TWO

THE FOUR GUERRILLAS kept their vehicle at as close to space speed as they could maintain under atmospheric conditions, pausing only once so that the Colonel could relieve Varn at the controls. Twilight had been well on when they had left the Connor farm, and Noreen's sky soon blackened into full night.

For five hours, they sped on through the darkness and squalls of rain until at last the floodlights of the spaceport brightened the horizon. Minutes later, they were within sight of the complex itself.

Normally, there was little life in the place at this hour, only the ights surrounding the starships and those in the buildings housing he night crews manning the port facilities and in the Garda office, vhere a skeleton force always remained in case of trouble or an mergency.

On a typical night, off-world visitors would mostly be asleep oard their vessels or amusing themselves on one or the other of em. Contests of chance were common among the crews of ssels berthed together on a quiet planet where there was nothing uch to keep them abroad.

That last was certainly the case in Noreen's port area. The ngle cantina closed its doors at midnight, and there was no erotic ouse to provide later entertainment. Bawdery was not illegal on oreen of Tara, but it was unprofitable. Traffic from the starlanes as not sufficient to support it, and the wildly scattered population ith their strict code governing personal relationships provided an en poorer client base.

At first glance, nothing seemed very different tonight, but the crowd of transports parked near the Garda station told that an uncommon number of people were awake and in the complex. Islaen had called ahead and summoned a meeting of all port and Garda personnel, as well as the masters of any vessels currently on-world. She had offered no explanation save to say that Noreen of Tara was facing a serious emergency. As they passed through the gate, she was very conscious of the curious, concerned transmissions of many minds. None appeared to be merely annoyed. That was to their good. It meant that everyone accepted the potential seriousness of the situation, as she had anticipated would prove the case. It was too well known that a Commando did not give an order like this lightly.

The flier came to a stop in front of the Garda office, where a space had been left free for it. The guerrillas had not finished securing it before the door opened and a tall man wearing the uniform of a ranking Garda officer came outside despite the driving rain.

"Colonel Connor?"

"Aye."

"I'm Commandant Curn McGra. My Captain in charge of the port area alerted me when she got your call. Everyone else you wanted is present as well."

"Good. —I'm very glad to have you here, Commandant. It'll make my job a light year easier." People simply responded better in a crisis to their own trusted leaders than to strangers, or virtual strangers, and she knew this man was well respected. She herself liked what she saw of him and the transmissions she was receiving from him.

The room inside, the common Garda office, was crowded, but those gathered there shoved aside to give the newcomers passage to its center where everyone could best hear them. Once there, Islaen introduced herself and her companions and then detailed the danger threatening the spaceport and planet.

"My unit will defend Noreen as best we can," she concluded, "but even with the help of every ship here, we're not likely to break the attack completely. A lot will be left for the port gunners—"

"Help!" exploded one of the four off-worlders, three men and a woman, standing by the door. "Colonel, you four may feel honor-bound to commit suicide in those two-man splinters yours, but a freighter runs on all burners from odds she can't handle. It's a lot healthier for herself and her crew that way."

The two other men with him nodded in agreement. The woman held herself impassive, giving no indication of what her thoughts might be.

Varn Tarl Sogan looked from one to the other of them contemptuously. "Clear, then," he said, dismissing them as one of the Emperor's guards would dismiss a whining menial. "We have enough to do without having to worry about protecting those of your ilk."

"If you're calling us plasma spines, Commando . . ."

"Enough!" the Colonel snapped. *Ease off, Varn. We don't need a brawl here. It's their right. Freighters fight when they must, but they're neither soldiers nor Patrol agents.* "Get off-world fast," she told the spacers. "If those raiders come sooner than we anticipate, you could be caught in the fire despite yourselves."

The four glared at the Arcturian, then at her. The men turned and stalked away from the building, leaving the door swinging wide behind them.

The remaining freighter master closed it to shut out the rain and leaned back against the jam.

Islaen studied her. She was thin and not much bigger than Bethe Danlo, with a sharp weasel's face and small, hard eyes. Her complexion was the dark, rich shade of well-made jakek, her hair darker still. "Well?" the guerrilla asked.

"I've knocked a few good charters out of Noreen. I guess I owe her something. I'll hear what you've got to say before making up my mind. —That only goes for me and my *Sunspot,* of course. My hands do their own deciding."

"Fair enough. They can lift with the others if they choose. You can arrange to meet them elsewhere." Assuming she or her starship survived the fight ahead.

"Don't worry if they go," Curn McGra interjected. "My Garda can all handle lasers and handle them well, and we have only the two five-class fighters. You won't lack for gunners."

Sogan looked at him with interest. "Captain Karmikel and I each have a brace of unmanned weapons bays. If your people are good, we could each use a couple of them as well."

Islaen masked her surprise. She nodded in agreement but said nothing.

"We have very little choice as far as tactics go," the war prince told them. "If the Patrol cruiser Colonel Connor mentioned gets here before the enemy, all we shall have to do is provide support. If she does not, we must reduce the force actually reaching the planet as greatly as possible. It could be worse. These Albionans are doubtless competent space hands, but I think few if any of them will prove as able as actual pirates in battle. They will not have had the same intensive experience."

"Or the same nerve," a Garda Sergeant put in. "From what you say, they're just port rats."

"A lot of port rats," the *Sunspot*'s master corrected. "Numbers make a difference. —You do have some idea of how five small ships are to do dirt to that pack, I suppose, Captain Sogan?"

"We must take them completely by surprise and knock as many of them out as possible in the seconds before they can bring up their defenses. Once they do, it becomes a melee with the odds distinctly in their favor.

"I propose we await them in Deirdre's system. Her whiteness creates a glare that will screen us well, provided we are careful. Our actual mode of attack depends in part on their formation and method of approach, but I believe we should hit them in three parts. Captain Karmikel's ship and mine are both heavily armed, and we will go after the biggest fighters, which we presume will be in the center. Let the Garda ships go for the right wing, and yours, the left, Captain . . ."

"Lambert. Sal Lambert." She nodded. "All right. I'm game."

The dark eyes remained on her. "It will be no sport, and there is little chance that any of us will be coming back."

"Life in the starlanes fosters an awareness of the odds, Captain. There wasn't much hope for Astarte, either, and we fought an armada there. Big ships." She saw his look of surprise and shrugged. "You wouldn't remember me. I was only a mate at the time. You never even saw me. Our citation wasn't first-class like yours, but my share of it helped me get the *Sunspot*, along with what I'd already saved."

"There will be another for this if we survive it," Islaen Connor promised.

"I'm counting on that, Colonel. She's a sweet little ship that I've got, but she needs a lot of work that I can't afford just now," her hard, dark eyes narrowed. "I know the kind of debris we'll be dealing with. Push them hard enough, and they'll run right into the next galaxy."

"Aye, it's a hope, but greed's hardened more than one spine. They'll have to take pretty heavy losses before giving up on those stones, particularly since they'll know if this is all Noreen has to send up against them, there's nothing much to stop them below. They'll also realize they won't get a crack at a haul like this again."

Islaen turned to Curn. "Commandant, give the order for the populace to go to ground, planetwide. Those sons could come in strafing from any direction. There's little we can do for the stock, unfortunately. Tell the people they have the next five hours in which to pasture them in the woods and forests, which should afford them reasonably good protection, and to move what stores and valuables they can, but after that, they must get under cover themselves. Have each family bring blankets, food, and water for a fairly long siege and a transceiver so they can keep informed of the situation and call for help should they need it."

"Those prisoners . . ." he began.

"I gave my orders concerning them. Tie them up in one of the warehouses facing the planeting field. Top floor. I don't want them exposed needlessly, but neither shall they enjoy any greater security than the people defending and running the port. Besides, we don't really have any better place to stash that horde during an attack. We can't afford to have them break loose during the fight."

"No," he agreed. "That, we can't. It'll be as you wish, Colonel."

"Thanks, though my wish is that none of this were necessary." Her mind touched the former Admiral's. *Sorry, Varn. That's the best I can do.*

You mean it is the worst you can do, he replied sarcastically, but he looked strangely at her.

The Commando-Colonel's eyes swept the room. "You people know how to run the spaceport and how to fight for it if it comes to that." Her gaze flickered between the Garda leader and Sal Lambert. "As soon as your ships are ready, we'll lift and get into position. Then I suggest we all set a watch and get some sleep. We'll need our wits awake when our Albionan friends finally arrive."

TWENTY-THREE

BETHE DANLO CHECKED her nets yet again and ran her eyes over the weapons controls in front of her. They would be her charge during the battle. Jake would concentrate on managing the *Jovian Moon* and aiding her gunners' efforts.

"Our new comrades are comfortable with their battle stations?" she asked.

"Aye, and suitably impressed. —They both look like they can handle their part well."

"They'd better," the demolitions expert replied.

Both fell silent for several minutes. Bethe watched her husband. His blue eyes were running over the instrument panel, checking and rechecking the *Moon*'s systems. She blinked back the tears that suddenly filled her own eyes as she realized the strength of her love for him and how soon it would probably be ended. "This has been the best part of my life," she said suddenly, "the happiest and most fulfilling."

"No regrets?" he asked softly.

"Only that I held off so long before marrying you."

"That was for the best, I suppose. Members of our ridiculous species set more value on something when they have to struggle a bit to win it. What we've had has been good. The Spirit of Space willing, there'll be more, and it'll be even better."

She nodded, echoing that hope and making a prayer of it, although she knew full well that only good fighting and better luck would bring it to pass.

They're late, Islaen Connor said.

They will not be late enough, the war prince responded.

Unless they were not coming at all, not to Noreen of Tara, the woman thought. Perhaps even now, doom was raining down on some other planet, a planet she should have been able to warn and defend.

Noreen is the target, Varn Tarl Sogan told her firmly. He did not have to read her thoughts to guess the direction of them. His own had run the same course often enough throughout this vigil, but always, reason had argued his doubts down. The evidence, once they had uncovered it, was plain enough. The assault would come, and it would come soon.

None too soon for the Arcturian. Although every moment of delay brought the help they needed closer, he still longed for an end to this waiting. His nerves were raw with it, and it was becoming increasingly difficult to screen his rising fear from his companions. There was no shame in this brand of dread with a hard battle before them, but neither should he inflict it on the others. They both had enough to manage with their own.

It was strange, he thought. He had no terror of dying when he contemplated turning his own blaster on himself, yet now . . . Maybe it was pride. His life was his, to use or to spend as he would. He did not grant any other the right to terminate it, certainly not vermin out of Albion's choking alleyways. Maybe he had just realized how little he wished to die, by anyone's hand. Whatever he had lost, he had also found great reason to desire life.

Sogan closed his eyes momentarily to give them a rest from constantly scanning the screens and instruments. As always, desire was of no significance. He was not being offered a choice.

He sighed to himself. He would not yield to the Grim Commandant without battle, but if he must die, at least he would not grudge the sacrifice. Time after time since joining forces with Islaen Connor, he had risked himself for planets whose peoples were strangers to him, occasionally strangers for whom he had very little liking. This time, they were defending his consort's beloved homeworld, fighting for her kin—people who filled her heart and mind and who had received him well and warmly despite what he realized must have been a sharp preference for Jake Karmikel.

He felt the woman's eyes on him. She smiled when he looked up. *Gathering stardust, Admiral?*

Aye, he confessed. *I was thinking of how fine a world Noreen of Tara is. It is a privilege to fight for her.*

You've had your share of that since our meeting on Visnu, she said ruefully.

His answering smile reached his eyes. *A war prince prefers that his life be a bit interesting, Colonel.*

He leaned over so that his fingers brushed hers. His consort had a right to strength from him and a show of reasonable confidence. She, too, feared, and she was not playing the coward before him. *I owe you a great deal, Islaen Connor, and I intend to see to it that we have the time to make you some return for it all. As your father made sure to point out to me before we left Kinkora, we have come through our troubles before now.*

I don't intend on enlisting with the Grim Commandant too tamely myself, Admiral, she told him tartly, but the softness never left her eyes or mind. *I love you, Varn Tarl Sogan.*

And I you. Both of you, he added as his hand dropped to cover the special netting rigged on the arm of Islaen's flight chair to secure the gurry. He could feel her little body trembling, although Bandit made no complaint. She had experienced war in space before and had not liked it. "I will do my best to bring us all through, small one."

Varn will save us! Varn's the best! Islaen, too!

Sogan laughed despite himself. "We shall try to live up to that accolade, Little Bandit."

Islaen's eyes flickered to the distance viewer. She stiffened. *They're coming, I think.*

The war prince fixed his attention on the place to which she pointed, increasing magnification and light amplification to the maximum as he did so. The oddly fuzzy patch she had spotted looked sharper, but it was still too far for even the *Fairest Maid*'s instruments to resolve into its individual components.

Jake had probably picked it up as well, but he doubted any of their three allies would be able to do so for many seconds yet.

Smart, he said softly, but then, he had not expected stupidity from this scum. L. George Thatcher had not been guilty of that save in his premature moves to eliminate them. There had been no flaw yet in any of his planning.

The raiders had swung about so that they had the denser starfields of the galaxy's center for a backdrop, dimming the little light they reflected by comparison. To judge by their present course, they would skip by Tara, seeming to take no interest in her planets, then whip around Deirdre, using her glare for a shield even as his party was doing, and rush to the attack before anyone on Noreen became aware of their peril.

The Arcturian's eyes glittered. That meant they would not be able to raise their screens until the very last moment, and Noreen's defenders were ready. He would see to it that these vermin got a strong taste of the surprise they had planned for their supposedly unsuspecting victims.

Five minutes passed. The cloud separated into forty-nine points of light, still tiny but discernible for what they were. Another couple of minutes, and he could make out the class of each starship and the fleet's flight arrangement.

The fighters were deployed in the classic convoy pattern even as the former Admiral had imagined they would be. The formation was sloppy and loose in structure, with the ships comprising it farther apart than any Navy pilots would have allowed; however, their attack would be effective, particularly with surprise on their side. The three ten-class vessels were in the center and a little forward of the rest so that their combined firepower would be concentrated on their targets, knocking out whatever defense might be raised in the first moments of the assault. Flanking these were approximately twenty five-class fighters. The smallest ships, the two-man fighters, were farthest out, ready to peel away from the pack to rake the planet on every side to prevent the organization and movement of any on-world assistance to the beleaguered spaceport.

Get set, Sogan whispered.

Bandit's ready!

"Good, small one, but stay out of our minds now. One stray thought could be enough to slay us all."

Bandit will be quiet!

Islaen's hands tightened on the weapons controls. Varn would maneuver the *Maid* so as to give her the best approach to her targets, but the responsibility for taking them out lay with her, her and the two Garda Yeomen sitting in the revolutionary stellar crystal weapons bays perched on the very hull of the starship.

Sogan quietly gave his orders to his gunners and to the other ships under him, then he settled back to wait.

The pletzars? the Colonel asked. Unlike surplanetary combat, they would maintain their contact during this contest, for the faster and closer the communication between them, the deeper their partnership, the more effective a fighting unit they would make.

No. Try the purple laser first. The more powerful weapon

would have wrought deadly havoc with their relatively closely packed foes, but the Albionans were spread out just far enough that too many of them would still escape. If he chose to fire the deadly banks, he would be able to do so only once, and loosing them would probably render the *Fairest Maid* incapable of playing any further role in the fight. He dared not deprive Noreen's defenders of their strongest ship with the battle barely begun.

For an instant's span, the renegade fleet was visible on both the distance and near-space viewers, then it disappeared suddenly from the former.

The images grew even sharper on the screen beside it. Every starship was clearly visible now, every detail sharp to their eyes. There was yet no trace of blurring to signal that the invaders had begun to raise their defenses.

Closer and closer they came, and still Varn held his small command in place. Islaen had to fight herself not to look questioningly at him. She knew the Arcturian was waiting until their foes were almost upon them.

Now!

The *Fairest Maid* leaped forward, seeming to double in size and brilliance as her screens activated around her. Even as she moved, her lazers let loose, lashing the utterly startled and defenseless center of the oncoming fleet with vicious whips of deadly light. Those raging to right and left were the familiar beams of incandescent blue. That emanating from the bridge was violet. It was not a cohesive beam but, rather, a seemingly gently drifting wave of purple-tinted motes so brilliant that the eye could not look directly at them.

For all its seeming softness, the energy comprising that wave was fast, and it was fierce, merciless as the strange particles sought their prey. The wee, dire hunters touched each of the three ten-class fighters in turn, and in a breath's space, each ship flared like a miniature nova. For several seconds, the glare remained, then only a glow as the cooling dust which was all that remained of the slain starships and their crews dimmed and dispersed into the eternal night around them.

The Commando-Colonel was aware only of the war she herself waged, but Varn Tarl Sogan was schooled to see not just his own limited part of a battle but the conflict as a whole, and a portion of his mind remained detached from his own efforts to monitor the fortunes of his crew and his comrades, as well as the fate of those they fought.

Thus far, the small Federation force was faring well. Each of his gunners had two of their five-class enemies blown, and he glimpsed the death glow of as many more to his right, victims of the Garda ships. Sal Lambert's *Sunspot* was proving as tough as her master and had accounted for three.

The surviving raiders pulled back even as their screens swelled and brightened around them. Their retreat stopped when they saw how pitifully few ships opposed them, and they advanced again, cautiously and under full screens.

The fighting was different now, a testing the strength and skill that could not be permitted to go on too long lest part of the raiders merely sidestep the struggle and continue on to their target, while their comrades finished the conflict in space.

No, the war prince decided after a moment's reflection, there was no danger of that. Having seen what the defenders could do given any opening, they would fear to come against them with anything but their full strength. They would fear even more to allow a force of this size, small as it was in comparison to their numbers, to remain in space to hound and maybe trace them after they had taken the stones. They would finish his command off first and then take Noreen at their leisure.

Two more of the attackers went up, but they had been severely damaged in the initial charge. There would be no more such easy victories.

Battle in space was a warfare of watching and waiting and of striking swiftly to seize any opening offered by an opponent. The screens defending even the smallest starship were incredibly strong, but they had to open at the moment of firing to give the vessel's own laser beams an exit, and it was at the firing ports and at the seams where the great plates of energy met above them that an enemy gunner aimed. Either he would hammer away at the place, striving to spring the joining despite the deep overlap generally designed into the screens, or, more commonly, he would wait. Having once seen her discharge, he would sight on his target, and when she next used or began to use that bay, he would strike, endeavoring to send his own beam through the narrow gap in her defenses and up through the firing port itself into the laser banks beyond. A large craft could sustain one such hit, or maybe several, and go on fighting with her surviving ports. To one the size of any of these combatants, a direct strike to any of the weapons banks meant utter destruction.

Despite himself, Sogan glanced nervously in the direction of his two auxiliary bays. Each was under its own gunner's control, and one error would be their death, whatever his skill or Islaen's.

The Noreenans made none. They might have been untried in space combat before this day, but they had trained for it since their first days in school, and they had continued training in the long War's aftermath. If the Arcturians were gone, pirates remained, aye, and had increased as a threat, and a wise people continued to hold themselves prepared to defend themselves and their own. He had known that would be the case, or he should not have considered accepting, much less requesting, their services, but there had been no way to test their nerve or judgment beforehand. Actual battle can do strange things to even an essentially sound soldier in his maiden encounter with it. The two Garda had held, or were still holding, despite the grim reality of the fight, and the war prince felt confident that the trust he had placed in them was well given.

Seconds later, his belief was rewarded by the sight of a fireball erupting on the starboard side.

After that, there was no more firing as bolt after bolt drove against the *Maid*'s screens, testing and endeavoring to force them.

The Federation starship made an elusive target. She moved fast, swerved so sharply and suddenly that she seemed more a living thing than a mere machine under human control. The war prince drew on all the power, all the astonishing refinement of movement, given him by the experimental controls and drivers with which the Navy had supplied him. He provoked battle where only passive defense should have been possible, confusing and confounding still further his already disbelieving foes. Such movement should not be possible. In a more conventionally outfitted ship, it would not have been, and it seemed to them that they were witnessing the violation of basic physical law in nearly her every maneuver.

Islaen fought as if she were an extension of the Captain's mind. She fired, held her port open while Sogan swerved the *Maid* away from the Albionans' answering beam, then loosed another shot, sending it tearing through the others' port before the renegades had ceased to discharge their own laser. She did not even notice the doomed fighter nova as she set her sights on another target.

Abruptly, the pressure on them eased. Varn's brows came together in surprise, then he realized what was happening, and his expression hardened. So. His counterpart in the renegade fleet was a better tactician than he had imagined. The Albionans had broken off the melee and were concentrating nearly the full of their attention on one of the Garda fighters, paying the other defenders only enough heed to hold them in play and away from the work they were doing. By hitting a single victim with all their power, they would soon batter her screens down or blast her through her ports if she tried to defend herself. It was not an original strategy, but it was dramatically effective when the force trying it greatly outnumbered its opponents, as was the case here. He had used it himself, as had Ram Sithe when the tide of the War had turned to give the Federation the necessary numerical superiority over the Empire's fleets.

A blaze of light, and the Garda vessel and those she had carried were but fiercely glowing particles already cooling as they spread apart, vanishing in the vast emptiness of space. The glow had not yet faded before the raiders turned on her sister ship.

Varn Tarl Sogan's face was hard and set. They could not afford the loss of that second fighter now. Her destruction would doom their hopes entirely even if for some inexplicable reason the remaining defenders were not eliminated in the same manner. They would simply perish a little more slowly in individual combat, leaving Noreen all but open to the raiders' will. The port unners would not be able to take out half of those that would be eft.

He could delay no longer. His lasers would not suffice now, lthough they were basically stronger than the attackers' defenses. e Garda fighter did not have the time to wait for him to batter em down individually, assuming that were possible before the *airest Maid* herself were blown. No matter. A far more powerful eapon was his to command. Their enemies, bunched as they ere and intent upon their sure kill, were vulnerable as they were ot likely to be again.

Vulnerable? They were nigh unto slain. No screens not specif- ally formulated to withstand the wild brand of energy generated a pletzar bank could do so for more than a few seconds, and ch defenses were possessed only by Navy or Stellar Patrol ssels. He could exterminate the entire pack within minutes after ning fire.

Minutes he did not have. The Arcturian knew his fight would be measured in seconds, and precious few of those.

Pletzar's were weapons of big ships. The *Fairest Maid* was simply too small to support even the streamlined bank the Navy had installed on her, as proven by the near disaster over Jade of Kuan Yin. Following that, her power systems had been augmented to help her bear the strain of their firing, but her master had no illusions as to the extent of her ability to support the awesome demands their discharge would make on her resources.

He had no more choice now than he had in the battle for Jade's infant colony. *Ready the pletzars. We are going in.*

Aye. Islaen's voice was steady. She knew as well as her consort the risk they were about to take, but she kept her fear locked within herself, concealed by mental shields as strong as the screens guarding the battlecraft they flew.

Take as many of them as you can, the man added unnecessarily as he sent his starship hurtling toward the invading wolf pack.

Islaen kept her fingers steady until they had reached optimum firing range, then they tightened on the sensitive rod.

For an instant, there seemed to be no change at all, but in the next, a strange, soft glow seemed to flow out from the *Maid*, pale at first but gradually brightening until it was visible throughout all Tara's planetary system and its environs.

Chaos erupted outside like a vision from a raklick roar gone sour. Two, three, six of the invaders exploded before their crews ever realized a terrible new danger had come against them. The rest seemed to go mad as they struggled to draw back, to get out of range of the war prince's deadly pletzars. Four more detonated almost simultaneously, even as they tried to pull all their screens aft in a futile attempt to bolster their defenses long enough to make good their escape.

It was the only maneuver that did offer the chance of gaining those few precious fraction seconds that meant safety, and all th raiders stripped away the screens from the most of their surface t set them, one atop the other, in opposition to the pletzars.

The *Fairest Maid* did not give chase as she concentrated o aiming and discharging her weapon. For better than a full minut she sent forth that terrible wave of energy, then the power bas sustaining it was gone, and the starship went dark. She froze i space as her engines died. The screens guarding her came dowr and even the air within her cabins and halls ceased to circulate . . .

Jake Karmikel had been little longer than the Arcturian in recognizing their enemies' battle plan and realizing the danger it represented. He watched the destruction of the Garda fighter with a wrenching sense of loss born of the kinship they shared as Noreenans in battle for Noreen herself, but he kept his eyes riveted on the *Maid*. Only one thing could save them now, baring the unlikely arrival of the Patrol cruiser. When Varn began his run, his hands hit his own controls. "Let's go! They'll be needing help!"

For an incredible minute and a quarter, the *Fairest Maid* was as an incarnation of some destroying god, sweeping all in the path of her withering hate, then the wild hemorrhage of her power overcame her.

The Noreenan's own heart seemed to die with her, but this had been inevitable. The needle-nose had held out longer than any of them had reason or right to expect.

He swore fluently. "I knew that demon wouldn't be able to resist using those damned pletzars!" Jake activated the *Moon*'s intercom. "Starboard, Larboard, keep the bastards off us. We'll cover Sogan from the bridge." The Albionans would realize soon enough that the *Maid* was now a painted target. They would get over their panic fast then, unless the remaining defenders could keep the pressure on them, giving them no time in which to think.

If Sogan was a master pilot, so, too, was Jake Karmikel, but the blue-eyed Commando-Captain flew his ship with a brand of daring different from that shown by the Arcturian, more aggressive and seemingly more careless of the result to his own battlecraft, yet never did he err in the execution of any of his attacks or feints.

He drew on every spark of speed and agility his *Jovian Moon* possessed as he dove into encounter after encounter, sometimes dueling, sometimes merely disrupting a fight already in progress, sometimes drawing or deflecting fire directed at a harder-pressed and less well-screened comrade. Through it all, he kept the crippled starship in sight, knowing an assault on her to be inevitable.

The other defenders were equally quick to seize the advantage the war prince had given them. The *Sunspot* dashed to the kill and took out two within minutes of beginning her run, a performance quickly matched by the surviving Noreenan vessel, although she had taken damage herself and dared not hunt actively.

The pace of their attack slowed as a full melee once again erupted. The Albionans had recovered some of their will to fight with the continued dimming of the pletzars and were battling well, although they were now on the defensive. At last, one of them, a five-class, gathered the courage to test the truth of the *Maid*'s seeming helplessness. She dived for her, spitting fire.

Fast as she came on, the *Jovian Moon* was quicker still. Jake threw his ship between the Albionan and his defenseless comrades.

Bethe Danlo compelled herself to concentrate on her weapons alone, to keep her mind off the wild, seemingly suicidal swerving of the battlecraft, off the performance of their Garda gunners, off the terrible danger to the three trapped in the lightless, eerily motionless needle-nose.

The Albionan fighter's bolt struck them squarely on the starboard side just beneath the bridge. The smaller ship's screens deformed slightly under the force of the impact, but they were Navy-strength, capable of withstanding many times that power before beginning to suffer stress even at their seams, much less on an unbroken front. The *Moon* did not so much as tremble.

The starboard gunner responded, doing no damage but revealing the location of his own port. It was an invitation not to be wasted. The raiders fired again, this time from their dorsal bay, hoping to ram their bolt through the Federation craft's discharging port.

Karmikel had anticipated that and whipped the *Jovian Moon* sharply to three o'clock.

Bethe stayed with her sights, riding with the movement and figuring it into her calculations. Her fingers tightened on the controls.

A sparkling stream of purple motes ran almost merrily back along the attacker's own beam. A second, and space brightened yet again to mark the death of another ship.

Ten of the renegades remained, but they had taken enough. They turned and fled, speeding back out into that part of space whence they had come.

Varn Tarl Sogan watched the battle from the bridge of his paralyzed warship. The *Fairest Maid* had done well before th lack of power had beaten her, he thought. Whatever the outcome for them, they had given their comrades the chance, not merely of delaying their foes but of victory.

He saw the fighter that would be his death begin her run. The war prince braced himself. A quiver of fear and regret he was not ashamed to own ran through him. This was an honorable fate and would be accomplished quickly, but there had been much that was good in his life. Above all else, he grieved that he could no longer shield those with him, the two he loved above all others and valiant gunners they had taken aboard for the battle.

His breath caught as the *Jovian Moon* cast herself in front of the attacker's laser and in the next moment sent them to the damnation they so amply merited, breaking the will of what remained of the renegade fleet.

His head raised. He was alive and as yet whole, and he was minded to fight while that held true. It was not in him to cede his ship and those aboard her to destruction until his own life and power to prevent her death were gone.

Islaen Connor was no more willing than her consort to meekly surrender their lives. The *Moon* had bought them time. It was theirs to seize and use it.

Emergency power's working, in part, at least, she reported calmly. *I can feel some air moving again.*

The former Admiral's hands played across controls so familiar that he scarcely needed Deirdre's reflected light to identify them. *The main system is gone,* he told her after a few seconds' useless effort.

Try the auxiliary coils.

I am.

Varn had put little confidence in those. The system was the brainchild of his chief mechanic on Thorne, who had liked the presence of the pletzar banks even less than Sogan himself. The idea was ingenious in itself, enough to intrigue the war prince and gain his approval for the experiment, but it had never been fully tested, and he doubted this or anything else would be much help in their present need. A starship whose power was gone was dead in space. They could only hope that one of their comrades would survive to tow them back to Noreen where repairs could be effected, or at least to evacuate them, assuming they made it through the remainder of the battle.

To his amazement, the *Maid*'s normal lights appeared at the command of the switch. With growing excitement, Varn let them dim again to conserve power and activated another, more essential control. Immediately, the glow of full screens took form around them.

He released the breath he had been holding and touched the intercom switch. "Larboard, Starboard, are you all right?"

He was relieved to hear an immediate affirmative from both. "Good work. —The *Maid* is partially disabled, but she is still alive and is apparently capable of at least passive defense. I do not know what else she can still do, but hold yourselves ready to fight if we must."

Sogan turned next to the transceiver, which operated independently of the starship's power. "Thanks, Jake, Bethe. That was fine flying and shooting both."

"You're all in one piece?" came the tense reply.

"Aye. We owe our mechanics. —We can hold on here. Go after them. Shove them on in the direction they are going. It is right in line with the *Free Comet*'s approach."

Jake grinned. "That would be the crowning surprise of what turned out to be a very bad day for them, wouldn't it?" He hesitated. "If they decide to double back, you folks could be in very big trouble."

They had been speaking on ship-to-ship over the frequency the war prince had chosen for his command so that their other comrades would hear his plans without having to wait for another transmission. Now, a third voice entered their discussion. "You and the *Sunspot* go on, Captain Karmikel," the Garda Corporal piloting the Noreenan fighter told them. "I don't think I'd like to chance a full chase after the battering we took, but we'll manage well enough here. We'll see to it that our flagship doesn't have any more problems."

TWENTY-FOUR

"I'D GIVE A year's credits to have seen their faces when they found themselves running smack up against the *Free Comet*!" Jake crowed.

The fleeing raiders had been concentrating so completely on the two starships pursuing them, either of which might let loose with pletzars at any moment, that they had remained oblivious to the big Patrol cruiser until the foremost of them had quite literally nearly smashed into her screens.

"What I still can't believe," he continued more gravely, "is that every last one of them surrendered. Not a single ship tried to make a break for it."

The demolitions expert, sitting beside him in the crew's cabin of the *Jovian Moon*, merely shrugged. "What more could you expect from a pack of port rats?" she asked contemptuously.

Justice would be quickly accomplished in this case. She and her teammates had just left Horus after having made their official depositions, but their testimony was hardly necessary. Their captors had given the raiders to understand that their on-world comrades had betrayed their coming to save their own hides, and the prisoners had sung in consort in their determination not to die alone.

Bethe shook her head. "It must've been some scene, all right," she agreed, savoring the thought. She looked up at him suddenly. "You're one hell of a pilot, Jake Karmikel. Totally mad, mind you, but terrific. I don't think even our Admiral would've tried to outrun that laser, much less succeed in doing it, not to mention some of your moves."

"Ah," he replied, "I couldn't let them get fried after saying we'd cover them. You might start thinking that my promises aren't worth a whole lot."

"Well, be that as it might, I still think you're pretty wonderful," she said, knowing he liked the praise. He also deserved it. "Now, if I can only keep those maneuvers of yours out of my mind while I sleep, everything will be wonderful."

Jake bent to kiss her. "Just concentrate on dreaming about me, Sergeant."

The slate gray eyes sparkled as she snuggled against him. "You still owe me part of a honeymoon, Captain Karmikel. We have a nice, long furlough coming up, and I have a few suggestions as to how we might spend it—all of them very traditional and quite safe."

Islaen Connor swung off the core ladder and entered the bridge. She would have needed no mind gift to know she would find the war prince here, stretched out in his flight chair with his eyes fixed on the stars glinting beyond the observation panels.

Varn had been aware of her approach and turned swiftly to greet her. *Welcome, Comrades,* he said, including the gurry, who was in her usual place on the woman's shoulder. *Everything checks out below?*

Aye, Islaen replied, smiling at the pleasure which rose in him at her coming. *Up here?*

All seems well, though I shall not be fully content until we are home and I can examine her properly myself.

The Noreenan's eyes danced. *How could those poor Navy mechanics be expected to do the job half thoroughly enough?* she teased. *They get so little practice, after all.*

Laugh if you will, Colonel, but as long as my life depends on how well the Maid *functions, I shall be the happier for keeping watch on her myself.*

Varn's right! Bandit doesn't want to die, either!

Sogan laughed. *See! Even our feathered comrade appreciates my precautions, and everyone knows that she has more sense than all the rest of us together.*

Her mention of dying brought darker images back to his mind, and the man fixed his attention once more, briefly, on the universe outside. "The Albionans will be executed?" he asked aloud after a pause.

Islaen had felt the shadow rise in him before his shields had slipped into place and was prepared for the change in the manner of their communication. "Most of them, anyway, and probably the whole lot. Certainly Thatcher," she added significantly.

Sogan gave her no response for a moment, not so much as a shrug or nod of his head. "It is over at last, then," he said in the end, "at least as far as we are concerned. The tribunal can be trusted to handle what remains to be done."

"You feel no better about this?" she asked carefully, although his own words had given her his answer. There had been no satisfaction in them, just submission. "No better about yourself?"

Varn turned his head away from her. "I will not raise my hand against myself."

"It means nothing to you, nothing at all, that you've helped save the Spirit of Space alone knows how many innocent lives, that throughout all this you've brought a small army of renegades to justice?"

"That is a significant accomplishment, of course, as well as our duty."

"It was so important to you to kill L. George Thatcher yourself?" Her anger was rising. Hurt was one thing. Blind, unremitting stubbornness was another. "The shame of this fate and of his failure is harder for him to bear than your bolt would have been."

Sogan still did not face her, but his eyes lowered. There was no real point in continuing the discussion. She would never understand. "The public executioner is not an acceptable second, nor can anyone else rightly stand in the place of one whose honor has been violated . . ."

"Damn you to all the hells, Varn Tarl Sogan! How many times do you have to be told that your honor is not tarnished? What you did on Amazoon was necessary, and most of what happened was expressly against your will . . ."

The man sighed deeply, with a weariness that seemed to consume him. "Whatever either of us would wish to the contrary, I am not the space mongrel Varnt Sogan, Islaen. I am Varn Tarl Sogan, war prince of the Arcturian Empire. My ways, my reactions, are those of my own people, so different from yours that our ultrasystems collided in a decades-long war despite our leaders' full knowledge of how costly such a conflict would be and l their honest efforts to prevent it. Whatever my desire or even y conscious will in this or in anything else of basic importance to me, I am going to respond in accordance with what I am, not by an alien code under which fate compels me to live. It is difficult enough to bend myself to its commands in mundane matters." His voice changed. "Maybe I am the worse fool even to try."

"Now, you're just whining," the woman told him evenly. "I expect better than that from you."

His head snapped around. The dark eyes were hot with fury, but that was preferable to his prior mood, and she met them calmly.

The former Admiral held his temper. His face and voice were cold, but he was in command of himself. "You are correct," he said. "I was pitying myself without right. We accomplished our ends, and we survived the fight. Even the *Fairest Maid* survived it. There are families on Noreen in deep mourning, whatever their pride in their dead."

He came to his feet and stood before the observation panels. All was quiet out there now, but awesome violence, human-spawned or natural, too often rent the serenity of the dark realm between the stars. "I wish we had been able to save that Garda ship."

The Colonel came over to stand beside him. If Sogan had not thrown off his bitterness and self-perpetuated shame, he was attempting to set them aside, to drive them into the past and chain them there. It was her business to help him.

He put his arm around her. Its weight felt good, and she rested her head against him. "Noreen's worthy of the sacrifice," she said, "but I, too, wish it never had to be made." Her throat tightened, and it was another moment before she went on. "They never had to face more than a few splinter-ship smugglers and an occasional rescue, but they pulled their part when the need really came."

"All your people did," he responded. "If I had a fleet manned by their like, I could conquer a galaxy, or defend one."

Her eyes lowered. Even through his shields, she could feel the intensity of the longing that momentarily swept him, and her own sense of failure rose to meet it. She could not give him the command he merited and wanted. She had not even been able to give him the vengeance she had promised . . .

Varn has us! the forgotten gurry exclaimed in genuine puzzlement that anyone could require more.

That's not enough, not always, Islaen said sadly, speaking in her closed mind. *Quiet now, love.*

The Arcturian did not hear his commander's answer, but he turned somberly to look at Bandit. "So I do, small one."

His shoulders squared. So much had happened to him that once would have been unthinkable. It was his to accept this taint on his honor as he had been forced to accept the rest, to live with it. There had never been a possibility of rectifying the damage from the moment the decision to act as he had done had been made, and now even the hope of avenging himself was dead.

He did have a duty to his consort, one he was not about to fail.

It had come to him on Noreen of Tara that Islaen Connor, too, was an exile, a voluntary one, perhaps, and one mercifully permitted to visit her own people and world frequently, but she was severed from any permanent return by reason of the work she did and had done since the day she had enlisted in the Federation Navy. Her kind's rejection of her might be gentle, but she was hurt by it, and that hurt was deep. He, an exile himself, could understand her pain and the isolation engendered by that severing. There could be no healing of it, but comfort and support he could give, and love in measure with that which she bestowed on him.

Sogan held her a little closer, then scooped up Bandit from the perch she had taken near to them. His acknowledgment of the Jadite's statement was a promise, a promise to them all. He did want a real life—not a shadow existence crushed beneath the weight of loss and fear—but he would have to make it, fight to make it, against himself perhaps more than against any other force opposing it.

A soft light touched his eyes as he looked from one to the other of his companions. He might win that struggle or be defeated in it, but attempt it he would, and with battle comrades such as these two beside him, he did not believe that he would fail.

279